ALSO BY JENNIFER MANSKE FENSKE

Toss the Bride

THE WIDE SMILES *of* GIRLS

Jennifer Manske Fenske

THOMAS DUNNE BOOKS

St. Martin's Press ❧ *New York*

THOMAS DUNNE BOOKS.
An imprint of St. Martin's Press.

THE WIDE SMILES OF GIRLS. Copyright © 2009 by Jennifer Manske Fenske. All rights reserved. Printed in the United States of America. For information, address St. Martin's Press, 175 Fifth Avenue, New York, N.Y. 10010.

www.thomasdunnebooks.com
www.stmartins.com

Library of Congress Cataloging-in-Publication Data

Fenske, Jennifer Manske.
  The wide smiles of girls / Jennifer Manske Fenske. — 1st ed.
      p. cm.
  ISBN-13: 978-0-312-37991-9 (alk. paper)
  ISBN-10: 0-312-37991-9 (alk. paper)
  1. Sisters—Fiction. 2. Accidents—Fiction. 3. Widowers—Fiction.
4. Maine—Fiction. I. Title.
  PS3606.E57W53 2009
  813'.6—dc22
                                                              2009007591

First Edition: June 2009

10 9 8 7 6 5 4 3 2 1

For Jonathan, now, always, ever

THE WIDE
SMILES *of* GIRLS

ONE

Arrival, Langdon Island

B efore Ruth died, before there was a fall or a push or a jump from the old bridge, she lived on Langdon Island and loved Hale Brock. Before she loved Hale, she lived in a large beach house with her two sisters, who were wicked like those sisters in fairy tales, and who mocked Ruth's choice of wide-brimmed hats and dramatic long skirts. Ruth felt as if she had been born in the wrong century and, like a lot of people who believed that, she sighed and read old journals and talked about what life could or should have been if she had lived one hundred years ago.

Hale and Ruth were married and lived on Langdon, which is a sleepy South Carolina island near Charleston that was starting to attract developers who like to take sleepy islands and wake them up. I moved to Langdon when my sister moved there but wasn't too keen on loving me anymore, and there was an accident and a lost love, and way more things to tell than I cared to tell. I tended to be a little closemouthed, a term that made me think of someone going around with their lips pursed and looking prunish and uncomfortable. I hoped I didn't look like that. If I was closemouthed, it was only because I liked to see what other people were going to say first. I wanted them to make the first move, to tip their hand a bit before I dove in with a thought or an idea. It's who I was.

March, my little sister, on the other hand, was openmouthed, openhearted, and lived life pretty wide open. She was the best and the brightest, and you never forgot March. I thought of March sometimes as being the same age as me, like we were twins, because I can't remember life without her. Even though I was two years older and felt every bit the big sister, March seemed to be ageless or timeless. Or at least she did at one point.

I met Hale when I was twenty-six and life was changing, changed, and different. He was grieving his wife, the lovely and talented Ruth. She was a costume designer for the theater, which meant she had fabulous clothes, daring dresses, and saucy hats. Around Hale's neat beach bungalow he had placed framed black-and-white pictures of his lost wife. I saw Ruth dancing, I saw her laughing. I saw her tousle-headed in bed and I saw her dipping down to kiss Hale's brow. She was a beautiful woman, with dark arched eyebrows and soft-looking lips. Her back was straight and she had long legs. Often, when I was over at Hale's cooking up a pot of pasta or shucking summer corn, I got the feeling Ruth still visited the bungalow. It wasn't a scary, ghostly feeling. It was more like a warm blanket. I asked Hale if he felt this. Mostly, I just tried to listen to him when he talked of her.

Hale knew all about me and March, and I thought I knew all about him and Ruth. But how much do you really know about someone who is gone? I knew March and I knew Hale, but Ruth would always be a black-and-white photograph. Someone else's memory. I could feel as if I knew her and her penchant for coconut-flavored lip gloss or her love of ice-cold watermelon plucked from the cooler at the Shop All, but these were memories told to me. Often, in those first few weeks of getting to know Hale, I thought I glimpsed his wife in the run-down corner grocery store up on our end of the island. There, there she was, her dark hair smoothed back in a turquoise silk scarf. There, there she was dipping her hands into the piles of apples and oranges. I would stop and stare at the women I thought were Ruth. I would take a step toward them, my heart pounding. If I found her, maybe she was never lost and I could return her to Hale. But then the woman with the scarf or the apples would look up and catch my eye, and I knew that it was not her. It was not the woman I thought I knew in the photographs.

I liked walking on the beach at sunset. I'm not a morning person, and for me, sunrise beach walks were few and far between. So, between the time the sun headed for the warm Atlantic and the last moments it dipped beneath the shelf of day and night, I would stroll along the beach. We lived at the east end of the island in a neighborhood that was shabby and perfectly isolated. As I trod over wet sand and spy fiddler crabs darting to and fro, I could see the tall condos farther down the beach. The crowds were bigger: there were more beach umbrellas closing up for the day, more people streaming out of the condo developments to observe the purple-pink sunset. Up where I was, I could catch the eye of maybe two, three people. Some of them are neighbors. They have taken to me, an interloper, someone from Upstate South Carolina.

What I tried not to look at while I walked was the old bridge, now coming down in sections where the highway department was dismantling it in what had to be the slowest road project in history. The old concrete bridge, like its newer, flashier replacement, spanned the bay between Langdon Island and the mainland. It was grayed and stained, a testament to another era when cars came over to the island one lane at a time. Back when the old bridge was built, the cars were slower, and who really needed to go to Langdon anyway? It was the place of some poor people, a few waterfront communities of ramshackle beach houses on stilts, and a tiny strip of commercial interests. A bait shop. An unused outpost for the county sheriff who was rumored to have never stepped foot on the island at all. Nope, Langdon was no one's idea of a beach paradise and the bridge was an old-fashioned concrete welcome mat, not seen until a person really needed to get across the bay. I found myself on that bridge, or the one that replaced it, one day, the day I first came to Langdon to see my sister March.

My dented sedan cheerfully pulled along a small, rented trailer full of clothes, a futon, and books, while I piloted down Highway 9. Langdon Island was a new home for March and me, and I wondered what the streets would look like, how the sand might sweep over the sidewalks, what we would find there.

I had left Atlanta and its tangle of interstates and commuters six hours ago. If I closed my eyes briefly, I could still feel the heat of the city and the thumping traffic, pressing against my head. I saw, and almost felt, the office I left in the glass building downtown. The air in my office was always too cool. I pictured my empty apartment. Within days, a new tenant would fill it up with her things. My brightly colored rugs and framed posters were in the trailer behind me instead of where they belonged.

Within a few miles of Langdon, I glanced at the map. The highway ran alongside the bay, eventually crossing the water and running straight into town on the island. The highway then terminated after faithfully carrying cars for hundreds of miles. On my map, the words "Road Construction" were stamped over the highway. I wondered if we would be delayed. But then I reminded myself I had no one waiting for me in Langdon. No one, unless you counted my sister. And it would be wrong to do that, because she wasn't waiting for me.

I ran my mind over our friendship, our sisterhood. Was there a way to go back? Maybe if I started at the beginning. Maybe if I stepped back to when we were young and life was more of a lark, at least for March. She always knew how to get a rise out of me and Mom and Dad. But for all of her missteps and passion, I knew of her sweet and open heart. I knew of her fierce loyalty and love for me. When did it slip away and become something I did not recognize? My heart beat a little faster thinking of my sister on the island ahead. Once, she ran to me to solve her problems. I could not fix her life now. I could not make her whole again.

Orange signs, barrels, and cones let me know that the road construction lay ahead. The bay appeared—beautiful, gray, and ringed with tan grasses and sticky mudflats. A few miles away, the town on the island waited. I slowed to the construction zone speed postings. Other cars and trucks slowed, too, as I made my way onto the slick, gray concrete bridge spanning the bay.

I am not a fan of crossing over water in a vehicle. I always think that some idiot is going to tap my car from behind causing me to careen over the side and die a watery death. How will I get out? I anxiously started across the water.

The source of the road construction was pretty obvious, even to a casual observer like me. I was riding on the new, wide bridge. An old, brownish concrete bridge sat off to my right, lower and swarthier than the current bridge just crossed. Its buckled concrete spans had weeds growing up through cracks. The highway powers were clearly dismantling this old bridge; every quarter of a mile or so, there were huge gaps that had been removed from the highway, revealing churning bay waters below. It was both scary and interesting at the same time. The highway was useless, I thought. Then I reconsidered because I saw the signs for the first time.

Someone had opted to use the old bridge as an art gallery. Or as a signpost to despair, to love. I sigh when I remember what I thought of the signs. I figured they were the work of a desperate, pimpled high schooler. Maybe a tech school dropout who lost his first love. Or a young husband longing for his wayward wife.

I laugh now, thinking of my ignorance about Hale's signs, but really I should have cried. Because when I saw the signs, carefully bolted to the side of each decaying section of decaying bridge, I was watching a man become unraveled, tube by tube of paint. Piece by piece of plywood. And when the bridge was through, when the old bridge petered out at the foamy shores of the island, that man would have told us all he knew.

Each sign, painted purple, painted red.

Miss Your Lips Ruth.

TWO

I don't remember a time when March wasn't larger than life. When I think of March, she is always louder and funnier and more vibrant than I ever was. Even as children playing in the fields, petting our horses and braiding daisies into their manes. Even in high school when no one knows his or her way. No one except for March.

On the eve of high school graduation, it looks like I have two choices: marry Barry "Little" Bittle or become a lonely librarian who wears dusty cardigans and purchases half-price cologne at the Save-Whiz. That is what Barry tells me when we crouch up in the knobby arms of the Tri-County oak tree. The tree stands on the grounds of our high school and suffered a cannonball shot during the War. A card-carrying member of the local chapter of the Sons of the Confederacy, five-foot-two Barry wants to touch the cannonball hollow before the sun comes up on graduation day. I agreed to go with him because everyone else is getting nastily drunk down below on the school lawn. I also know I can keep an eye on my younger sister from the tree. Make sure she doesn't get into trouble, or if she does, scrape her out of it. It is what is expected of me. Our parents are older, slower, and more inclined to believe March is forever falling into trouble because she bears some sort of unlucky stamp. Actually, March's problem is that she's too lucky.

"Mae Wallace? Are you up there? 'Cause if you are, I'm coming up."

I lean out over the edge of my whorled tree branch. March is clumsily clawing for a piece of the old oak. She wears a mortarboard even though she's not due to graduate from Tri-County for two more years.

"Stay down there, March. You're drunk. You'll fall."

"Let her come up, Mae Wallace. What's the big deal?" Barry appears at my elbow, grinning like a moron who's had too much hooch. "Everyone knows two sisters are better than one."

"Barry, you just this minute were telling me that I was your one true love and we should 'get married and start making babies.'"

Barry gives me a long look and wipes some spittle out of the corner of his mouth. "I said that, huh?"

"My other choice, according to you, was to become a librarian and spend my days with romance novels so that I would know what I was missing."

"I think I'm in love with you, Mae Wallace Anders." Barry

9

makes a gigantic show of caressing my face with his dirty, tree-climbing hands. His breath is predictably stale and sweet at the same time.

I scoot back on my limb away from Barry and keep one eye on my tipsy sister, who has finally found a branch to support her weight. I hear the branch groan and then start to crack. My sister falls at least ten feet to the warm ground below.

"March!" I turn to scramble down the tree. My fingers find holds, my feet scrape bark, and then I am on the ground next to my prone sister. The party stumbles on near us; no one notices two sisters, one small and worried, and the other large and fallen.

March is a big girl. She's really huge—overweight, fat, heavy. Whatever you want to call it. And a person might think that I am her protector, saving her from the taunts of cruel classmates. They would be wrong. March is her class vice president ("More power than you think," she'd whispered to me on election day), captain of the track team where her shot-put record will never be beaten, and the inventor of four flavors of ice cream, one or two of which nearly every American probably has in their freezer right at this moment.

I kneel at March's head, gently prodding for signs of life. Barry bellows something from the tree's midsection.

"Little, shut up. My sister's hurt."

"Oh, March can take it. Remember when that horse kicked her at your farm?"

In spite of the situation, I have to laugh. My parents used to run a dairy farm and when we were younger, an ornery horse popped

March right in the backside. She hauled off and gave that horse what for. The story is what I love about March: don't try figuring her out because it will be a waste of time.

Take her boyfriend, for instance. She is at the senior party at the invitation of Ray Dale, the coolest guy ever to walk across the campus of Tri-County. Ray started shaving in the seventh grade, wears black Elvis Costello glasses, and dresses in vintage clothing. Ray talks differently and walks differently than anyone else in town. And he loves my sister. The two look like quite a pair: March with her arm slung around Ray's thin waist, her large hips swaying from side to side clad in a full skirt. "Why must you wear those skirts?" my mother likes to plead with March. "Look, in the catalog for *Today's Big Teen*, all the girls are wearing pencil skirts. Just look!"

"Mother," March would answer wearily, "in case you haven't noticed, I am not a pencil. I'm more like a jumbo marker."

Little battles like that go on all the time at home. My mother mostly leaves me alone. I like to read, ride horses, and play with our four dogs. I've been told I'm kind of pretty, in a traditional way. My medium-length brown hair holds streaks of blond highlights from long horse rides under the summer sun. The braces came off in eighth grade, so now I don't mind smiling if someone says something funny. Once in a while, I'll ask for some money so I can go to the Henderson Mall for a sweater or a skirt that I saw in a magazine, but usually I don't give a fig about clothes.

I've become more confident in high school, maybe because I've found something I'm good at—volunteering. I just like doing things that help other people. Last month, before it was really hot and the mosquitoes were biting, I helped build an outdoor pavilion for a local summer camp for poor kids. I loved learning how to use the circular saw to cut lumber. I even got to roof a little once the foreman saw that I was serious and not goofing off and drinking lemonade all day like some of my classmates.

Boys hold some fascination for me, but not enough to really do anything about it. Not March. She loves dating—boys, old men, young men, babies. And they love her. People gravitate toward March, even the thin, pretty ones you would think might ridicule her. Would this happen in a big city and not just a small town like Henderson? I'd like to think so. I'd like to think star athletes, drama-class stars, band geeks, chess champions, and debate nerds could all live under the umbrella of happiness that March opens over her part of the world. It makes a nice story.

"Mae? Mae Wallace?" March is coming to, groaning a little bit under my hands. I try to keep her head still in case she has a broken neck. I've seen the paramedics do this on TV. "Why can't I move?"

"Oh, March, March. Stay right here. I've got to get help. And everyone is drunk." I can't believe my sister is injured. My parents are going to freak out.

Instead, March sits up, swatting away my hands. "I can't move because you're pressing on my neck. Ouch, it hurts. Thanks a whole bunch."

I help her stand, no easy task, but in a moment March is dusted off and ready to rejoin the party. "I think I'll skip the tree. Doesn't seem made for a real woman of generous portions."

"It survived a cannonballing in the War," Little calls to us from above.

"Thanks, Barry, thanks a lot," I call up to him, hoping he can see my angry glare. "March, I'm tired. Do you want to go home with me? Everyone is so sloppy drunk—it's not fun anymore."

March pretends to consider my request. She has hours left in her sixteen-year-old body. She and Ray could head up to his parents' lake cabin and make out in a rowboat. They could stop by the Pancake Griddle for a late-night snack. They could smoke clove cigarettes while listening to the college jazz station. The night is very, very young for March.

The main lawn of the school still rages on with partiers. I see a few girls I've known since I was in elementary school being hosed down with whipped cream. Jason Lane, a kid who used to kiss me before xyla-chimes in third grade, runs by, pursued by Dixie Crumb, who is stumbling in her high heels. Graduation is at noon tomorrow. I wonder briefly who will clean up the used balloons, fast-food wrappers, and shaving cream littering the front lawn.

"Think I'll find Ray, Mae Wallace." March gives me an apologetic hug and a sticky kiss on the cheek. She's been drinking wine coolers, her favorite. Because she's so big, March has given up trying to get really drunk at parties. It takes too long for the alcohol to travel through her system. Now she settles for a weak buzz. Ray Dale does not drink, something else that sets him apart from almost every other high schooler in town. He told me once it "interferes with his thinking." Whatever. I wish I were drunk. It would take away this feeling that I am passing wearily from one high school event to another. Except this one has a definite ending. There was a beginning, four years ago, and now, there is this: graduation.

It's not like the end of high school sneaked up on me. I was aware of the slippery last semester of my public school career. The year opened with the gentle chill of a Southern winter; moved on to the Valentine's dance where a guy from chemistry class clung to my hips with too-sweaty hands; segued into a short Spring Break that crossed over Easter; and finally, ended with a round of exams that wrapped everything up. Still, I sit here on the littered grounds of my almost former high school, and I want to go back and do it all again. Enter the dented metal front doors painted a dull brown and rewind the tape.

"Mae Wallace, will you marry me?" Little calls down to me, bleating a drunken proposal before he vomits all down the side of the poor oak tree. I wait to see if he is going to choke on his own waste before digging around in my shorts for the car keys.

The graduation ceremony will be in less than ten hours. There is a dress to pull out of the closet. I need to make sure the camera is loaded with film. I might even file my nails and apply clear polish. Turning away from the party, I trudge across the grass to my waiting car. It's time to go home and get some sleep.

Summer unrolls the next day, once the senior class has wriggled out of their caps and gowns and dutifully shown up at barbecues and picnics. My parents take me to Garrison's, the nicest restaurant in Henderson. A few years ago, we might have been at a lake-side picnic celebrating with hot dogs and cold beer. But ever since my parents made it rich from ice cream, they take us to nice places with white tablecloths. March and I sit in starched dresses, the backs of our necks still damp from showers, while waiters buzz about with pitchers of sweet tea. I've gotten used to it.

"Here's to Mae Wallace, high school graduate," my father says, and lifts his glass.

I duck my head, raising my glass. It seems silly to make such a big deal out of graduating from Tri-County. Most people in town have done it. What mattered next was college, everyone knew that. If I could handle four years of longer papers and harder tests, then we could celebrate. I thought of my as-of-yet unassigned roommate for this fall at Mary Gossett, a small liberal arts college down off the coast of Charleston. What if my roommate was a mean girl? Or didn't like me?

I try to picture my future dorm room. I have already decided that music posters are too immature. I plan to hang black-and-white pictures of faraway places that I want to travel to one day. Maybe Africa or India. I am going to ask my mom to buy a bunch of black frames. That would be a cool look—kind of like the art gallery in downtown Henderson. Mom and Dad have purchased a few pieces there—Dad is a fan of landscapes—and I tagged along.

Imagining my room, my thoughts turn to the desk. Would it have plenty of room for my books? I knew college texts were huge and expensive. I might have to get a shelf unit. Or perhaps there were inset shelves in the dorm rooms. That made sense. College students had oodles of books.

"Oh, pooh, Mae Wallace," March says as she touches my glass with her half-empty one. "You're in another world, worrying over an exam that some random professor will give you five months from now. Relax, it's summer!"

As usual, my sister is correct. She knows me, probably better than I know her. It is comforting, though, realizing that someone else can get in my head.

"Mae Wallace, here's to your summer at Cream Castle, and then to a productive first year at school. We love you, honey." Dad takes a long sip of his iced tea. My mother does the same and then we look down at the menus. Chicken, I usually get the chicken. It comes with a sprig of rosemary and a little dollop of raspberry coulis. March is unpredictable—she might order the honey ribs or the jerk pork. One time, she asked the chef to make whatever he thought she would like. Eating out is an adventure for March.

"Honey, what day do you start at Cream Castle?" Mom asks me, reaching for the breadbasket.

"Odelia told me to report first thing Monday. She said to enjoy my last few days of freedom before I started working."

"She would say that," Dad harrumphs, although I know he is secretly pleased. His secretary is a smart woman and tough—but supersweet inside.

My parents had us a little later in life than most of the families we knew. They thought they couldn't have children, and then like a sweet peach falling off a tree, my mother often told me, I arrived. My mother didn't even know she was pregnant until she felt the slightest stirrings of something sliding delicately under her skin. She had trouble zipping her skirts and then a firm bump made its way out from a place one-and-a-half inches under her belly button. March was another surprise, two years later.

When we were three and one, my father decided he wanted to farm the land and get back to some sort of vague roots he felt deep inside. My mother, happy to be remaking her home with two little girls, followed him willingly to a dilapidated historic blueberry farm on the outskirts of Henderson. We bought the place from the estate of a farmer who dropped dead over breakfast one day, leaving a terribly ticked-off wife and no life insurance.

Needless to say, my father was a horrible farmer. The dead farmer's horses, chickens, and cattle had funny ideas about things. They wanted to be fed or watered or milked every day. Dad, on the other hand, might have had in mind that day to try out a new melody on his classical guitar or snap pictures of wildflowers. We nearly starved.

"Hon, are you in there? David wants to know your order. Do you want the chicken?"

"Yes, please," I nod to David, a stoner turned professional waiter. He graduated two years ago from Tri-County. I wonder if seeing us and the other celebrating families makes him feel wistful for his own high school career. Or maybe he is happy to get the large parties and generous tips.

At about the time when the family savings were running out, a real estate agent approached my parents about buying a portion of the back pasture. My father laughed at the man for wanting the hilly, ravine-choked land that was long overgrown with thistle and kudzu. My mother, interested in feeding her children, encouraged Dad to sell but cautioned him to do a little research. My father did, and he learned the agent worked for a large developer who had plans for a three-mile stretch of Henderson that bordered our farm. Neighborhoods, coffee shops, parks—the developer had an entire world planned right outside our scrappy pasture. My dad wondered why they didn't make an offer for the entire farm, but my mother pointed out it would have probably provoked suspicion. Our historic blueberry farm featured a barn built like a real castle, complete with a turret and shallow moat. The place was a wreck, of course, but history buffs were constantly coming out to the farm to measure beams and take photos of architectural details. Any sale of the farm proper would have made news in the rabid historical community—something a discreet developer bent on buying up land cheap would not want in a million years.

So, Dad countered the agent's offer with one quadruple the price and the man did not bat an eye. Armed with cash, Dad decided what he really wanted to do was invent something. He said he looked to us for inspiration, and seeing my rabid desire for ice cream, and all the poor, unused dairy cows and neglected blueberry bushes, he set about concocting the best blueberry ice cream ever.

Our food arrives, and I dig into the chicken. It's as tasty as always, and I am thankful for the predictability of small things, like the tart and sweet raspberry coulis and tender chicken. I think I never want to leave my family. Dad is making Mom laugh about something, and March is sipping her soda, rolling her eyes at David, who flirts with her. I love these people, and I think it's kind of cruel to make me go away to college. Even if it only is a few hours away, down near the coast, maybe I don't want to go. Ever.

"What if I stayed home next year, you know, kept on with Cream Castle and helped out Dad?"

My parents stop laughing and look at me. David scurries away and March glances down at her half-eaten shepherd's pie.

"What do you mean, Mae Wallace? Of course you're going to college. Mary Gossett is a great fit for you. Remember all the schools we looked at?" My mother looks concerned.

Last summer, we trekked up and down the East Coast, visiting about nine colleges and universities. I lost track. We kept to the small, private ones. I had already decided I wasn't a rah-rah football fan, so huge state schools were out. I didn't want to be in the cold of the extreme Northeast, so we stopped around Virginia. When it came down to it, I think I was kind of scared of living somewhere too far from home. I loved the blueberry farm—now the main offices for Cream Castle—and I knew I would miss my horses and March. Mary Gossett offered a great solution. It was elite enough that my father was pleased, and small enough so that I wouldn't feel lost. I secretly hoped March might want to follow me there. She would probably laugh at the idea. March was most likely destined for some California school or a pottery studio in Greenwich Village. I sadly knew a small college like Mary Gossett was not her style.

"I know we looked at lots of schools," I say, stabbing a baby

Jennifer Manske Fenske

carrot. "But now I'm wondering if I am ready for college. You know, a year in the real world might not be such a bad idea."

"Mae Wallace, you are going to college, and that's it. At eighteen, we don't always know what we want." My father wipes his mouth with a cloth napkin.

"That's true," Mom says. "When I was eighteen, I almost ran away with a carpet salesman."

We all stare at her. Even my father.

Mom laughs, sweeping her brown hair over her shoulder. "Haven't I mentioned this before? Harry installed carpets at Tri-County. It was the old building, the one they tore down to make room for that boxy addition you girls have. Anyway, he and I hit it off, and he asked me to run away with him once the carpets were installed. I think he was from somewhere down in Dalton."

"Whoa, Mom, you fell for the carpet guy?" March looks excited.

"It seemed very exotic at the time." Mom shrugs her shoulders. "He had been to Atlanta. He was twenty, and I thought Harry had seen the world. I was very enamored."

"But then, your mother took that ill-fated Shakespeare class and met me, the new transfer student," Dad says.

"No, actually, after Harry, I had a few more boyfriends. You and I met later that year."

March and I look at our mother, take in her crow's-feet and the slight sag to her lower chin. I start to think I have found the fount of March's fabled magnetism. I always figured it was my wildly creative father, maker of lullabies and childhood forts fashioned from old camp blankets.

"And when we met, you were smitten for all time?" my father says, with a slight questioning note in his voice.

"All time. Absolutely."

The rest of the dinner passes without a ripple of dissent from me. Of course, I know I have to go off to school. It's what is expected of me. It's what I guess I really want to do, deep down. But leaving home means leaving everything I love, including my sister. March can be frustratingly optimistic, wildly enthusiastic, and cleverly charming. She is more fun to be around than even Dad.

I've always towed the older-sister line, with all its responsibility and trappings of seriousness. Being silly never felt comfortable to me. Even when we were young and life was generally about games and frivolity, I was more likely to be found with my nose stuck in a book, or quietly contemplating a spider web edged with morning dew. I was slow to catch on to jokes because I took everything very deliberately. March, on the other hand, flitted through life like it was a lark. Even though we were so very different, I never doubted for a second how much my younger sister loved me.

When we were ten and twelve, March wrote a short novel. She based the title character, a girl with superpowers and a clear, strong soprano voice, on me. She liked to bake me little cakes sprinkled with powdered sugar. As a preteen, I found her crying after an underwear shopping trip. "I'm sorry my breasts are bigger than yours," she sobbed. "It should be the other way around because you're older." My sister is a magical person. I wasn't sure how many magical people I would find at Mary Gossett.

The dessert is brought to the table. It is Cream Castle, of course, served with delicate vanilla cookies. Dad raves about the flavor, Peach Pizzazz, and eats every bite like he hasn't spent the week tracking sales in Asia, worrying over rising fuel costs and dairy farmer strikes.

"I don't think I've had a better dish of ice cream," Dad says, licking his spoon.

"Nor I." Mom brings a small bite to her lips. She is meticulous about her figure, so half of the bowl will go uneaten. March will swoop in before too long. My parents still caution my sister about her weight, but it's almost like they do it automatically. March has never been anything but big, from about six months of her life. She cheerfully accepted it years ago. It has taken me and my parents a little longer.

I might have spent some part of my childhood being embarrassed about my bigger sister who wore larger everything and couldn't run the mile in gym class. But I barely remember if I did. March had a way of turning things to her advantage. When she figured out running the mile was beyond her, she approached the coach about filming the athletic progression of her junior high colleagues. Her documentary, *And They Lifted Up Their Feet*, is still played on public television a couple of times a year.

With dinner winding down, my father nudges Mom, who reaches into her purse and brings out a small box wrapped in light pink paper. The present looks like my mother—spare and elegant. If Dad or March had wrapped it, they would have used the comics pages or ads ripped from magazines. "Why buy wrapping paper?" March liked to say. "There're tons of paper everywhere."

Everyone looks at me while I open the box carefully. I slowly fold the wrapping paper off to the side and roll up the satin ribbon. March is about to blow her lid—she rips into presents like a tornado.

Inside is a small velvet box and when I open it, I find a gorgeous diamond and ruby pendant. It is beautiful, and so nice that I think I will never wear it. "Turn it over," Dad urges.

Mae Wallace, you are loved always. The date is scripted below in tiny, fine strokes.

"This is too expensive!"

"Not for our girl." Mom smiles and reaches for the box. "Let me put it on you."

The weight of the diamonds—one large one, surrounded by five smaller stones and then encircled by what looks like a dozen rubies—is heavy around my neck. But I love it.

Standing up, I walk over to my parents and give them hugs and kisses. David discreetly delivers the check. I notice March is quiet. "I'm really going to miss you, sis."

"Me, too." I am choked up like it's the last day of summer instead of the first.

"I've got something for you, too, but it's more handmade." March looks uncharacteristically shy and unsure. She pulls a present from her leather bag, wrapped in Cream Castle coupons. "It just seemed to work," she says, grinning.

March has given me a sky-blue fabric journal. My name is stitched onto the front in yellow yarn, and inside, she has already pasted a few pictures of us smiling and mugging for the camera. There's a picture of the restored barn on the Cream Castle farm. One is of us dressed up when we were little; another of the two of us, one thin and one bigger, wearing matching bikinis when I was fourteen and March was twelve. "Ugh, I can't show this to anyone," I protest. I look like a stick, scrawny and unfeminine. I never wore a bikini after that summer.

"You'll fill out one day, Mae Wallace, I promise," my sister says solemnly, the corners of her mouth turning up into a smile.

My family walks out of the restaurant. *This is a perfect night,* I think. Although it's not in my nature, I try to relax and look at the rest of summer with a casual, lazy eye. My internship at Cream Castle will take half of my days, but then I can hang out at the farm, ride my horse, go to the lake, or just chill out with March when she's not spending time with Ray. Although college looms ahead like a big, scary thing, maybe I can enjoy the next two months.

On the way back to the house, March reaches over and squeezes my hand. "Let's go for a ride when we get home, okay?" She keeps her voice low so that our parents in the front seat don't hear her.

I am surprised, but I don't let on. March is one of the most energetic people I know, but she rarely exercises on purpose. She's not lazy by any means, in fact, she's usually a whirling dervish of motion, but choosing to saddle up her horse and ride from Point A to Point B is not her game.

We pull onto the farm, bumping down the lane toward the house, angling away from the historic barn on the slight rise of a hill. Seeing the wooden turrets standing tall and serene across the main pasture fills me with a sense of calm. I am home, for now.

When Dad made that first batch of blueberry ice cream years ago, he did something not many ice cream makers were doing at the time. He added things. To the blueberries he added crispy chunks of topping that made it taste like blueberry cobbler. To chocolate, he added chocolate-covered raisins and malted milk balls. He gave the flavors crazy names and then offered them for sale at small cafes and bistros all over the South. It was a perfect combination for people with a little extra cash who were soon to figure out they liked paying four dollars for a cup of fancy coffee. Premium ice cream was the new rage.

With the Cream Castle profits, Dad expanded the business and brought on savvy businessmen and -women. He built Mom her dream house on the blueberry farm property, and he bought us girls horses. March's mount was a sturdy quarter horse and mine was a beautiful glossy black gelding that I was forbidden to name Black Beauty. Instead, I called him Razzle, after the candy every- one was eating that summer, Razzle Dazzle. As I grew older, I just called him Raz.

We change into jodhpurs and T-shirts and head to the barn. It's nearly four o'clock and the horses whinny with happiness when they see us. That joy soon fades because they realize we're here to make them work instead of feed them an early dinner.

While I brush down Raz, March goes after her horse, Butter Sue. Butter is ridden the least of our four mounts. The part-time groom who takes care of the barn tries to ride her at least once a week, but he is partial to Dad's horse and he loves Raz. Everyone does. Butter Sue is kind of obstinate. She throws her head in the air when March approaches with a halter. "Blast it, why can't Henry ride her more? She's a spoiled brat!"

I slip away from Raz, who clearly loves my brushing, and help

March with her horse. It is another fifteen minutes before we are all saddled, bridled, and mounted. We start down the lane toward the back pasture at a walk, the horses throwing mournful glances toward the barn.

I love the first few minutes of a ride, the horsey sway pitching back and forth when you're reminded your legs are wrapped around twelve hundred pounds of muscle. I couldn't count the number of hours I had spent on Raz's broad back, exploring the farm and the neighboring acreage adjacent to ours. As soon as school let out each summer, I rose each morning early for a ride. It was just the two of us, Raz and me, before the day ran away with heat. He and I would find a quiet spot; then I would dismount, unpack a snack from the saddlebag, remove his bridle, and let him graze in tall grass while I settled down with my book. From time to time, Raz would flick his deep brown eyes over to me while I read, checking to make sure I hadn't left him. I always packed two apples—one for me and one for him.

The farm is quiet, the dairy cows pent up for milking and the hay mower in the back pasture is silent. A few cars slip away from the Cream Castle headquarters up on the hill. As Raz and Butter take us farther down the lane, the shadows thrown from oak and sycamore trees give welcome shade. I can sense March wants to talk about something. It's my way to let things happen on their own, though, so I don't say anything.

Butter tromps along beside me and Raz, her honey-colored coat looking shiny and healthy. I know Raz appears much the same way. Henry is a wonderful groom, giving the horses more attention than any of us can. Butter shakes her head, looking over at me knowingly. I smile at her. She's a handful, but still a good horse.

"I sometimes think Butter understands me. Do you ever think that way about Raz?"

Nodding, I agree. "He seems to know what mood I am in, what I'm thinking about. I used to tell him all my secrets."

"You didn't always tell me." March says this matter-of-factly, with no accusation in her voice.

She's right. While my sister is an open book, I tend to hold things inside. I mull them over, and then decide if I want to talk about them or not. Like my feelings about going to college. March was probably surprised when I mentioned staying home next year. She thinks the idea of college—lots of young men and women thrown together like a wacky version of summer camp—is a grand way to go about things.

"Mae Wallace? Have you ever been in love?"

"Nope, not really."

"There's not been anyone—someone that you kept a secret?"

I flick a leaf off of Raz's big shoulder. "You know all my boyfriends. No elaborate romances here. Not yet, anyway."

"Yeah, but you've had some wicked crushes. That soccer player was smoking hot."

Closing my eyes, I think of my impossible, six-year devotion to Lance Duberre, Tri-County's all-star goalkeeper. Raz stumbles, and I open my eyes to find March staring, a little smile playing across her lips. I try to change the subject. "I'll bet I meet my future husband the first day of freshmen orientation at Mary Gossett. It's a little predictable, but we'll stare deeply into each other's eyes in line at registration and then we'll just know. You know?"

"What about Little Bittle? He seems really into you," March teases.

"Yes, any day now we'll tear off to the Methodist church downtown and you'll be my maid of honor."

March's shoulders slump a little in the saddle. Butter tries to rub her off on a young sapling, but March applies her leg and a firm rein.

"I think I may be in love, Mae Wallace."

I figured this conversation was getting around to Ray. He was her most serious boyfriend to date. I think they had been together for almost a year. March had two scrapbooks dedicated to their relationship filled with movie stubs, pictures, and empty candy wrappers. I thought Ray was a bit much, kind of a poser in a town that didn't know a fake when they saw it, but he made my sister happy.

"What are you going to do—with the semester over and Ray going to Rhode Island for school?"

"Ray?" March keeps her eyes on the path in front of us. We have left the lane and are riding through the woods between the main pastures. The path is well worn from trail riding. The horses plod on, no doubt scheming about how they can return to the barn and to the loving attentions of Henry the groom.

"I'm not talking about Ray, Mae Wallace. Sure, he's okay. But he's kind of immature."

I pull up Raz, forcing March to rein in Butter. Two birds fly over our heads, calling to one another with faint chirps.

"I've been seeing another guy. A man," March continues. "I think he's the one, the real love of my life."

I try to think of places where March could meet a guy without my knowing it. There were plenty of options. She volunteered at the community food bank. She worked at the local movie theater. March was even allowed into the bar near the Save-Whiz because she could sing karaoke better than the regular inebriated patrons. My parents were unaware of that little fact.

"Dan is the best man, besides Dad, I've ever met. He's funny, kind, and he really, really believes in me. He says I can do anything."

March digs her heels into Butter's side and trots down the path. I follow, Raz only too eager for a challenge. "Wait! Where did you meet this mystery Dan?"

March picks up her right rein and prepares to kick with her right leg. I know we're seconds away from a rocking canter back toward the barn. The horses will go nuts and we'll be taken for a fast ride.

"Dan? Oh, him?" March calls from ahead of me, laughter in her pretty voice. "It's Coach Dan to you."

I am left in her dust as Butter gets the signal to canter. Her haunches dig into the South Carolina red clay, and March and mount rattle down the path. I feel Raz smoothing into a nice canter, his specialty, as he tries to catch up with his barn mate. I am barely hanging on, avoiding branches and watching for holes. Coach

Dan from the track team? Cute Coach Dan, straight out of grad school, with the cute *wife?* March has gone off the deep end. I am speechless, angry with her, in shock—all sorts of strong things. As I race to catch up with my younger sister, I give Raz a sharp kick. His ears shoot up and he takes me on. We ride faster, faster, and then we are gone, streaking past the silent trees in the forest.

THREE

From my open third-floor bedroom window, I can see my housemates traipsing back and forth across our gravel parking lot. SUVs are loaded up with beach chairs and towels, coolers and tennis rackets. Doors slam. The two house dogs bark and run up and down the scarred stairs in the old Victorian mansion, beside themselves that they might get left behind.

I sit down on the window seat, the one where I have read my anthropology case studies and conservation histories. Classes ended today for Spring Break, and most of my twelve housemates are clearing out this afternoon for points all up and down the East Coast. Angela is even headed to the Bahamas with her family. My plans are a little more humble: March is driving down to Mary Gossett tomorrow from her school in North Carolina. She ended up going to a smaller college than I thought she would, but one that was chock full of crazy theater majors, home-brew fanatics, and "enviro-wackos" as March liked to call them. She and I will spend the week on Tap Island, a short drive from Charleston. My parents bought a house there, not long after the ice cream money started rolling in. I think I've crashed there at least once or twice a year since I started at Mary Gossett, or as most of us call it, just "Goss."

My room is on the top floor of the most creaking, battered, and well-loved off-campus house. I spent my first three years in the college's dorms. They were okay, but I have adored living in our house that we call The Swan because of its wide, white porches and graceful atmosphere. Despite its weathered appearance and gently sloping floors that creak constantly, the house is beautiful.

A knock at my door announces Clarissa, who has the room next to mine. We share a tiny bathroom. Of all of the women in the house, I would have never guessed Clarissa and I would have been close. She is the opposite of me in every way. While I have chaired Red Cross relief drives for various natural disasters, Clarissa raises money for each weekend's kegger. When I found a Sudanese refugee family in town to sponsor, Clarissa donated a string of pearls and two pairs of black pumps. Although I think she can be clueless and selfish, Clarissa complains I am uptight and predictable. For some reason, it works.

"When are you heading out?" Clarissa is already wearing her bathing suit under a terry-cloth dress. She is driving to Tap Island as well, with a few other friends. They have a condo not far from my parents' beach house.

"I'm waiting on March, remember?"

"Oh, yeah." Clarissa scratches her nose absentmindedly. She had it done for her birthday and she likes to touch it occasionally. For the record, I think it looks pretty much the same as it did before the surgery.

"Is Ellis coming with y'all?"

I feel a little stab, but it isn't Clarissa's fault. I was supposed to go with Ellis, my boyfriend of the past two years, on a trip helping to rebuild homes in Pensacola, Florida, that were damaged in a huge hurricane last summer. At the last minute, though, March had miraculously freed up a week from her insane schedule and begged me to go on a sister vacation with her. Ellis was pretty steamed. He said he didn't understand how I could be so "irresponsible."

"You're turning into your sister, MW." Ellis stood right where Clarissa was standing now and crossed his arms over his "Feed the Hungry" T-shirt. Ellis liked to shorten my name. No one in my family ever did that. To them, I was always Mae Wallace. It is my mother's middle name combined with a great-grandmother's last name on my father's side.

"What's that supposed to mean?"

"Dropping out of this trip—just to go lay on the beach with your sister who never lifts a finger for anyone. You really surprise me. I expected better."

We had had this conversation last night, when the rented van pulled up to the house and Ellis gave me one more chance to hop onboard. It was tempting—March would get over it, I knew. But for once, the lure of roofing in ninety-degree heat or dragging piles of storm refuse did not win out. I wanted to feel hot sun on my face, loll in the waves if the water was warm enough, and eat lots of seafood.

Ellis eventually stormed off to his van full of people with purer hearts than mine, and I started packing for the beach. I missed him, and I didn't.

So I tell Clarissa, "No, he's off to Florida to save the world."

My housemate laughs. "It's good that you're doing something for you." She stretched and glanced at the clock in my room. "Better get going. I want to be in the pool by sundown."

"I think you can make it," I say, giving her a hug.

"Who's taking the dogs?"

"Evette's hauling them to Wilmington. She says they'll like the sea air."

"That sounds like her." Evette is always rescuing cats and dogs. We put a limit on two dogs for the house, and no cats because Clarissa is allergic to them. When we graduate in a few months, Evette has already put dibs on the dogs. They will be the start of an enormous collection, I am sure.

Mary Gossett has been the opening of an entire new world for me, one that I enjoy turning over and over in my mind, like a pretty keepsake. I arrived here unsure of college life and have emerged almost four years later in love with the perfectly kept grounds of the historic school, the Sunday lunch tradition where men and women wear white, and the way I seem to know almost everyone I run into on a simple stroll across campus.

Away from home, where Mom and Dad were famous and March was infamous, I learned to be a leader. It turned out that predictable, organized women were always needed to predictably organize festivals, relief drives, and special teas and parties. I have been president of four clubs and revived the annual philanthropic ball. I made friends and more friends. College life has been deliciously perfect, like the round pearl I wear pinned to my white cotton shirt. It was a gift from Ellis last Christmas.

The house is almost quiet. Evette will probably be the last to go, after me. She runs all the wildlife society functions, and networks up and down the South Carolina coast to find foster homes for abandoned dogs, but when it comes to organizing herself, she can be a little scatterbrained. I decide to see if she wants to get something to eat. It's nearly dinnertime.

Evette's room is right below mine on the second floor. I find her on her twin bed, scratching the two house dogs, Tandy and Blitz. The dogs, card-carrying mutts, beat their tails happily when they see me, but stay where they are. Evette is their queen. Her room smells a little like wet dog.

"Want to get dinner? We could walk over to Taco Hour."

Evette wrinkles her nose. "Didn't Tez find a fingernail in her taco salad last week there?"

"Oh, yeah, I forgot." Tez lived on the first floor and was engaged to a law student. She had a flair for the dramatic. Finding body parts in a meal is the kind of thing that would happen to her.

"I've got pizza from lunch. We could heat it up." Evette stands up from her bed, pushing past the two dogs. "Do you have any soda?"

"Let me check my shelf." Since there were so many roommates

in the house, all of us subscribed to a long-ago invented system of colored shelves in the kitchen, bathroom, and laundry room. My shelves were purple. The rule was: if it's not your shelf, hands off. For the most part, it worked. No one wanted to be known as a food thief. Of course, if one roommate had something you wanted, any girl in the house would give it to you. All you had to do was ask.

While we heat up pizza and pour soda into tall tumblers, Evette tells me about her hopes for Spring Break. There's a guy, but he might have a girlfriend. My mind drifts for a minute, and I am thinking about Ellis. No doubt, my boyfriend is probably coaxing his crew into extending their first day of work. Showers, dinner, and drinks can wait, he'll say. Isn't it better that we get to a good stopping point?

I met Ellis officially two years ago at an off-campus party at the home of Owl Joe. Owl Joe was nuts about owls, and he was showing a DVD of the plight of some endangered birds. "My brethren," he called them. Amid the beer and stale pretzels, the DVD played in a continuous loop on his computer screen. At some point, Ellis and I ended up in Owl Joe's bedroom, listening to a CD of owl hoots, and drinking Kool-Aid and vodka.

"Know any owls?" Ellis asked me. I could tell by the way he looked at me that he was a little interested.

"Not personally."

"I think Owl Joe is a tad bit nutty."

I raised my glass. The punch was making me tipsy. "Nutty for the birds."

I knew Ellis from around campus. We ran in the same save-the-world circles, but had never really worked together. I noticed he always had a lot of help with his particular causes, but not a ton of close friends. I dated here and there—an aspiring minister who tried out his sermons on me; a wannabe-blues guitarist who needed to practice more; an undeclared major who fell in love with me after two dates. I wasn't crazy about any of them.

After that night, Ellis gave me a call from time to time. I think I gave him my number. He swears we kissed the night we met, but I find both of our memories unreliable from that evening. Plus, I would remember if I got kissed. It doesn't happen all that much. I would remember lips.

I wonder if true love often starts out in this low-key manner. It doesn't for March. She runs pell-mell into it, tossing her head at love like a runaway horse. I can't count the number of boyfriends she has had. Dad used to wonder if she let her heart be claimed too easily. Lucky for March, Dad never found out about some of her more clandestine affairs—like the one with Coach Dan. I harped after her for weeks that summer to break it off before his wife found out and their marriage was ruined. I didn't care if Coach Dan was fired and strung up on a pole at Homecoming. I hated thinking about sweet Molly finding out about her husband's treachery and running her car into a brick wall or something. I can't stand seeing other people get hurt.

March wailed at me over and over again that I was a spoilsport and unromantic. Didn't I see that his marriage to Molly was a sham? They didn't even sleep together, Coach Dan said. Their union was more like a comfortable friendship. He was waiting until the right time to end it for good.

And then near the middle of the summer I graduated high school, when I was beginning to despair that my sister was the devoted home-wrecking type, March ran into Molly in the produce section of the grocery store. Coach Dan's wife had a nice, firm bump under her sensible school secretary denim jumper.

March later reported to me that she had dropped a bag of apples, and poor, pregnant Molly bent down to get it. She handed it to March, who promptly dropped the bag again. "You're having a baby," she said.

"Yes, yes I am." Molly must have looked puzzled. Normally, my sister was blessed with the gift for gab.

"You're having a baby."

I picture Molly eventually making excuses while rolling her cart away and leaving my sister there in the produce department, a sack of bruised apples at her feet. March's memory is kind of fuzzy. She says she thought she stumbled out of the store, she thought she called Coach Dan and cursed him out. She thought she would be a better judge of character the next time. I hoped so.

I never had that headstrong type of love March has experienced on more than one occasion. Ellis was more like a comfortable pair of shoes, the kind you wished would last forever, nice and broken in. The thing with shoes, though—and I knew it— was that no pair will last an entire lifetime. No matter how well made, shoes were shoes. They would wear out.

After dinner, I walk around the neighborhood, a perfectly safe thing to do both on and off campus. Most of the houses are dark and the driveways are empty. Everyone has taken off for Spring Break. It makes me a little lonely. This time next year, I'll be somewhere, working a job. I think about Ellis. Will we be engaged, off rescuing some endangered species, or rebuilding coastal houses together? Try as I might, I can't picture my books on his shelf, and his CD collection mingling with mine.

Early-blooming azaleas crowd the driveway of many of the houses. Left unpruned, they turn into beautiful, wild things with heavy-bloomed branches spilling onto the sidewalk. I drag one hand through a pink bush. Its simple elegance is comforting. Here is something that makes everything else look easy: a few hundred blossoms, working together in the near dark of a pleasant spring evening.

The next morning, March roars into town like only March can. For starters, she pulls up to the house driving one of Dad's vintage convertibles. I groan, thinking of how many strings she had to pull to get the Thunderbird. It's his absolute favorite. The baby-blue body is paired with perfectly polished chrome. The leather seats are without blemish; you'd be hard pressed to find a piece of lint on the floor mats. We're going to have to swerve to avoid bugs—I cannot even imagine soiling, denting, or otherwise marring this perfect vehicle.

March wears a long white scarf and cat's-eye sunglasses, like a 1950s movie star. Her generous breasts spill out of a white halter top. It's quite a sight. I haven't seen her for a few months—since Christmas—and although I wish I didn't still do it, I take a quick inventory of her body. She seems a little lighter, and that makes me happy. March developed diabetes last year, and I worry about her long-term health. My sister, however, is not worried, and she tosses me a matching pair of cat's-eye glasses.

"For my big sister. Live a little."

I cram the glasses on top of my head, and go back inside to get my small suitcase. I have packed lightly, just a few shorts, T-shirts, one sundress, a pair of leather sandals, and a bathing suit.

We hug, and I feel the happiness I do when I am near March. Her body, big and bold, is comforting to me. We're from the same flesh and I am silently grateful for her friendship. Making quick work of packing some snacks, we fill up an ice cooler and throw in last-minute beach supplies like towels, sunscreen, and a deflated hot-pink raft, a cast-off from one of my housemates.

The trip to Tap Island is a quick one, a little less than an hour. I drive, out of nervousness that March might hit a pothole or sideswipe a tree. She cheerfully reminds me she drove three plus hours by herself to get to Goss and pick me up.

"How in the world did you get Dad to loan you this?" I ask nervously, adjusting the rearview mirror for the eighth time. The top is still down, teasing my hair into a matted clump. March has another scarf wrapped over her long dark hair, every bit tucked away from the wind.

"It was easy—I just told him that you had requested it."

My mouth drops open, and I reach one hand over to swat March's arm. "What? I said no such thing!"

"I know. That was the genius of it. You weren't there to plead your case, so I did it for you."

"But I didn't want the car—"

"I know. But I did. This will make our trip much more memorable. It will be one for the archives."

"You didn't bring your video camera, did you?" March had gotten more and more into her documentary/filmmaker/auteur phase. The girl loved to film things.

March digs around in her bag for some lipstick and I know I've got my answer. Well, if she wants to have her head pressed up against a digital camcorder all week, that's her choice. I plan to settle into a beach chair, open a book, and rest. My mind takes a swing at making me feel guilty. No doubt, Ellis is on a ladder by now, pounding away his frustration at the imperfect world. I mentally bat away his image, and lean over to turn up the radio. Dad replaced the old radio with a satellite one, and we have it tuned to big band classics.

"Pennsylvania 3-5-0," March sings at the top of her lungs. Her scarf swirls in the wind. Hulking oaks arch over the two-lane highway, draped in Spanish moss finery like expectant brides. The air is heavy and humid—summer is on its way and will not be turned aside.

"Do you ever think you were born at the wrong time?" March asks me, pulling off her glasses and cleaning them with the hem of her halter top.

"I don't think so. What do you mean?"

"This music—it makes me think of another era. Ladies dancing, men smoking thin cigarettes. Romance. Everything seems so elegant, you know?"

I glance down at my faded T-shirt, jean shorts, and cheap flip-flops. "Yeah, I think I do. Elegance is something we don't see every day." But as I speak the words, I realize that March is elegant, pretty, sophisticated in a way that I am not. She's more like Mom—eager to try the latest makeup brands, more comfortable in a skirt than pants. She is earnestly feminine.

Sighing, March slides her glasses back into place. "Men today—they don't really get it."

A sports car passes us, a college-age guy at the wheel. When he pulls alongside, he gives both of us a long stare and then roars off. "Take a picture! It lasts longer!" March yells after the car, giggling at her middle-school insult. "See what I'm talking about? No romance."

Nodding, I glance over at my sister. I can sense she's holding something back. She has a look of concentration on her face, and I can only guess what she's dying to tell me. She's dropping out of college? She's pregnant? She's found the cure for cancer? None of these would surprise me. As she's gotten older, March has only become more excitable, more dramatic, more *alive*. I find myself trying to keep up so that I won't be left behind.

The Tap Island house was opened a few days ago in preparation for our arrival. The house's caretaker, a middle-aged man named Romero, unshuttered the windows, brought in a cleaning crew, and stocked the fridge with a pleasant selection of nonalcoholic drinks. March laughs when she opens the refrigerator door. "Ha! I'll bet that was Dad's idea. No beer. Well, I guess I'll have to find someone who is twenty-one to do the adult beverage buying."

I smile at March's naked hint. "We'll hit the Piggly Wiggly first thing."

I unpack my suitcase in the Yellow Room, while March selects the Pink Room across the hall. We've stayed in these rooms since we were girls. They are named after the dominant color of the room when my parents first purchased the house, but over the years, Mom has redecorated fairly extensively. The Yellow Room is more like a yellow and blue room, with a woven grass rug covering the hardwoods and deep-blue broadcloth curtain panels hanging from silver curtain rods. March's Pink Room has become more of a light pink and white, still girly enough for March, but not too sticky sweet.

I pour a glass of water and walk out onto the porch off the main living room. March joins me with a diet soda, and I feel us both start to relax. The ocean pounds mere steps in front of us, and the sun is still high in the sky, and I feel a million miles away from school, meetings, rallies, and Ellis. It's nicer than I thought it would be.

"Do you miss him?" March asks, reading my thoughts in that way she does sometimes.

"Ellis? I was just thinking about him."

"Well?"

I sit on a weathered Adirondack that Romero has outfitted with new, green cushions. "He was pretty ticked about me not wanting to go to Florida. I think he thought it showed a character weakness or something."

Waving her glass toward the ocean, March says, "Oh, tell him to get bent. Life's not always about slaving away for the oppressed."

I feel the urge to defend Ellis, but I realize March is right. I am right. It is good to get away for a little bit. I do miss his strong arms, though, and the way he can make me forget about everything on my to-do list with a soft kiss. I try to picture Ellis here, but I draw a blank. He and March don't really get along. "That's why I'm here, dear sis. I have my own mind. I am not owned by the poor and downtrodden, right?"

March clinks her glass against mine and settles into another chair. "I'm glad. You work so hard on the rare salamander thing, the misplaced immigrant workers, the homeless deer—I just think you should have more time for you."

I laugh at March mangling my on-campus causes. "You're one to talk. How many clubs are you in these days?"

"Ah, but there's the difference between you and me. I'm no longer running the show like I did in high school. I participate, I pitch in. I don't necessarily *lead*."

"There's a difference?"

"Oh yes, big sister." March takes her last swallow, knocking the ice cubes against her nose. "I have more time for my art. For Sanders."

"How is the mighty, mighty Sanders anyway?"

March stands. "Well, you know, it's here and there."

I take the hint, and stand up. March isn't ready to spill her beans. "What do you want to do?"

"Let's go swimming. And then to Dirk's for she-crab soup. Afterward, drinks at that new place where I can never remember the name? Down by the pier?"

"Jammer's." I wince at the tacky name, and the ten-dollar umbrella drinks it conjures. March loves those beachside bars with thatched roofs. I prefer a small, out-of-the-way place serving microbrews. "Okay, but if the water's too cold, I reserve the right to loll about in a beach chair until the sun sets."

"Deal."

We follow March's plan to the letter with one exception. While she reads a magazine on the beach, I give in to a restless feeling and decide to take a stroll. "Suit yourself," March shrugs and plants her feet in the sand. That's okay with me—sometimes I like being by myself. I take the time to think about everything: life, school, Ellis, graduation plans. Life after college will come, I tell myself, so I am forcing myself to think about it, just a little bit. Graduation is a mere three months away.

The sand is hard and the wind whips, full of springtime vigor. The water is a little cool, and my bathing suit is still damp from our brief swim. I hug my arms to my chest, and wish I had slipped on a T-shirt. Walking quickly, I look back over my shoulder. The sky is a gray-blue, and the ocean rolls by endlessly, showing off whitecaps. I am so glad we are here.

In recent weeks, Ellis has begun dropping our future plans into the conversation. He'll say things like, "When we're in grad school," or "When we both get our first nonprof jobs." At first, I felt a warm blush when he made comments like that. It seemed perfect— weren't we the couple everyone said was made for each other? We painted banners together, raised money for orphans side by side, and hammered on Habitat houses in the blazing sun. We made sense.

But then one day, after Ellis teased me about being a trust-fund kid, my hackles were really raised. "When we're married, you can just write checks to the causes I support and call it a day," he said, leaning forward to swipe a bite of my ice cream cone. We had met up on campus near the bookstore a few weeks before Spring Break.

"Excuse me?" I grabbed my cone out of his reach. It wasn't Cream Castle ice cream, so it wasn't any good, but I didn't want to share it with him.

"You know, if you're busy with other things. We'll just dip into the Ice Cream Trust Fund and support a small country or two."

Ellis was usually pretty cool about my family money. After all, I could touch maybe twenty bucks of it before I turned thirty-five and was allowed access to my trust fund. The family wealth had no presence in my daily life other than my school expenses being paid and I had a newish car to drive. My parents had made sure I knew the value of a dollar. And Ellis had always seemed to understand that for my family, money was just one of the things that made us who we were. But now, he was acting like a total ass. "So, what's this about me being busy with other things? I expect to have a job, you know."

"Sure. For a while, anyway. Hey—I know it's not a very fashionable thing to say these days, but a lot of women choose to stay home with the kidlets." Ellis stopped talking because he could see my face, but then he decided to be a total idiot and kept going. "So, if that's what we want you to do, I think it's great. You'll make a wonderful mother."

I stopped mentally planning my future with Ellis that day. I still loved him—he was my first real boyfriend—but I was starting to glimpse why people rarely married their first real boyfriend. Then I began to play the "what if" game. What if Ellis grew up a little, I grew up a little, and we worked things out? We had so much in common. He made me laugh, he was supercute, he had passions for things when most college guys just cared about beer. I knew all those things mattered, but I didn't know how much yet. On what scale did I need to measure my love for Ellis?

But for now, the beach is wide and I am practically alone. The large beach houses are my only companions and I give in to the urge to run down the gray sand, back to my sister, legs pumping over the hard, gray beach side by side with the saltwater. March is a tiny spot, way down the beach, and I run to her. When I am a hundred feet out, she lifts her head, spots me, and starts waving like we haven't seen each other in years. Sand kicks up on my back, on my hard-pumping legs. I run and run and run until I cover the distance between us.

Later, at Jammer's, March dumps her surprise on me. We carry two of the ten-dollar drinks, umbrellas included, as we migrate to one of the outside benches on the porch. Luckily, it isn't too crowded yet. Thumping popular music bleats out of the salt-encrusted speakers.

"I'm getting married, Mae Wallace," March tells me, her eyes sparkling with an early-drunk easiness. Since high school, my sister has figured out what cocktails will put her ample frame into a state of alcohol-fueled relaxation. She drinks one now, something with pineapple and rum.

"You're what?"

"I'm getting married! I mean, I think I am."

I glance down at her left hand even though I have been with March all day and I would have known if she were sporting a new engagement ring. Her hand is empty, except for a mood ring displaying a rosy pink color. "Sanders proposed? I thought you weren't that serious." I had only met Sanders Patterson twice, and that was enough. He screamed "old Southern family" with a side chaser of guns, hunting, and golfing. I wasn't sure what March saw in him.

March smiles, and shakes her head. "It's not Sanders," she says.

March has always loved surprising me. Once when we were kids, she and the groom saddled up our two horses. She then led them up to the house and lashed them to the hitching post out front. Pulling together a picnic full of strawberry soda and Pixie Sticks, March then sneaked upstairs to find me reading. With her round, brown eyes, she pleaded for me to come outside. When I did, I was tickled. She had even braided a few daisies into Raz's mane.

But now, March's surprises are bigger. And not necessarily improved.

"Who is this mystery guy?"

"Don't get a tone," March snaps. "I'm telling you the best news of my life and you're pulling a tone on me?"

I put down my drink and extract the miniature umbrella. Setting it aside, I turn to face March on the bench. "Why don't you start from the beginning?"

March gets a look on her face that can only be described as "lovestruck." Seriously, that's the word I would use. Her eyes are half-closed and her lips are slightly wet from the drink. I think her mouth even trembles. There might be something to this, I think.

"Well, I met Alex this semester in my film class."

"You met him this semester?"

"You've got that tone again."

I take a quick sip. "Sorry. Go on."

"He's like the best student in the class. He's made three short films already, using money he raised on his Web site. And he's brilliant. So deep. We really get each other, and our art."

"That's great, March. Really. Where's he from?"

"This little town in North Carolina. He sat next to me in film class and we just bonded right away. We have similar families and we look at life the same way."

I try to picture this movie-making Romeo who has clearly swept March off her feet. She falls hard, but even for my sister, this sounds a little serious.

"So we flirted all the first part of the semester, and then we were assigned to work on some scenes together. We spent long nights casting, rehearsing, and filming. It was thrilling and romantic, because I could feel that we were developing some intense bonds. Finally, one night over takeout, he just blurted out that he was thinking of me as more than a film-class buddy."

"What about Sanders? Did you break up with him?"

March wrinkles her nose and sips her drink. "Oh, him. Well, we just never had a spiritual connection, you know? Not like me and Alex. I swear, it's like we have the same brain sometimes."

"And?"

"No, I haven't told him. Not yet. I want to, but he's so traditional and all. It will probably break his heart. And I didn't want to dump him right before Spring Break."

This plan makes sense with what I know of March's romantic tangles. She usually keeps one or two guys waiting in the wings. She might not necessarily date them, but she develops emotional attachments so when Guy Number One is out of the picture, Guy Number Two steps into his spot. "Where is he, anyway?"

"Alex? He's in New York at an alternative film festival."

"No, I mean Sanders."

Sighing, March drains her drink. She's wearing dangly crystal earrings that sway when she talks. "Oh, he's probably climbing down from a deer stand about now."

"So, what's this about getting married?"

"Right. That's the best part. Before I left school to go home and borrow the car for our trip, Alex took me to our favorite little Italian bistro. They have the best eggplant parmigiana and little buttery rolls. Anyway, he pulled out a ring from his pocket—it was his grandmother's but he said I could have any ring I wanted one day when he had the money—and he asked me to marry him.

He even had a small camera going that captured the whole thing on film."

"What did you say?"

My sister gives me a look. "Well, duh, I said 'yes.' True love only comes along once in a while and when it does, you have to grab it."

The cocktail waitress takes our empties and March asks her to bring us another round. Without thinking, I calculate the sugars in the tall drinks. March doesn't count her carbohydrates like she should.

"So, why aren't you wearing his ring? Have you told Mom and Dad?" The big sister in me rears its head.

"One, because I need to release my current boyfriend before I announce my engagement—it's the polite thing to do—and two, are you nuts? They'll just say we're too young, we have two years of school left, blah blah blah."

A drunk-looking frat boy starts to walk over to our table. I turn my head quickly away, shutting off any opportunity for conversation. The guy gets the hint and walks on. "Not to be a fuddy-duddy, but Mom and Dad would have a point," I say. "Why not date for another year or so and then get engaged your senior year? Is there a big rush?" A huge part of me is relieved that March isn't going to be pulling on a white gown anytime soon. But another part of me is secretly entertained by her love life. My own is a watered-down imitation compared to hers.

"Mae Wallace, I don't expect everyone to understand, that's why we'll keep our engagement a secret. But you're my sister, okay? Try to be supportive." March's eyes fill with tears.

"March, being supportive doesn't mean not questioning you. Sometimes a big sister asks tough questions—in her own way."

"But we're so in love!"

"I know, and I think I understand. Well, sort of. I just don't know why you have to label it with such a huge commitment. Getting engaged is pretty big, you know."

The ocean seems calmer tonight, although the sea breezes are quick and warm. More tipsy people are crowded around us, waving glasses in the air and lighting up cigarettes. The music cranks up another notch. I don't know how much more Jammer's I can stand.

"I guess I feel like our love is powerful, and it's not going to change, so why not just embrace it? Just as we pursue filmmaking, we're pursuing our love." Shoving a lock of hair behind her ear, March gives me a direct look. "Does that make sense to you?"

It really doesn't, but at this point, I know better than to say so. I'll have to meet this Alex. Maybe he and March will have a storybook relationship and live in the clouds far above us sweating mortals. Maybe I'm jealous. I never think of Ellis the way March is thinking about Alex.

I decide to leave March's love life for safer topics. The alcohol can only fuel her dramatic side. I watch her dig around in her bag for a digital camera. She leans back to catch the attention of a guy in a red polo shirt and asks him if he'll take our picture. March and I wrap our arms around each other and tilt our heads to the center of the picture, like we have done for hundreds of shots. When she downloads the pictures and e-mails me a copy, I know what I'll see: our white straight teeth, the wide smiles of girls who are out for the night, and the open, sunny face of my sister. Mine will be a bit more closed, more suspicious as I consider the surroundings, the picture taker, and my own distracted thoughts on this night beside the sea.

FOUR

Life after College

The ladder sways as I climb to the top. I clutch the aluminum rungs, sure that my sudden death will come before the end of my shift. I just don't want to fall in front of Mrs. Banks or her three young children. I've climbed plenty of ladders, but that doesn't mean I like it.

"Then, just scoop up the leaves and drop them down below," I call out, using my gloved hands to clean out the clogged gutters. Big clumps of wet and decomposing leaves and sticks fall to the ground. Mrs. Banks probably has about six months of leaves up here, and her gutters are completely blocked. When I climb down from the ladder, she gives me a look.

"I ain't going up there."

"It's not so bad. Here, you try this gutter up front. It's easy to reach." The house is a few miles from downtown Asheville, in a new subdivision of ranch homes. Skinny poplar trees dot most of the small yards.

"My father, he could come over and do it for me," Mrs. Banks says, eyeing the white-painted gutters.

"I know, but didn't you say he has a bad back?"

Mrs. Banks sighs. "Yeah, he does. It wouldn't be right to ask him. I just wish Derek was around to do this for me. He used to take care of our rental, kept it looking nice."

I am quiet, knowing that her husband Derek has been dead about a year. Mrs. Banks is starting to see that she has to keep up her property on her own. Her gutters are useless, and the water is backing up, pouring off the house, and draining into her basement. She looks upset, but I have learned the look on her face will soon be followed by one of acceptance. It's one of the best things about my job. I help people keep and maintain their new homes—usually built by nonprofits for reduced prices and a long-time low interest rate—so that they don't lose them to foreclosure or neglect.

I teach homeowners not to ignore a five-dollar hose leak on a refrigerator because it could turn into a five-hundred-dollar repair if the floorboards rot out. I also lead seminars about financial matters—like the importance of paying the mortgage on time, every month. I work with immigrants to explain simple things we all take for granted: what temperature to set the thermostat, how to load a dishwasher so it is used most efficiently. Last week, I helped a woman with two small children cut back the overgrown weed trees by her front porch after a neighbor complained. It turned out the homeowner just didn't have the correct tools to do the job.

Mrs. Banks climbs the ladder unsteadily, and manages to clean out one section of gutter. She is breathing heavily when she comes down, but she looks pleased. Her oldest son offers to try, but she tells him he can when he's older. I work with her on a few more sections until I feel she gets the hang of dragging the ladder, extending it if necessary, and then climbing safely.

"Thank you, Mae Wallace, for spending your Saturday morning with us. I guess I just needed a kick in the pants. Waking up yesterday to all that water in the basement was a little scary," Mrs. Banks says.

"I was glad to come out. It's funny how a few leaves can mess up everything."

"You want some tea? I made a pitcher this morning." Mrs. Banks looks tired.

"I'd better get going. I have to work in the office this afternoon, answering the phones."

"All right then, you take care. I'll try not to call too much."

I walk to my car at the end of the drive. "Call anytime you want. That's why we're here."

Driving back to the office, I take a short detour to grab a sandwich and a brownie at June's Sandwich shop on Pack Square. June gives me extra pickles and a wink. "Working again?"

"That's right," I say. "Looks like you are, too, or I wouldn't have lunch made."

June wipes her forehead with the tail of her apron. "How else would I spend a Saturday? Don't have any use for relaxing."

"We're in the same boat. A day off—what's that?"

June laughs and goes back to the sandwich counter. Saturday is a busy day for tourists in Asheville, in town for tours at the Biltmore House or just shopping the art galleries and stores downtown.

Two blocks down from the square, I pull my car behind a renovated one-hundred-year-old bank building. Housing Help is located on the first floor. I gather up my lunch and push through the front door. The bell rings, startling Zelda, my coworker.

"Geesh! You scared me. We haven't had anyone come in here in more than an hour."

"Sorry, it's just me."

Zelda stands and gathers up her purse and day planner. "How'd it go with Mrs. Banks?"

"Pretty good. I got her on the ladder, and I think she can take it from there."

"Don't count on it. I'll bet she calls here again next month pretending not to know how to clean out her gutters."

I keep my head down and settle into my cubicle. Zelda is pretty cynical. She usually has to be talked into seeing the best in our clients. It was an eye-opener when I took the job right after college. Until then, I had only worked with idealistic students—myself included—and we thought we could save the world. Zelda has figured out we really can't. I still like to believe we can change it, if not save it entirely.

I've been with Housing Help for about a year and a half, and I still get excited when I work with a new client who is learning about home ownership. The nonprofit got its start when our founder,

Shana Wilkinson, discovered some people who have been approved for homes through well-meaning charities and other organizations are often unfamiliar with the basics of home ownership. My job is to work with new clients and basically do all the grunt work. Zelda writes grants and interacts with clients the least. Shana fund-raises and is the public face of Housing Help. Another staffer, Dean, does what I do, but he's been here for a few more years.

I take a bite of my sandwich and wave good-bye to Zelda. I'm not upset to see her go. I've described her to my family as someone with a little cartoon black cloud hanging over her head. I've never met anyone who fails to see the bright side in anything.

Shana has left a brief to-do list; other than that, all I have to do is answer the phones and help any walk-in clients. It's usually pretty slow, which can be good or bad. When I first started, I missed Goss a lot. I thought constantly about how the light on campus looked at a certain time of day, or what the air smelled like in the fall. I pictured my clubs and meetings going on without me, and it made me sad. I longed to be back in school. Maybe I should have stayed on for my master's? I thought like that all the time. Sometimes I was heartsick over missing school and my friends.

I even missed Ellis, even though we had broken up by the time we graduated. We spent the last few weeks of school hammering out our breakup. It was exhausting. Both of us knew, I think, that we just weren't right for each other for the long term. It was easy to think that, but telling our hearts to give up on companionship, comfort, and habit was another task altogether. I left Goss first, to head home for a week's vacation with my family before my job began. Ellis stayed at Goss for a few more weeks, wrapping up some fund drives and grant proposals. He then took a job in Florida for an Everglades reconstruction project. We exchanged a few e-mails and then one or two awkward phone calls. After that, nothing. If I am honest with myself, I know I still crave his companionship at odd moments. I wonder if he does the same.

The phone rang. "Housing Help." I chew frantically on the pickle crammed into my mouth.

"Sister!"

"March." It's so good to hear her voice. I haven't made a ton of friends yet in Asheville. College was different—people your same age were clustered everywhere. In my apartment building here in Asheville, there are maybe two other women my same age and neither one seems like she's looking for a friend. I have only dated two guys—both briefly. It was nothing to write home about, really.

"I was hoping I would catch you at work. I'm in Asheville!"

"No way."

"I'm telling the truth. Kowalski wanted to catch part of the film festival up here this weekend. Apparently, Daphne Crowder is going to be there and Kowalski practically worships her. I've never seen her work, but if it's anything like they say it is, I want to be there. Plus, my big sister lives in Asheville. Do I need an engraved invitation?"

I have no idea who Daphne Crowder is, but I don't care. I'll have company tonight. "Do you need a place to crash?"

"Of course. It's me and Kowalski and Vince."

"You and Vince are still together?"

"Yes and no."

I smile into the phone. I know there is a story coming. It will have to wait, but I can still look forward to it.

"Okay, I get it—trouble in paradise. Say no more."

March laughs. "You've got it. Did I ever tell you Kowalski and I were born on the same day? And only six hours apart."

"March, keep your eyes on the road. Please do not flirt with Kowalski with your boyfriend present. It's bad form."

"Oh, Kowalski? He's just a friend. You know, more or less."

"Come by Housing Help when you get downtown. I'm done at five."

"See you then, big sis."

"Can't wait. Bye, March."

We end up at the Fine Arts Theatre where Daphne Crowder is set to introduce her latest film. The crowd is a mix of Goth types and film nerds. We grab some local ale and settle into velvet seats near the front. Kowalski, thin, tall, and easy going, doesn't want to miss a glimpse of Daphne. March teases him, but I can tell she is a little jealous.

Vince and I share a bucket of popcorn. I like him. March has dated him on and off for about a year. He's not a film major like her ex-fiancé, Alex. I say a silent prayer of thanks. Alex turned out to be more of a drama queen than my sister. We found out shortly after Spring Break last year that Alex's grandmother's engagement ring was really from a pawnbroker and it had been slipped onto the fingers of more than one of his girlfriends. March made sure his camera was turned off when she had the pleasure of throwing the ring back in his face, literally. I think the ring left a scratch on his nose.

Vince, on the other hand, is an earnest marketing major with a good sense of humor. We get along, and he seems to genuinely care for March. "How's the job?" he asks me as the crowd hums around us. Miss Daphne is running late, to Kowalski's consternation.

"It's going well." I take a swig of my beer, a pale amber bock. "I like what I do, most of my coworkers are pretty cool. It's a good job."

"Think you'll stay there for a while?" The house lights dim and the curtains roll back.

"I probably won't. There's no place to move up. We're all kind of at the same level, except I got there last."

Vince grins. "Ah, low man on the totem pole."

"Exactly."

Daphne Crowder finally takes the stage. Kowalski inhales sharply and looks ahead. The filmmaker is striking. She wears a slinky black dress and thin slippers with some sort of embroidered jewels on them. Speaking into a microphone in low, hushed tones, Daphne begins to explain her art using words like "juxtaposition." When she uses it for the third time, I tune out. Glancing down our aisle, I notice Vince is listening patiently, Kowalski looks like he's been transported magically to heaven, and March is watching Kowalski. Poor Vince. I feel a surge of pity. Before the weekend's over, I fear he will be history.

The movie starts. I'm no film major, but I think it's about a train traveling on a long, black track in the middle of winter. Lights keep going on and off on the train, and after a while, the camera cuts to the inside and a sleeping woman in a berth. There is a burst of laughter when the train sways and the woman falls out of her berth. But the next shot reveals a man, not the woman, and he is holding a white pigeon. I don't get it.

March nudges me in the arm and sticks out her tongue. I nod in agreement. "Let's go talk in the lobby."

"This blows," she says, easing out of her chair.

We buy a couple of overpriced decaf coffees and find chairs in the movie theater lobby. "I know I should probably be all impressed, but I don't get films like that," March says.

"Won't you get kicked out of film class for saying such things?"

She laughs. "Probably. I don't care. I was thinking of changing my major. What can I do with a film degree, anyway?"

"March, I don't think you can switch your major with only one semester to go. Just a thought."

March sips her coffee and looks glum. "You're probably right. I hate it that I got so into films when I was dating Alex. It kind of set my career path, and now I don't know if I want to do that at all."

"Well, what do you want to do?"

"Marry Kowalski."

I look at my sister. I think she's probably half serious. My parents have asked me to tell on her if I ever hear again that she's engaged to a guy she's known for three months. Or to tell them if I think she's using drugs, drinking too much, or not taking her diabetes medication. When they first asked me to tattle on March with the Alex disaster, I nodded noncommittally. Now, I think I want to pick up my cell phone, place a quick call home, and tell all.

But instead, I try to play it cool, like I am a globe-trotting sister who dispenses sound wisdom. "Mrs. March Kowalski, huh? What's his first name again?"

"Heywood."

"Mr. and Mrs. Heywood Kowalski request the pleasure of your company at their son's baptism."

"Hey—I'm not thinking about kids, yet, sis. Just a little cottage for the two of us, surrounded by flowers—"

"Since when are you a gardener?"

"Since I hired a gardener in my little fantasy. You have a problem with that?" March gives me a pouty smile.

"No, just wondering where all this money is going to come from for the cottage and the flowers and the gardener. Just curious."

Rolling her eyes, March polishes off the rest of her coffee. "It might have escaped your notice, but Mom and Dad are loaded. Just a little bit."

March and I have always differed in our opinions of the family cash stash. I tend to think of it as a savings account, something for a child's college education or to purchase a first home. March likes to think of the money in our trust funds as financing the rest of her life. I have tried to tell her there's not enough money in the funds to do that, but she doesn't listen. She thinks that when she runs out, Mom and Dad will just lead her over to a hole in the backyard and dig up a few hundred gold ingots. At least, that's what I think she thinks.

I try changing the subject. "So, what about dear Vince, who thinks you are in love with him?"

March really tries to look contrite, but I think we know she's beyond it. "Dear Vince. I really do care for him, really I do." She stops, rubs the squinty part of her forehead. "But he's a little more like bread and Kowalski is a croissant!" She claps her hands together, delighted to have figured out her problems.

I think of Vince, abandoned in the dark movie theater, watching a movie about a train and a pigeon. I usually don't care about my sister's dumped boyfriends, but I truly like Vince. The few times I have met him, I could tell he was more special than the other March castoffs. There's something about his soft, brown eyes and kind smile. Kowalski seems like much more of a crowd-pleaser—the kind of guy who makes people laugh and then orders another round of beer.

"So, when does the big breakup happen? Not tonight—please don't make me suffer through a night of happy Vince and despondent Vince. Play nice this evening, okay?"

March looks down at her hands. She wears a plain, silver band on her right hand and a daisy ring on her left. "Well, I don't think I'll be doing anything tonight about this little problem."

"Why not?"

"Vince asked me before we left school if I would move in with him."

"Move in as in move in? Like live together, get engaged, end-of-story move in together?"

"That's how he made it sound."

I think I may be making the emergency call to Mom and Dad sooner than later. March has never lived with a guy before. She's always broken up or moved on before things got too serious. Alex lived in the dorms, so setting up housekeeping was never an option when they were engaged. I can't see March living with someone else, honestly. She is a closet hog, doesn't really like to cook or grocery shop. And she usually dates one or two people on the side until she moves them into first place. But also, knowing her, she'll move in with Vince, break his heart, and then move out to live happily ever after with Kowalski or whoever comes next.

"What do you think? You're not saying anything."

I stare across the small café table. "You can't be serious. You're talking about picking out china with Kowalski and you expect me to say you should move in with Vince?"

"I know, I know, stop making me feel guilty. It's just that he's offering something more than anyone else. Who knows if Kowalski even has feelings for me? What if I am having just a big crush?"

"The point is not whether you might make it work with Guy Number Two or not, it's how you feel about Vince. Do you love him? Do you want to marry him? Is living with him going to help you decide?"

"I don't think I want to marry him, not right now, anyway."

"Then, you know it's not fair to lead him on."

March examines her fingernails. "I guess moving in would kind of send that signal, huh?"

Sighing, I nod. March has a big heart, but she doesn't always put it in the right place. When we were kids, she would bring home ownerless dog after dog, or collect money for starving kids in Africa. But then she wouldn't feed the dogs and the donations would end up sitting on her dresser for months. My parents were always trying to instill some sort of responsibility in March, with less-than-stellar results. Still, March tended to draw all types of people to her and for good reason: she was the organizer, the go-to person, the "big idea" girl. It was her follow-through that was lacking.

"I think," I say carefully, "that you ought to end things with Vince, if that's where your heart is leading you, and then after an appropriate time period of weeks, not days, you should explore your feelings for Kowalski."

Shrugging her shoulders, March says, "There's not much time left in the semester for all of that."

"One day soon, your world will be ruled by years, not semesters or tests. It's called life, dear sister. You'll be one of us, soon."

March rolls her eyes and glances over to the concession counter. "Want some jelly beans? They have those gourmet ones you like."

"Come on, March, those things are loaded with sugar. You shouldn't have them."

For an answer, March stands and walks to the counter, where she orders a regular soda and a box of jelly beans. This makes me mad or sad, I can't tell which. I try to remember my mother's rules for dealing with March: one day, she'll take an interest in her health. One day, I'll save the world, I think to myself.

More and more people walk into the lobby from the theater, escaping the clutches of the art film. I catch sight of Vince looking for March. When he sees her, he looks happy and relieved. I feel for this nice guy and hope that March figures out things pretty soon.

The three of us gather near the restrooms to discuss the night's plans. I'm up for a late-night dinner. March wants to wait for

Kowalski and find out what he wants to do, and Vince suggests a stop at Blue's Taproom.

"They have about thirty kinds of microbrews," he says. "March, you could get that wheat beer you like so much."

"Yeah, I guess so," she says, flipping a piece of hair over her shoulder.

I figure March is still mad at me, but then I follow her gaze. Kowalski is in the lobby now, and he's not alone. He's leaning in closely to Daphne Crowder, filmmaker extraordinaire, who appears to like the attention.

March snaps her gaze back to Vince and me. "Let's get out of here, I'm tired of waiting."

If Vince has noticed my sister suffering from a serious case of the green-eyed monster, he's playing it cool. He nods and offers to carry March's tote bag for her. Seriously, he does. I watch all this in disbelief: March's jealously of Daphne; Vince's adoration for March; Kowalski's smitten, shy smiles. I feel like a scientist, calmly exploring the mating rituals of my companions.

We hurriedly decide on Blue's Taproom, where they serve both beer and pizza, so we'll all be able to get what we want. We tell Kowalski our plans. He mentions an "after-after party" but I can tell from my sister's face that she would rather die than attend a party where Kowalski and Daphne will be canoodling. We leave, with March in a huff. Kowalski leaves, too, with his arm around Daphne.

At Blue's Taproom, I try to comfort March without letting on to Vince why she is upset. "We don't really need an after party, you know. I'd rather be with good friends than a bunch of film nerds, anyway," I say.

Vince nods. "I can only hear the words 'my art' and 'juxtaposition' so many times, you know?" He shoots a glance over at March, who has her mouth turned into a permanent frown. She looks away.

I laugh, louder than is probably needed. March seems so glum. I tell her I need to use the restroom and give her a look, which she ignores. Since she won't follow me, I sit back down.

"Thought you had to use the little girls' room," Vince says, lifting his first glass of dark ale. Around us, waitresses dart in and out, delivering trays of microbrews and steaming pizza.

"False alarm."

March sips her wheat beer. "I don't get why people fawn all over that woman's work. I mean, a train? Like, who hasn't seen that metaphor a dozen times? It's like, 'Oh, my womb is birthing blah blah blah.'"

The bar is getting crowded. I hope our pizza comes soon because I am famished. Vince talks loudly over the crowd. "Yeah, trains. That was kind of dumb."

"You stayed for the entire thing, if I remember correctly," March says darkly, staring into her beer.

Vince swallows once, and then twice. I can tell he doesn't know how to handle the sullen side of March. I feel for the guy, like I do all of March's soon-to-be-discarded loves.

"I didn't want to horn in on your sister time," Vince says, his face a little flushed. "You two seemed to be bonding or something."

"Why don't you go get cozy with Daphne, maker of stupid train films? Everyone else is."

"Don't get mad at me. I didn't do anything wrong," Vince says.

I fight the urge to defend Vince. His only fault that I can see is being a bit of a doormat around my often flighty sister. I wonder if March will end it with Vince soon, now that Kowalski is out of the picture. My guess is she won't because of his offer on the table—moving in and setting up house is going to look tempting at this point. I sigh, and take a long sip of my hard apple cider. Sometimes, March wears me out. Since we didn't attend the same college, I only saw her love life from afar. Seeing it up close and personal makes me ill, like when you witness a minor car accident. You see the cars getting ready to collide, and your head screams, "No! No!"

Before long, March stops talking and Vince reacts by drinking more. I try limited attempts at conversation, but they fail miserably. Vince replies in one-word answers and signals for another beer. March fixes her gaze above my head. Finally, she grabs her bag and says she wants to go to my place and sleep. I nod and get out my wallet to settle up, ever the dutiful sister, but Vince stops me. "Hey, I want to stay here. Why don't you drink another round with me and then we'll meet up with March?"

"Whatever." March turns to go.

I am torn between wanting to help March and also realizing that there's nothing I can do. She's worked herself up into a fit—not over her boyfriend but another guy who apparently has his eye on someone else. My second apple cider makes me feel a little less like caring about March's drama right now. I throw my house keys to her. She has about six blocks to walk and the streets are full of people. March can take care of herself.

Later, when Vince grabs my hand in front of a darkened storefront and pulls me toward him, I will think, "I don't do things like this!" But I am a little buzzed, the apple cider in my belly making me feel oh-so-mellow. I don't do these types of things, no sir, but then I am, kissing, kissing, kissing my sister's boyfriend. Although I don't think of him like that because technically, March has moved on. I do recall this thought: *March can take care of herself.* Vince is drunk, upset, and tastes like wheat and pizza. I drink in his kisses and fumbling gropes because I miss this, I miss the kisses and sticky breaths, but most of all, I think if March can take care of herself, then I can take care of myself as well. It's fuzzy, ale-cloaked reasoning, but I grab it and run. Vince kisses me harder, my back is up against the metal security gate, and for a while, for a few sweet moments, it's all I know.

FIVE

After Asheville: Atlanta

From the twelfth floor of the World Matters building, downtown Atlanta spread out like a wild quilt of metal, concrete, and the city's fabled tree cover. A tangle of highways bordered one or two major construction sites that were sidled up next to the skyscrapers and high-rises. After a year on the job, I knew most of the buildings by sight. I imagined they had what this one contained: tall, glass elevators, numerous security personnel, hundreds of cubicles, even more workers working quickly and quietly.

My cubicle did not have a view. I was catching this glimpse of Atlanta courtesy of my boss's office that, like all the other bosses' offices, was situated on an outer ring around each floor. These offices had windows, doors, and space. The cubes, on the other hand, lived in an inner ring and were beige, doorless, and certainly windowless.

I missed windows, but I loved my job. I worked in the domestic area of World Matters, an international nonprofit development agency. My department enlisted big corporate firms to partner with us as we built homes. On any given day, I might talk to a vice president at a global high-tech firm or the marketing folks at the country's largest coffee-shop chain. The companies' large donations funded our work, and they received positive advertising and press for their contributions.

"Mae Wallace? Any word from Saber Auto?" My boss, Andreas, glided into the room. Andreas was beautiful. Her olive skin was touched with a bit of bronzer and lip gloss, and her suit was a perfect plum color. I sat up straight, hoping the touch of mustard I glopped onto my skirt at lunch wasn't noticeable.

"Just got the word. Our contact said they weren't sure we were the right fit for Saber's charitable 'angle.'"

Andreas frowned and settled behind her desk. I flipped open a notebook and sat in a chair opposite the desk. "That's great," Andreas said. "So people having decent housing is an 'angle' now?"

"Something like that."

"Did they happen to say what they wanted instead?"

Trying to stifle a small laugh, I checked my notes. "My contact suggested they might want to donate a vehicle from last year's line to a worthy recipient."

Andreas sighed heavily. "So, we're used to working million-dollar deals with companies and Saber wants to write off a used car? Give me a break."

"I thought our presentation clearly showed that we were looking for a serious partner for next year. Instead, we got shut out."

Andreas looked pensive. She swung her chair around to face the large windows overlooking downtown. "When are you taking off for your trip home again?"

"I was going to leave right after work. It will only take about three hours to get to South Carolina. My parents' retirement party is tomorrow evening."

"Why don't you get out of here an hour early? It will help you beat the traffic."

"Thanks, Andreas, but I want to work on this account. I have an idea."

My boss turned around, surprised. "If you have some other thought, go for it. I'm stumped—we made our best presentation and the president seemed to be on board. I just don't know what happened. I thought it was a done deal, to be honest."

"I'll let you know what I find out," I said, heading back to my cube.

The rest of the day flew by and soon I was headed up I-85 toward home. My red suitcase was placed squarely in the trunk, and my garment bag holding my dress hung neatly in the backseat. For the first time today, I allowed myself to think of the weekend and what I might find.

March would most likely be home by now. The house was probably bustling with caterers and flower deliveries. The retirement party was tomorrow, and tonight we would just have a small family dinner. I was looking forward to seeing Mom and Dad, but when I thought of my sister, there was a small pause.

The interstate narrowed from six lanes to two and soon I was rumbling through the Upstate of South Carolina. I passed the exits for Anderson, Clemson, and before too long, I turned off toward Henderson. It had been a while since I went home, and the feeling was surprising. I couldn't wait to see our house, and the castle. My horse Raz would be out in the pasture, and since he's in retirement, I wouldn't bother him for a ride.

Atlanta was exciting, bustling, fun. I had made friends there, especially at work, where I found a lot of people like me. We all wanted to save the world and working at World Matters seemed like a good way to go about it. There were a lot of nonprofits in Atlanta—I was always running into someone who worked for health care, housing, disease prevention. The loneliness I had in Asheville was slipping away. I knew that Vince had a lot to do with that.

After our impromptu make-out session that night almost two years ago, Vince and I became a couple. Unfortunately, he lives in Charlotte, and we don't see each other as much as we want to. He's making his way in banking, and although there are plenty of banking jobs in Atlanta, we haven't really broached that subject. If he moved here, we both know we would be taking a bigger step. Bigger than both of us, really.

March still hung in the air between us. After that night in Asheville, we slinked down to my apartment, my face red from Vince's light beard stubble. We even held hands, although it seemed like a horrible thing to do. But I was stubbornly unmoved about March's feelings that night. Something inside of me did not want to be the good sister who made all the bad things go away.

March, of course, was oblivious to our guilty looks and furtive glances loaded with some sort of meaning. She broke down in front of me and Vince, crying about Kowalski and how he had hurt her. Vince took it stoically, tried to comfort March with awkward pats, and then suggested they part ways. March agreed, to my relief, and when she had crashed on the couch, Vince and I slipped out on the balcony to talk about our future plans. I felt awful and wonderful. We kept seeing each other, and I only told March about it much later, later than I knew was right and fair.

My cell rang with Vince's ringtone. "Hey! I'm a few miles from home."

"Excited about seeing your folks?" Vince's gentle voice came over the line.

"Yeah. It should be a busy weekend. Wish you could be there." I stopped talking because we both knew why he wasn't on his way from Charlotte to meet me.

"Well, you know how things are. You'll have to fill me in on how much ice cream was consumed."

"What are you doing this weekend? Got a game?"

"I'm afraid soccer will have to wait. I have to work all weekend. End of the quarter reports and all."

I laughed. Vince worked hard and was on his way up at the bank. "I'll think of you when I'm stretched out in the chaise lounge in my parents' study, reading a book and eating bon bons."

"The life of an ice cream heiress. We should all be so lucky." Vince inhaled sharply. "I miss you a lot, Miss Cream Castle. Can you come up to Charlotte next weekend?"

"I think I can. Let's talk more on Sunday. I'm home now." We said our goodbyes and hung up.

The castle came into view, and with it, the pasture and the house. I was happy, happy to be home and happy to celebrate with my parents. They sold Cream Castle to a national ice cream company, and they were retiring. I was proud of them—not everyone gets to follow their dream the way they have for all these years.

Still, it would be strange not to have the ice cream company in the family. But neither March nor I wanted to be a part of the business. After college, March landed a job like only March can. She met Martin Trambeaux, a renowned documentarian who was getting ready to launch a three-film series about the plight of an endangered coastal duck. March was hired as his assistant, but she's already moved beyond that and will actually direct some filming, besides doing all sorts of other documentary stuff like fund-raising and marketing. I don't always know what she is doing, but I know she's happy doing it. Martin is a safe, crusty sixty-year-old, so I don't anticipate hearing that March is running off with him any-time soon.

The last time I talked to March was about a month ago. I was busy, she was busy—I could make excuses, but the truth was, Vince had cast a shadow between us. It was something that I felt guilty about one day, and indifferent the next. After watching my sister explore two dozen relationships a year, was it so bad that I wanted a little piece of that happiness?

To be honest, I never saw the thing with Vince lasting this long. After that weekend in Asheville, he finished his semester at school, sneaking up to see me almost every weekend. We didn't tell March even though she had moved on to her next boyfriend, the bean roaster at the local coffee shop. She seemed to be over

Vince, a fact that Vince himself knew deep down, even when he asked her to move in with him. He told me he was searching for something that would keep her close, something that would get her attention.

My mother walked out of the house and waved happily. My dad was not far behind her. When I put my arms around my parents, I was reminded how much I love them, and how they felt frailer to me. Their aging surprised me from time to time. I still saw them as they were when I was eighteen and heading reluctantly off to Goss. They knew better, they usually did, and I felt a rush of gratefulness.

"Mae Wallace, did you have a safe trip? We're so glad you are home." My mom kissed my cheek and hugged me close. Dad followed, grabbed my luggage, and we walked back toward the house, arm in arm.

"We're having a fish and oyster stew in honor of your sister's documentary. But no duck—I promised," my father laughed.

"Is March home? I don't see her car in the drive."

"She ran into town to refill her prescription," my mother said, and her lips twitched just a bit. "She forgot her medicine. She left it in Orlando."

I let this bit of information slide. What it meant was that March showed up at the house without some or all of her meds— high blood pressure, diabetes, you name it. My mother asked and now March was at the drugstore. I felt a rush of irritation. March still hadn't learned to handle her health. As she got older, it worried me more. For a minute, I allowed myself to see our younger selves riding across the main pasture astride Butter and Raz. Our ponytails bounced in rhythm to the horses' canter. We were so close, or were we? Was childhood something I made up, or did it really happen as I remembered?

The house smelled delicious, and mom had decorated for fall with gourds and leaf wreaths. My parents seemed relaxed, happy. I thought retirement would agree with them. In the kitchen, I joined Mom for a glass of wine. "So, any first retirement plans?"

"I believe we'll do a few projects around the house, for starters. I've wanted to redo the downstairs bedrooms and that awful half bath near the living room."

"I thought you would travel—you know, see Bora-Bora and Paris, stuff like that."

Mom took a sip of her wine. Her hair was highlighted a pretty brownish-red and she still had her trim figure. I made a silent wish to age as gracefully as she had. "After so many years of being in charge of a company like Cream Castle, I think just dropping everything and traveling would be hard on your father. He's used to having a list of things to do, and people to supervise."

I laughed. "You just don't want him to supervise you like a new flavor rollout."

"It has crossed my mind that too much togetherness could be a bad thing," she said. Mom stirred the stew and checked the bread in the oven. "So, are you and March talking more?"

I groaned inwardly. My mother had made no secret of the fact that she wished March and I would kiss and make up. I had told her it's not that easy. I wanted to explain that I was stubbornly holding on to something wonderful, something I had never had, even if it rankled my sister. And I couldn't explain that I thought

March was enjoying playing the role of the victim a little too much.

When I finally told March about Vince, she took the news hard. I drove up from Atlanta and found her packing to move home from school for a few weeks before her job began. I stood in her apartment, folding shirts into boxes and wiping down the counters, looking for a way to start the conversation. Bart, her coffee-bean-roaster boyfriend, had just stopped by to take a few pieces of discarded furniture. "See you later, baby," he said, pulling her close. As he walked out of the door of the apartment, Bart pulled a folded piece of paper out of his back pocket. "I wrote you a poem. Read it later, okay?"

"That was sweet," I said, when Bart had left.

"Yeah, he's always writing me poems and little stories for me. I told him he could be a writer, a real writer, but he doesn't have that much ambition, you know?" March went through a stack of film scripts, tossing ones she didn't want.

"Guess you won't be seeing him again?"

"Probably not. We both knew it wasn't something that was going to last. At least, I knew it. I think Bart did, too. He'll probably seduce a sophomore summer school student next week." She gave a small smile.

"Are you excited about learning all things duck?" I settled down onto the couch.

"Yes and no. I'm thrilled to land this job—I know how lucky I am—but I'm also nervous. Martin is famous, sort of demanding from what I can tell, and we'll be spending a lot of time in hot, sticky swamps. I'm not sure about that, you know?"

"You'll do great. You always land on your feet," I said, meaning every word.

"Hopefully so. Hey, you know, I think I'll get to Atlanta a lot and we can see each other. Martin has several investors there and we have to schmooze them from time to time." March sat down on the couch beside me.

My heart took a downward turn. I needed to tell March my news, or she would show up on my doorstep and find Vince eating breakfast. "Hey sister, I have something I want to talk to you about."

"What's up? Tired of moving my junk around? We can go get lunch. I'm starving."

I took a deep breath and then just said it: "March, I have been seeing Vince for a little while. I think we're probably going to keep dating. I wanted you to know."

Outside in the parking lot of March's apartment complex, cars and people went by the window. Everyone was moving boxes and furniture. Girls wore halter tops in the sunshine, every guy had on an old ball cap, or that's the way it looked to me as I stared out of the window. I wondered idly if March was going to take the pretty blue flowered curtains.

March leaned toward me, her brown hair swinging over her shoulder. "Vince? You're kidding. My Vince?"

This reference bothered me. I knew they dated for a semester, but he had been mine for just as long. Not since Ellis had I been in a relationship that meant something. "Yes, we're seeing each other."

"Is this why he broke up with me? He was dating my *sister*?" March fairly shrieked the word.

"March, you know that's not true. You broke up with him in

Asheville the weekend you came to visit me with Kowalski. Remember? You cried all over my living room in front of Vince."

My sister waved her hand impatiently. "Vince knows that's how I am. I have crushes. Kowalski was a crush."

I did not want to get into their past, but March was dragging me there. "Look, March, you had one foot out the door when things blew up with Vince. I didn't take your boyfriend."

"Sounds like you were waiting in the wings." March sniffed and looked away, toward the window with the blue curtains.

I had already decided not to tell March about kissing Vince before they were technically broken up. "I wasn't. Vince and I started dating after that weekend, after you were through with him and onto whoever."

"Bart. I started dating Bart. Who is a damn sight more loyal than my own sister."

I felt tears prick my eyes. This was going as badly as I thought it would. March liked to be the center of attention. Her older, quieter sister couldn't have something more torrid, something more racy, could she? I knew the answer was no. And that's when a small gulf between us began to open and pull apart a little farther until it was two years later and things weren't terrible, but they weren't the same.

Since that conversation, I deliberately had not flaunted my relationship with Vince. I had gone about my life, mentioning him from time to time, but never bringing him home for Christmas or family celebrations. When March visited me in Atlanta, Vince stayed in Charlotte. We didn't speak of him, which made me sad. Vince was a huge part of my life: he was funny, smart, thoughtful.

I knew we were heading toward an engagement, but I couldn't even think about how it would work. Part of me knew that March had made this huge mythology of their past relationship and she had forgotten that it was a bit shallow, a bit grasping. Vince never pulled any punches about this with me. He told me how infatuated he was with March and how she delighted him with her vivaciousness. I could see it—a lot of guys fell for March that way. But Vince told me he trusted me in a way that he did not trust March. "She was always looking for the next guy," he said.

My parents' front door opened and I knew my sister was home. I left the kitchen where my mother was ladling soup into earthen bowls and walked quickly to the entry hall. March took off her coat and tossed her keys onto the black wooden hall table.

"Hey, sis," I said, waiting to see March's mood.

"How was your trip up?"

"Nice, the usual boring I-85."

We stood there, and I saw the quick glance March gave my left hand. There was no ring there, of course, but she checked to be sure.

"Did Mom tell you? I adopted a dog," March said.

"No way! That's so cool. What about traveling, though? What are you going to do with him while you're on the road filming?"

A look of annoyance flickered across my sister's face. "Her name is Posey and she's going to stay with Mom and Dad this fall while I travel. After that, I'm thinking of giving the duck project the heave-ho. Crawling through swamps is getting old."

"What kind of breed is the dog?"

"She's a mutt, but she doesn't know it, so don't tell."

I laughed for the first time, and I reached my arms out for March. She returned the hug, and I inhaled the clean, shiny smell of her hair. This was my beloved sister; I just didn't know how to make things right again.

Dinner was everything I knew about home: warm soup, crusty bread, good conversation. My parents were in great spirits. I thought they might be a bit melancholy over seeing their life's work sold to a faceless corporation, but they seemed remarkably reasonable.

"Cream Castle was a wonderful ride, but with you girls in the duck and house business, I knew there was no one who would care about it quite like I would," Dad said. "It was better to sell."

"And you got like a ton of money," March giggled. I never asked my parents the terms of the deal, but apparently my younger sister did.

"March, that's tacky," Mom frowned.

"Still, it's true. When can I get a villa in France?" March reached for another piece of bread.

"When we're dead and gone and you inherit the gold bars hidden under our bed."

"Ooh! Gold bars! Excuse me, I have to go upstairs to your bedroom and look for something," March said playfully.

Dad laughed. "Hold on, toots, we plan on being around for a long, long, time."

This felt more like my family, and I held a hope that March would tease me again like she used to, instead of regarding me as the person who wounded her beyond measure. I wondered if she was dating anyone. There was no way I was going to ask. I missed hearing about March's crazy man exploits. It used to be a way we bonded until I crossed the Vince line.

"So, what are you girls wearing for the party tomorrow?" Mom asked over dessert of sliced mango and strawberries.

"I have a red dress cut down to here," March whispered, pointing to her belly button. She giggled again.

"I brought a black dress I wore in a wedding last fall."

Mom nodded. "Are you still going with me to Fred's in the afternoon?"

"As long as he doesn't give me a bouffant like he did for my first prom." March shuddered.

"Yeah, well, at least he didn't burn off your bangs with a perm in the fifth grade," I said.

Mom and March laughed. "That was pretty bad. He's much better now," Mom said.

"I hope so." I played with my slippery mango slices. "Do you need any help in the morning?"

Mom shook her head. "I decided to splurge a little. We have a party coordinator and caterer, and all I have to do is show up in my own living room."

Half of the people in town, plus employees, had been invited to the party. It would be one of the biggest social events in Henderson.

"Hey, March, where's your dog?"

"Posey's in the barn. Mom said she had to stay there until after the party."

Mom said, "I had the house cleaned from top to bottom this week. Dogs are invited to party in the barn until Sunday morning. Then they can come inside."

"Poor Posey." I stabbed the last piece of mango.

After dinner, March and I wandered over to the barn. The tall clapboard castle glowed softly under the spotlights, and the Cream Castle flag snapped back and forth in a persistent evening breeze. I heard a low whinny. Raz knew we were here. After him, Butter neighed in reply.

We both struggled with the main gate, rolling it back on the hundred-year-old hinges. A few dog yelps greeted us from the first stall. March released a brown and white fur ball that leaped to kiss her on the mouth and then fell at her feet in submission. Bending down, March rubbed Posey, cooing to her all the time.

"Isn't she beautiful?"

I couldn't really tell. Posey was all motion, fur, and tongue. When she finally discovered there was someone else besides March, she walked over and sat, regarding me seriously, her tail beating a swath of sawdust.

"Hello Posey," I said, and like that, I became her new best friend. She nuzzled against my leg, her tail beating the air relentlessly. "Where on earth did you find her?"

"In a swamp. Where else do I hang out?"

"Seriously?"

"Yeah. We were going into this place where some new duck had been spotted or hadn't been spotted—I can't remember; the details run together—and I heard this whimpering from a burned-out cypress tree. I nudged our boat closer, sure that we were about to get attacked by some sort of man-eating bat, and there was Posey, hiding in the tree, soaking wet, lost, and miserable."

"That's awful! How did she get in the middle of the swamp?"

"Some bastard put her there. It's the only answer." March's face was set with a flash of anger.

"Thank goodness she's loved now." I sat in the sawdust, petting Posey's soft fur. She began to make low grunts, and closed her eyes.

"Careful, she'll follow you home now. She's already forgotten me."

"Nah, she's your baby. I'm just an available pair of hands."

March sank down beside me. I could sense she wanted to talk to me about something. Part of me hoped she'd spill the beans about a new boyfriend, but those days seemed far behind us now.

"So, how's Vince?" March traced a pattern in the sawdust, and avoided looking into my eyes.

"Good. He's been promoted at work again."

"He was always smart."

"Yeah."

From another stall, Raz thumped his door, making a hollow sound. He wondered why we hadn't brought the party to him. I pictured his handsome face with his now-gray muzzle and sighed. We were all getting older. It didn't seem fair. Even March had a gray hair or two tucked behind her ears.

"So, are you two getting serious?" March looked over at me. I couldn't read her expression.

"I think so." I took a deep breath. I was not sure how this would go. "We have talked about making things more permanent."

Coaxing Posey into her lap by clucking softly, March rubbed her hands roughly through the dog's fur. Posey opened her eyes, surprised, and then surrendered. "What a life she has, this dog," March said.

"March, I don't know how—" I began.

"When we were on the trail of the coastal duck down in Florida, Martin could sit for hours not talking. At first it drove me crazy, and I would make up things to talk to him about. Or I would bug the cameraman, Len, just to hear another human voice. But after so many months, I grew to appreciate the silence. It has a life of its own, silence."

Crickets chirped outside the wooden walls of the barn. I knew the sound was the same heard more than one hundred years ago. Perhaps two sisters sat in this same place in another century, scratching a dog and talking. Maybe there was something between them, something they didn't talk much about no matter what happened.

I let it go. That's how I was. I didn't dig too deeply, even though I might have wanted to. For years, I had let March set the pace of things: the family discussion, the night's events. I had even let her set this painful rift we had occurring right between us. Did I not care? I knew I did, but sometimes leaving things up to March seemed easier. I found myself taking that easier path now, winding my way up and out of sight.

I woke up the next morning in my old room, stretching under the covers. The heat was on, giving the bedroom a cozy warmth. It must have gotten chilly overnight. I turned over, hoping to sleep a little more. From downstairs, I heard the whine of a vacuum. My mother, no doubt, had discovered some forgotten corner of the house that did not get a thorough cleaning. I should really help her, but the bed felt so comfortable. I curled on my side, enjoying a real mattress for once. At home in Atlanta, I slept on a ratty futon mattress. It was all I could afford right now on my do-gooder salary.

The vacuum shut off, and I heard my father's voice and then what sounded like a deliveryman. A truck backfired, and doors slammed. Sleep was a memory. I sat up in bed, rubbing my face. It was a little after nine. I wondered if Vince was awake yet in Charlotte. I glanced over to my cell to make sure it was turned on. He probably wouldn't call me, though, since he might find me with March. He didn't like to come between us, even if it was a phone call. Vince had only seen March once or twice since they broke up and it was as awkward as anyone could have wanted. Part of me wished they would both get over it, but March seemed to like playing her part and Vince was so gentlemanly as to let her. It was my own little private drama. I contemplated sinking back under the covers.

March was probably still sleeping. She had a week off from Duckworld and I would bet she was dreaming soundly, glad to be away from the swamps and editing rooms. Maybe I would make some waffles. As kids, March loved it when I made breakfast. She would pour the orange juice and sit at the kitchen counter while I baked scones or muffins. She was part tester, part spectator.

I pulled on an old fleece robe from my closet. Even though I had been gone from this house for years, some of my old clothes still lingered. One day, I should clean out my old stuff, but I thought my mother kind of liked having part of us in the house. Wrapping the robe around me, I shuffled downstairs, hungry and needing a cup of coffee. Mom passed me on her way upstairs, smiling and showered. She loved parties and was looking forward to the house being packed tonight. Dad, sitting at the table reading the paper, was a little more ambivalent. I would bet he would have been happy just having a few friends over to celebrate.

"Morning, sleepy. There are some scones on the counter."

I grabbed a scone and poured some coffee in a brown mug with yellow flowers. "These mugs are new?"

"Your mother threw those."

"Pardon?"

"Her ceramics class. She made four mugs like that. Don't tell her, but I think they look a little retro. Too 1970s for my taste."

I considered the mug in my hand. "I think it's charming."

Dad shrugged and went back to his paper. I knew he was secretly pleased with Mom's interests, from flower arranging to quilting. She was always looking for something new to do, a hobby to conquer.

"These scones are great. I'd better put them away or March won't have any," I said, reaching for my second.

"March? She's up and out already. She went to see Butter. Took her a mess of carrots."

This surprised me. March liked to sleep in. Plus, it was cold outside. I could feel a chill in the kitchen from all the windows that faced the pasture. My thoughts turned to Vince. Maybe this would be a good time to call him—when I didn't have to worry about March walking in on our conversation.

Walking over to the French doors off of the kitchen, I took in the pasture and the long sloping hill toward the barn. Autumn had touched the nearby woods with a perfect hand, each tree blazing with yellow, red, or ochre. The barn stood tall on the hill. Before long, a tourist or two would invariably drive down the lane to take a few pictures.

From my viewpoint I could see Posey barking with happiness as she trotted out of the barn. March was right behind her, but she was riding Butter. That was March, always surprising me. The most surprised creature had to be Butter. Even from the house, the horse looked fat and out of shape. She was probably in no mood to take a ride this morning. She knew Raz was tucked inside his stall, munching on hay while she was going to be clipping through the damp pasture grass. Poor Butter.

"Look, Dad, it's March. She's riding Butter."

Dad frowned and glanced up toward the window. "I wish she wouldn't. Butter hasn't been ridden since spring or before. Your mother said she was starting to act senile."

"Can horses be senile?"

"You know what I mean. She was acting like she didn't have any sense. Horses are like people. They can get irritable." Dad stood from the table, leaving the paper open to the opinion section. "You're not going out on Raz, are you?"

"Nope. He's in retirement." I felt a chill and tightened the robe around me.

From the window, we watched Butter duck and shy at a few

birds that flew up and out of the pasture. March dug in her heels, sitting in her seat squarely and confidently like we were taught. Posey ran ahead of them as they broke into a trot across the field. I thought they were planning to come up to the house and ride past the kitchen windows. March knew I would be awake by now, and she probably wanted to show me how she was her own person. She didn't need me to make her waffles anymore.

And then we saw, my father and I, Butter shying once again in the middle of the pasture. Posey flushed out something, maybe a fox, and she pounced, delighted. But Butter was having none of it. She balked, March dug in her heels, and then Butter did what I thought an old, chubby horse with barn envy could not do. She bucked once, then twice, and she was rid of her childhood friend. March's head slammed back against her shoulders and I felt, rather than saw, her body falling over the horse's broad rear end. Butter gave one more buck and March was free, free to fall into the brown and green grasses covering the field like a morning gown. March sank down into the grasses while the brown mug I held shattered against the kitchen floor.

SIX

My first home on Langdon Island was a beach bungalow on Sea Street. The front of the home looked lovely, with camellias and fragrant gardenias spilling over the front walk, but the back, where I lived, was a dump. My section seemed ready to fall off into the sea-oat covered sand dunes at any moment. The floors didn't just creak, they moaned. And the electricity flickered with any breeze strong enough to move the dozens of wind chimes anchored under the eaves. Hale insisted my house had character; I said I was waiting for it to fall down or burn down, I wasn't sure what would come first.

I rented it over the phone, before I moved down to Langdon, and I often regretted it in those first few days. But my cautious nature did not want to show up in a new town without a place to stay. Having my name on a lease, however long distance, seemed preferable to rolling into Langdon and just knocking on doors. Hale laughed and said this was a sign of my proper upbringing. He, the type not to write prompt thank-you notes, probably moved to Langdon with nothing more than a tent and a gallon of fresh water. Hale nodded when I told him my theory. "Didn't even need the water," he said.

But I ended up keeping the house. For one, the rent was super cheap, and I was living off my scant savings. I didn't want to sponge off of my parents after everything they had been through with March. For another, it was at the end of the beach, far from the strip and the summer crowds. I felt free to stay in my pajamas until four in the afternoon if I wanted to. Or eat chocolate chip cookies for breakfast without troops of cheery tourists tromping past my windows on the way to the beach. Up at our end of the island, there was just a bunch of retired neighbors in weather-beaten houses, and Hale.

Development had arrived on Langdon Island. The new bridge was a response to the acres of new condos on the west end of the island. Already, a shiny new grocery store had planted itself off of Sea Street. It was flanked by a video rental store, a nail salon, and a fast-food restaurant or two. I tried to avoid going that way, unless I had to leave the island, and I didn't really even need to do that. All of my business was concentrated on the eastern end of the island.

"We should all band together and save our neighborhood from

the roar of the bulldozers and the din of the nattering crowds," Hale told me one morning a few weeks after we met. I was sitting on the back deck, looking at the waves roll one after another at high tide. With only a thin scrap of dunes between my house and the ocean, I felt as if the Atlantic was in my backyard. Tall sea oats rattled in the wind, joining the chimes on the house.

"You, me, and who else?" I asked.

Stretching out on the weathered porch boards, Hale leaned back on his arms. "Our neighbors, the OFDs." Hale liked to call our neighbors the Old Fuddy-duddies. While some people had colorful and loving older neighbors, kind of like foster grandparents, we had crusty types who complained if your grass looked the least bit shaggy.

"Are you kidding? The OFDs will sell out the first chance they get."

"I wouldn't be too sure," Hale said with a lazy smile. "After all, they like most to muck up the works. If the developers want a piece of our little neighborhood, then the OFDs will delight in telling them 'no.'"

"Well, I don't own this house, anyway, so I guess I have no say."

"Yeah, well I don't own mine, either, so I guess I would need to take it up with my landlord, Mr. Forrester. I just think we should fight it, you know? This little street, all ten houses, could be bought and torn down for some skyscraper of a hotel. I would rather die. I like it quiet and peaceful. That new bridge is bringing way too many people to the island. It's like a welcome mat: 'Hey—we have a faster way to get to Langdon now, come on over.'"

Then we were quiet because I think I knew what Hale was

turning over in his mind. He was thinking of the new bridge, the old bridge, and what he had lost. The bridge was just miles away, but it loomed over us; it was a part of every thread of Hale's life.

I decided to change the subject. "Forget developers. What do you want to do for lunch? I'm not due out at the Sea Villas for two hours."

"Today physical therapy or aqua art therapy?"

"Neither. This afternoon she's getting a haircut and a mani-cure. I get the same treatment, too. It's supposed to help her feel normal."

Hale sat up, rubbing his face. He chose his words carefully. "That sounds, well, strange, but interesting."

"I know. I am willing to go with whatever they say at this point. Nothing's working, so why not try whatever?"

We decided to hit the taco stand three blocks away. Senor Taco was run by a Coast College dropout named Terrence. He appar-ently bought the taco stand and all of the equipment at one of those postal auctions where they sell off stuff that was undeliverable. He also got a truckload of stuffed animal panda bears at the same sale.

"Hale! Mae Wallace! What's going on?" Terrence bent down to the screened window, not an easy thing to do with his tall frame.

"Just looking for something for lunch," Hale said, smiling.

"Man, you've come to the right place. I got tacos, tacos, and more tacos."

As Terrence started working on our meal, Hale and I helped ourselves to the vat of sweet tea on a nearby picnic table. I was so new to the island that the saltiness, the rawness of the air, still took me by surprise. Goss was about an hour from the ocean, so the smell was familiar, but Langdon was right on top of the Atlantic. The air held a flavor that was at once immediate and clingy, like a dress worn for too long or a pair of too-tight shoes. I was still figuring out if I liked it.

We sat down at one of the weathered picnic tables. I found Hale's company reassuring. So much of the past six months had been foggy. I had wandered the halls of three hospitals, one rehabilitation center, and the offices for March's out-of-state health-insurance headquarters. March was getting the best care in the country, had been seen by the best specialists for spinal cord injury. Her prognosis was clear, but it was something my parents could not handle. On some days, I accepted it while on others I wanted to scream at the gray ocean outside my house. I was learning that sometimes, that was the way things worked out. Your only options were seeing things for the way they were or yelling until your throat turned raw.

"I love this place," Hale said between mouthfuls of his crunchy taco. "You know, if the developers dance their evil dance, Terrence's landlord will sell out and throw him off this little plot of land. No more tacos."

I looked around the little scrap of land near the gas station and an old Laundromat with a fading vintage sign. Hale was probably right. The land would fetch way more than the rent for a battered taco stand that ran on a gasoline motor.

"What are you working on this week?"

Hale said, "I've got a commission for the Garden Club. They

want a painting for over the mantel at their fancy garden clubhouse. I've been told to match the sofa and the drapes."

"Ah, art by committee, how lovely. Very deep."

"Oh, you know, chintz is very fashionable. I'll be cutting edge."

Laughing, I took a sip of my sweet tea. "You should just paint the room, you know, paint the couch and the drapes and give that to them."

"I don't think they would get the irony, but it's a good idea."

Hale lived as an artist, which is to say he lived cheaply with few creature comforts. He rented a small bungalow on the end of Sea Street where he had lived with Ruth. The house was painted a deep red and had a crushed shell driveway and several hearty palmetto trees. The best feature about the house was the back deck where Hale sometimes sat for hours, looking at the ocean. That's where I first met him. I lived next door, and my second night in the house, the power went out. I found out later that I had tripped a breaker when I dared to use the microwave and the toaster oven at the same time.

After poking around the kitchen and looking for the circuit panel, I was stuck. I couldn't find it anywhere. I went out onto my rickety deck to think, and to my right, I saw Hale sitting on his deck next door. He had what looked like a drawing pad in one hand and a piece of charcoal or chalk in the other. I waited for him to begin to draw, but he just sat there, looking over the waves. I didn't know him yet, of course, didn't know the burden he was carrying. I probably thought he was just lost in thought or making his grocery list in his head. To be honest, I was so wrapped up in my grief that I failed to notice other people had problems or needs.

But I did want my power back on, so I called out to my neighbor. "Hello!"

Hale didn't hear me at first, so I repeated my greeting. "Hello!" His head snapped up and for a moment, I caught a glimpse of sadness in his face, a naked and unshared part of whatever it was he was thinking. I felt awkward and wished I could rewind the last minute or duck back inside. But he had seen me waving from my unpainted and haphazard deck to his painted, tidy one.

"Can I help you?" Hale was polite, but even then, he seemed to be on autopilot.

"Ah, I was hoping so. Do you know where they keep the circuit box in these old homes?"

At this, Hale smiled a bit. He put down his sketchpad and stretched his arms over his head. "It depends. Some of them are in the attic or under a cabinet. Most of the houses on Sea Street were built before such helpful things as codes or common sense."

"I think it might be a mystical thing. It appears I don't have a circuit box."

Standing, Hale asked, "Do you want me to come over and take a look? It would be no problem."

There is something about the laid-back nature of a beach community that makes me relax. In Asheville or Atlanta, I would have never solicited help from a complete stranger, even if he were a neighbor. But with the roar of the surf in my ears, everyone seems like a friend. I waved him on over.

Hale introduced himself and we shook hands. "Have you met your Mrs. Pelham?"

"The landlord? No, I rented through an agency. Why?"

Shaking his head, Hale laughed, "She's nutty as a loon. She stays in the front part of the house when she comes to town. Lives over in Charleston in a huge home, just her and two maids. I think she keeps this house just to stay in touch with the little people."

"Well, then I guess I am the little people. My name is Mae Wallace."

"Nice to meet you, Mae."

"Actually, my first names are Mae Wallace. My last name is Anders."

"Oh, I get it. You can call me Hale. Just one first name."

Looking back, I can see that Hale was probably teasing me. He has a way of poking just a little bit of fun, but not in a mean or hurtful way. I liked him immediately, and was glad to meet him. Since moving March into the Sea Villas nearby, I was lonely.

March was paralyzed. It hurt me to say it. Her legs didn't work and it didn't seem that was ever going to change. The accident had robbed her of walking, running (not that she ever did), and the independent life she had lived. In time, March could function independently, we were told, but until then, there was physical therapy, rehabilitation, and "life skills" training.

My parents, numb for months about the accident, had selected Sea Villas Rehabilitation Center as one of the best places in the nation for March to stay for the foreseeable future. Although no one asked, I volunteered to go and live on the island to be near my sister. My parents stayed behind in Henderson, and visited every so often. I think if they lived here, they would be driven crazy by seeing March hurting so much all of the time.

We all missed March terribly. Sure, we had her body and her glossy brown hair and the long fingers she used to swish through the air when she was particularly excited. But March's face, her eyes, her mouth were gone as if they were washed away. It was as if Butter's last kick had tossed March off and into space. Where her brown eyes used to laugh, they were dull and tired. Her mouth, which used to spell out her hijinks, was silent. March hardly spoke to anyone at all. To me, she said the least.

After our taco lunch, Hale and I strolled back to Sea Street and waved good-bye. He walked into his house and the waiting commission painting for the Garden Club. I briefly envied him for having a job to do. Since leaving my position at World Matters, I missed that sense of identity. I liked having a long list of things to do, people to call, and meetings to attend. I knew I was one of maybe six people in the state of South Carolina who enjoyed business meetings, but I did and I sometimes missed them. I longed for the simple things, like picking up dry cleaning and strolling to the bakery near my apartment. I missed my favorite coffee shop with its chunky ceramic mugs. I missed Vince.

I slipped on a pair of freshly washed capris and a white T-shirt, and jumped in the car for the quick trip to the Sea Villas. The rehab center was in five gray buildings that were clustered around a parklike center. The parking lots were off to one side, hidden behind climbing wisteria, confederate jasmine, and towering oleander. The place was overlandscaped with bushes, shrubs, and plantings cropping up every two feet. From the top floors of the three-story villas, you could see the ocean. March was in a private room on the third floor of the Sea Oat Villa.

I signed in, greeting the receptionist, a sixty-something woman named Alice who always asked me how March was doing. Her concern never failed to annoy me. I wondered if I resented someone outside our family knowing about March's condition and then quizzing me about it. But Hale knew about March, and I didn't mind him asking questions in his gentle manner. Alice seemed greedy, like she enjoyed hoarding bits of information.

"You let me know if you see any change, honey," Alice said to me, squinting her eyes in what I guessed she thought was a sympathetic manner.

"Will do." I ducked past her and jammed the elevator button. Anything to get away. Lately, everything I did seemed like running. Moving to Langdon. Not answering Vince's letters. Failing to return my parents' phone calls.

On the third floor, two patients in wheelchairs talked to each other. I knew the younger of the two, Marla, who was recovering from a water-skiing accident. I said hello. Marla lifted her chin and nodded toward March's door. "We tried getting her to come with us to the dining room, but no luck."

"Well, thanks for asking," I said and then took a deep breath before pushing open the wide door to March's room.

I always tried to be breezy and upbeat with March. I would come quickly in her room, drop off a bouquet of fresh flowers, open the curtains, and comment on the weather. That was the role I played. March couldn't have cared less. She would sit in the bed or the wheelchair, her robe wrapped around her shrinking frame, and stare off into space. If the curtains were closed, she just stared at them, her back to the door.

But today, I didn't feel like being breezy. I felt like packing up my little house, hopping in the car, and heading back to Atlanta. I was not sure why this feeling hit me today, rather than last week or next week. But it did and I felt mopey and out of place. Langdon Island was starting to feel like home, but it wasn't quite there, not yet.

"Hey, sister," I called out to March as I entered her room. The room was decorated in beige and light peach. Beach-type paintings and peach curtains completed the bland, feel-better-soon atmosphere. Even though the Sea Villas were private and upscale, the place still held on to a hospital vibe. And no matter how sorry I was ever feeling for myself, seeing the patients rolling around the floors with shaved heads and staples arching across their skulls, or teenagers learning to walk again on crutches, always made me put a stop to any pity party.

"Hi, Mae Wallace."

I smiled at my sister, who was seated in the chair closest to the bed. "Ready for our beauty treatment?"

"Yeah, I sure do need to be dolled up for my night on the town later." March said this without a trace of interest or caring. I noticed she hadn't brushed her hair today.

"Come on, it'll be fun," I said, opening the curtains and throwing away a few used tissues.

March didn't say anything, so I decided to act quickly. I wheeled her chair over to where she was sitting. I held out my arms and March leaned forward. I felt her soft skin and smelled a slight acrid odor, like she hadn't bathed in a few days. March put more of her weight on me and I held her as she inched up and over, as I swiveled toward the waiting chair. Helping her move was getting easier with each passing week. With little access to junk food, alcohol, and oversized portions, March was shrinking before our eyes. She didn't seem to care or notice.

The spa was on the first floor. Norma, the spa manager, walked over with peppy steps to greet us. "Hello, darlings! Are you ready for a little pampering?"

March said nothing, so I smiled. "My nails are raggedy. Let's see if you can do some magic."

Pei, the nail tech, wheeled March over to the special pedicure station for patients. It had a raised hot tub for people in wheelchairs. I settled into the massaging chair next to March and picked up a magazine, like I might do in Atlanta. The Sea Villas were big into making life very much like every day. The problem was we all knew life was never going to go back to normal. March was not going to keep dating the world and coming home "in love" every other month. She was never going to ride Butter again. Poor Butter, I thought, remembering the look on my father's face when he and I rushed out to the pasture on that day. The horse had wandered a few feet from the fallen March, the stirrups hanging uselessly from the glossy leather saddle. She grazed uneasily, eyeing us for signs that we might try to ride her. My father raised his hand and took a step toward the beast. Butter rolled her eyes in fear and took off. A neighbor caught her later in the day and took her to his barn. To my knowledge, Butter was still there, waiting for one of us to come claim her. I knew my father never would. Posey, my sister's sweet new dog, was given to a college friend of March's who volunteered to take the dog until March wanted her back.

The massaging chair dug into my back. It was uncomfortable and pleasing at the same time. Norma scrubbed a maple foot rub into the soles of my feet and I closed my eyes for a moment. It was nice to stop for a few minutes. It was nice to be touched. Other than the occasional hug from Hale, I hadn't been touched in weeks. I missed Vince. I wanted his arms around me.

"That feels good," March said, looking over at me.

"Sure does," I replied, giving her a smile. It was nice, bonding a little bit. Then I noticed March's private smirk and she turned her face away from me. She couldn't feel a thing.

"Sorry."

Pei worked quietly, while Norma chatted on and on about her new condo on the other end of the island. I could tell March was getting agitated, but when Norma said, "And I told the contractor he would install the correct tub I paid for or I was going to get upset," I saw my sister lose it.

"Hey Norma," March said. "Why don't you shut your gob hole about your stupid condo. No one cares. No one here, anyway. We'd rather walk, thank you. Last time I checked, the people in this place had real problems."

Pei's eyes widened, but she kept her head down, buffing March's toenails. This only irritated my sister, who jerked her upper body back and forth. I knew she wanted to pull her feet out of the tub but she could no longer do so.

Norma stood up and backed away from our chairs. "March, I'm so sorry. I was just going on. My dumb mouth. I'm sorry." She looked horrified, her hands wet and soapy.

I quickly stood and shoved my feet into flip-flops and then helped March back up. We wheeled out of there fast, Norma still apologizing.

When we were in the hall, March said simply, "I want to die."

"March, don't say that." I knelt beside her. "You're just having trouble adjusting. We all are."

"It just occurred to me that I wanted to go outside, run down to the beach, and get the hell away from this place." March closed her eyes. "But I can't because I have a catheter bag that will need to be emptied before too long, and I have several sores on my ass that really should be healing, and oh yeah, I can't really run anymore. So, I think I do want to die. Or just roll away. Something that takes me out and up, up, up."

An ice machine rumbled at the nearby snack center. The waiting room outside the spa was perfectly straightened. Fresh flowers were arranged in clear glass vases. Current home decorating magazines were stacked precisely on a wicker coffee table.

It was the most March had said to me in weeks. Maybe since the accident. That's how I rated everything in life now. Before the accident, I had a job and a serious boyfriend. After the accident, I had grieving parents and an angry sister. No job, no boyfriend. I wasn't feeling sorry for myself, I was just being honest. Life was different now, in all its shades and complexities. But for March, life was unbearable, and I felt myself sinking into the ground with her, being pulled slowly under the tide of her agony.

When March fell from Butter, there was the crash of the hand-made mug as I dropped it. Then there was my father, running and running and running. Someone was screaming. My mother was upstairs, fluffing pillows and nodding contentedly at the perfect vacuum arcs in the carpet. I was fumbling for my cell phone before realizing I could use my parents' cordless phone. And then there was March, lying in the grass, dew splashed up on her pants, tiny bugs studded on her wet arms.

Her spinal cord was injured at a location they called T-10, and in a heartbreaking diagnosis a few weeks later, her specialists called it "complete" rather than the more hopeful "incomplete." She was a woman broken with no way to make it right. But I knew we should have made it right before the accident. If March wasn't so ready to show me she didn't need her big sister, didn't care if she was digging in for a war that was unwinnable, didn't seem to notice we missed each other, then I knew instantly March would have never ridden her childhood horse. Never would she have taken out a feisty, lazy horse who wanted oats and could not suffer a ride. I wished we could go back in so many ways, and undo hours and hours and minutes and minutes. Because when March fell, she didn't just hurt herself. She took all of us with her.

SEVEN

Vince's letters were all the same. He knew I didn't have a computer on the island, so he wrote longhand on thick sheets of stationery an elderly aunt gave him years ago. The first paragraph always offered details about what he did that day. He told me what he ate for lunch, how boring work was, and then what he planned to do that evening: soccer, watch a Netflix movie, or join his favorite married couple for dinner. I thought Sarah and Michael felt sorry for Vince since I left, and they invited him over for black bean soup or lasagna.

The second and third paragraphs told me, pleaded with me, insisted that I come home. Vince told me March would be fine on her own. That my parents didn't need to lose two daughters. That March didn't seem to care if I was there or not.

The fourth and final paragraph told me how much he missed me. Vince was not the world's biggest romantic, and I knew this part of the letter was hardest for him to write. His handwriting cramped up, and some of the words were hard to read. These words also made me cry. I wondered how long it would be before he stopped sending them.

"You've got to be kidding," Vince said when I told him I was moving to the coast to be near March. "Why?"

We were in my apartment, eating Chinese takeout. As usual, I had gobbled down my egg roll within seconds of unwrapping the food. Vince liked to savor his and would make it last for another ten minutes.

"I'm her sister, that's why. She needs me."

Vince was not impressed. March had been at turns angry, ugly, and dismissive toward me in the months following the accident. Where there was a slight standoff before, now there was a full-on silent war. And I felt as if I were drowning in it, unable to touch bottom. March raged on at the world, but it was me she seemed to hate the most. I had the job, the boyfriend, the legs that worked. I thought I was an easy target, and Vince kept telling me to stand up for myself.

"Oh, that's easy for you to say," I spat back at him that night. "Your sister isn't lying in a hospital bed blaming you for putting her there."

"Mae Wallace, March does not blame you."

"Sure she does."

"Have you asked her?"

"No," I sniffed. "But I know she rode Butter that morning just to make a statement. She was mad at me then, now it's a million times worse."

"Cut the melodrama, okay? March and you had that weird tiff going because she was pissed off at you for dating me. But wake up, Mae Wallace, she had like two years to get over that." Vince was practically yelling, which was a big deal for him. He was usually pretty laid-back. It took a lot to get him worked up like this. "I don't get why you couldn't just talk about it. Women are so strange, you really are."

I paced back and forth in the space between the kitchen table and the cooling Chinese food. Thinking about the weekend of my parents' retirement party always gave me a sour taste in my mouth. What if the night before the accident I had just walked into March's room with a bowl of popcorn and sat down? What if I said, "We need to talk about this. I miss you. I miss my sister"?

Pulling out a kitchen chair, Vince sat down and started scooping steamed rice onto his plate. I took this to mean he was done talking. But I was wrong.

"Bottom line, Mae Wallace? Your sister took out a horse alone. And not just any horse, but an obstinate, overweight, unhappy horse that wanted nothing more than to doze out her retirement. Even if March thought you were the worst person on the planet, it still doesn't change the fact that she did something dumb and reckless."

The rest of the meal was strained. I agreed with what Vince was saying, for the most part, but it didn't make March stand up and walk. Together we had battled pneumonia, skin sores called decubiti, bladder infections, and depression. She was hurt, I was hurt, and nothing was taking that away anytime soon.

We finished our supper, barely speaking. When Vince left, I tossed the brown paper food bag into the trash can. Our two fortune cookies were at the bottom. I threw them away, not even tempted to read what luck was ahead of us.

So I didn't really answer Vince's letters. I might send a postcard or two with a picture of a sunset or a marsh view. I wrote short sentences. *Nothing's changed. March is still the same. The doctors say we should accept it.* Last week, I wrote, *My house is falling down. I really should find somewhere else to live.* I hesitated before sending that postcard. I was really just searching for something normal and everyday to tell Vince. It was true, my house was a wreck. Mice and squirrels were camped in various nooks and crannies. The power still went out on a whim. But I loved my end of the island. I had friends there. Okay, well, I had Hale, and I wasn't ready to tell Vince about Hale.

I knew he would be hurt that I had found someone so easily who gave me companionship. There was nothing romantic going on with Hale and me, of course, but I knew it wouldn't look good. *Vince? I eat lunch with a widower every day and oh, yeah, he's cute and funny and talented! Isn't that great?* I wasn't that experienced with guys, but I knew telling Vince about my new friend was a good way to never see Vince again.

Hale was in almost all ways the opposite of Vince. He eschewed the good job, the stable life, the pattern most of us fall into after school. He told me once that he had always marched to a different tune, but after his wife died, he abandoned marching altogether. "I don't know, Mae Wallace," he told me one day when we were crabbing near the ruins of the old bridge, "when something that major happens to you, it's almost like you have permission to go crazy. There's not much anyone can do to you. So you lose your job or your house. Big deal. You already know those things don't matter."

I plied my net silently along the still water under the bridge, trolling for crabs and listening. Being around Hale gave me an anchor. Here was someone who had gone through something much worse than my family—after all, March was still alive—and he could still find humor in life. He still ate lunch. He washed his clothes. He shopped for organic apples.

Vince wanted me to shake off my sadness and guilt; he wanted me back, happy and puttering toward marriage. But how could I pick out towels and sheets or order china patterns when March was broken down, stuck on an island away from home? I thought of our childhood together, the whispered secrets and tattered stuffed animals. I could picture our sleepovers in each other's beds. I woke up beside March more times than I did alone. We were sisters, and sisters stuck together, or that's what I thought sisters did.

I found myself constantly thinking back to better times. Did I invent the closeness I remembered with March? Did we really giggle and play pranks on Henry, our stable groom? What about the time our father bought us matching bikes? I remembered riding them for hours, the streamers on the ends of the handlebars fluttering out beside us as we careened down the farm roads.

Hale would listen to me as I dissected my relationship with my sister. He usually repaired a broken fishing pole, or stretched a canvas while I talked and talked. When I was done, finally finished examining small details from years ago, I always felt slightly embarrassed. I joked once he should charge me for therapy.

"Nah, it helps to talk about it. Makes it real."

Vince was more of a fixer and to him, talking about it was like a road map. Find the problem on this part of the map and then fix it over here, on this map quadrant. It seemed to me like Hale's philosophy was to hear about an issue, mull it over, and then approach it like a friend. Carefully and thoughtfully.

He was the one who told me to allow March to rage. "Let her cry, scream, yell, whatever," he said the other day. We were stripping the husks off of sweet corn, standing shoulder to shoulder at his kitchen sink. Two pounds of boiled shrimp filled a chipped ceramic bowl on the kitchen table. We planned to roast the corn on the grill and then eat the shrimp with a couple of beers.

"March is hurting, and she needs to take it out on someone. Let that be you."

"But she's nasty to everyone—her shrink, doctors, nurses, nurse's aides, you name it. I'm just one more person."

"Isn't she the worst to you?"

I had to admit he was right. March seemed to be snottier, more cutting, and downright ornery when I was on the scene. I attributed it to her anger at me. Vince's response was that March should get over it. Hale told me to take it and ask for more.

"I guess I just figure that one day March will forgive me. And then we'll get back to the way things used to be."

Dumping the corn husks in the trash, Hale smiled at me. "I think things have changed with you and your sis forever."

I moved toward the kitchen table and swiped a fat shrimp. Part of me wanted to be angry with Hale for putting things so simply. Of course, he was right. But if I rewound our lives together, maybe I could get something back. Maybe I could make it right again.

Hale buttered the corn and placed it on a tray. He didn't give me any nuggets of wisdom. I waited, impatiently, until he turned toward me. "Are you going to stop obsessing and help me grill these things?" Instead of waiting for an answer, he walked outside onto the deck, his flip-flops slapping the wooden boards.

And then one day, when I had been on Langdon for about three months, Vince showed up on my doorstep close to sundown. He rang the front door of the rental, which boasted an old-fashioned doorbell that sounded like a trumpet blast of metal gears and grinding noises. Of course, I could hear the thing all the way on the other side of my part of the house. I had just started folding a load of sheets and towels when the bell clanged.

Since I couldn't access the front part of the house from my apartment in back, I walked outside and across the deck and peered toward the front porch. I saw Vince's VW Beetle in the shell-packed drive and my heart did that fluttery thing it liked to do when presented with my boyfriend. *Ex-boyfriend,* I reminded myself. Vince hadn't been too supportive of my move down here. Our relationship seemed to have skidded off into oblivion.

The bell clanged again. "Vince?" I had to shout because of where I was standing and the crash of the waves. "Is that you?"

For an answer, Vince came around the corner. He was wearing a shirt and tie, as if he had come straight from work in Charlotte. I did the math. He must have started driving around noon or one, and floored it all the way to the coast. His hair was shorter and kind of lighter than when we last saw each other. "Did you get highlights?" was the first ridiculous thing I asked him.

"No," Vince said, giving me a funny grin. "I took a spring trip to Barbados. I had a ton of frequent-flyer miles that I needed to use."

I pictured too-skinny girls wearing too-skimpy bikinis falling all over Vince and practically gritted my teeth. *Keep it together,* I reminded myself. *You gave up the right to be jealous.* But there it was: a mental image of a ditsy poolside gal rubbing lotion on Vince's slender but muscular shoulders. Her name was probably Fawn or Dawn or something awful. I hated her.

"Mae Wallace? What are you thinking?" Vince tilted his head toward me.

I stepped back from the edge of the porch and motioned for him to join me. "Come on up."

Vince hesitated, and I realized he was thinking about his overnight bag still in the car. We both tensed and then he seemed to make a decision and walk up on the porch. "Nice place. I can see what you mean about it being condemned."

I swatted his arm. We were just a few feet away from each other now. "It's not that bad. I probably exaggerated."

Looking around, Vince rolled up his shirtsleeves. "No, it really is that bad. Have your parents seen this place?"

I ducked my head and walked toward the sliding glass door.

"Want a tour? And yes, they've seen it but they only have room in their heads for March's problems. The walking daughter can take care of herself."

I felt rather than saw Vince take in the stained plaster walls and pitted wooden floors. "You mean your parents are so consumed with Miss March that they can't see you're living like this?" Vince pulled at his tie and sat down in a beach chair next to the rickety kitchen table. He was angry; it was the fixer in him.

"Look, Vince, the place isn't great but it's home for now. I don't spend much time here anyway. I go see March, I crab, swim, you know, I do stuff." *Stuff with Hale*, I thought a bit guiltily.

He pulled a hand through his hair. "Fine, whatever. I just don't like to think of you living here all by yourself when we could, you know, be hanging out back home."

"Whose home? Atlanta or Charlotte? The last time I checked, we weren't exactly firming up our relationship," I said with more heat in my voice than needed. I wasn't making anything easy for Vince. Life had become such a rolling burden of chores and sadness that I didn't have it inside me to help him out. And feeling that only made me sink deeper inside my coal-black mean little brain.

"Don't blame me. I didn't ask you to move to Langdon," he said.

I swung away from Vince, arms crossed over my faded MTV T-shirt. This couldn't get any worse. My mind helpfully conjured up pictures of Vince and me walking hand in hand down the beach instead of hurling insults. His kisses were perfect, the best I had ever known. Now he would be taking those lips back up the highway. I tensed, expecting to hear his footsteps retreating back over the porch.

The ocean lulled for a moment. I had come to enjoy these hiccups in the surf roar. The waves would die down for a bit and then seem to start back up again. When I would hear it, I sometimes imagined a huge switch turning off the sea. All of the waves would fade away and the roar would trickle down to just the thump thump thump of the shore meeting water.

Instead of listening to Vince walk away, I heard him sigh. I knew talking about his feelings was hard for him, but I was almost numb to anyone else's pain other than mine and my sister's. And I wasn't sure what March's agony was these days. It could be self-righteous anger, pity, or flippant rage. I was worn out from trying to figure it out.

"Mae Wallace, I came down here because I miss you. I can never get you on the phone, I can't even e-mail you, and when I try to write letters, I feel like the words just don't ever line up the right way. I work all day and then go home, but a thousand times a day I think of you. I wonder what you are doing, and I hurt for you because I think you are wasting your time."

"How can you say that?"

"It's been three months. How many times are you going to go into March's room and take the crap she's throwing at you?"

"It's not all bad," I said, moving over to the worn-out sofa in the living room. "Sometimes, when we paint pottery in craft class, she laughs at jokes I make. Last week, I even got her to take a beginner knitting class with me."

"That's great, Mae Wallace. Why don't you move home?" Vince sat down on the sofa. He reached for my hand. His fingers were warm. "She'll be okay, I promise."

"You forget—you and I would still live more than four hours apart. Moving back to Atlanta doesn't really get us on track or anything." I felt a little stirring of emotion after all these months of stoically taking blows from March and hurting from what had happened to my sister. Tears began to pool in my eyes and I had that tickle you feel right before sobbing. I wanted, needed to cry.

Vince slid closer to me. He cleared his throat and looped one arm around my back. "That's what I wanted to talk to you about. Maybe you can come back and I can move to Atlanta or you can move to Charlotte. We need to start over again, Mae Wallace."

I thought of my parents and how they liked Vince even though I hadn't really brought him around many times. We could visit them more often now, I began to form the thought in my mind, *now that March isn't around.* I pictured packing up my car and leaving Langdon, leaving March, and heading home. I could smell the rehab center smell—one part cleaner and two parts soap—and I imagined my sister by herself with no one to comb her dry, brown hair and no one to snap off the dead buds in her flower vases.

"I just can't leave her, Vince," I said. "She needs me. She doesn't act like it, but she does. My mother would be here but I think she just can't take it. Dad is a wreck, too. Maybe they'll come around later. But for now, I think I need to stay here."

Vince moved away from me. His jaw was tight and his eyes did not meet mine. "I don't understand how you can pick living this way. I don't want you to choose me over her, that's not it. I just want you to be happier and you don't seem to know how to do it."

My cell phone rang. I glanced at it sitting on the kitchen table. It could be the hospital, it could be March's doctor. It could also be Hale, and I didn't want to get into that at the moment. Vince was riled up. He didn't need Hale tromping into the picture.

Watching my eyes, Vince nodded toward the phone. "Go ahead, I know you want to take it."

It was Hale's number. I opened my phone and said, "Hey, can I call you back?" He probably wanted to get a late dinner.

Instead of Hale's cheery voice, I heard silence and what sounded like water or waves.

"Can you come down to the bridge? They found her ring. Her wedding ring." Hale's voice faded, his words a thread on the wind and the surf. I nodded, even though he couldn't see me. "Yes, I'll be right there."

Vince stood up. "Guess she's calling for you?" He looked at me. I wondered if he was already driving home in his mind.

"No, it's not March. It's a friend. A new friend I made on the island." My mind was all jumbled. Ruth's ring had been found. At the bridge. In the water? Who found it? And why now when Hale was moving on and healing? But the voice I heard on the phone was thick with grief.

"Well, what does she want? You look like you're about to cry."

I met his eyes. "It's not a she, it's a he and he's gotten some bad news."

Outside, the ocean lulled in its march to the beach. I heard the waves stop for one second, two seconds, three.

"What's going on with you, Mae Wallace? I can't get you on the phone, you don't write—you don't seem to care about us anymore." Vince stood, fishing in his pants' pocket for his keys. "So, I guess this new friend has been taking up your time. Sorry I bothered you."

I shook my head, thinking of Hale, thinking of what he must be going through. For the first time since I met him, I realized the gulf between us. His wife was gone; my sister still lived. It was not the same at all.

"You can't even say anything?" Vince said. "What's happened to you?"

I looked around for my purse and keys. They were on the counter next to a half loaf of wheat bread. The bridge, I had to get to the bridge. But Vince was standing in my way, blocking the door. "I can't talk about this right now, Vince. I want to, I just can't."

Vince's face flushed as he turned away from me. "Yeah. I can see that. You know what, Mae Wallace? I thought I knew how to reach you. I thought if I could just come down here, you would see what this is doing to me, what it's doing to us." He threw open the sliding glass door and looked back once with sadness. "I'm going home now. I won't be coming back."

EIGHT

The way Hale tells the story, Ruth was never supposed to be his. She would have never met him and would have ended up married to a banker, polishing her stainless-steel appliances until she turned sour like a spoiled carton of milk. This is how Hale puts it. Ruth would have been half mad with boredom. She would have wondered where she went wrong.

"But what if this banker lover of mine ended up being a real prince and I lived happily ever after in my mansion on the hill? What then?" she would ask, and I guess, plant a kiss playfully on Hale's forehead. I have to make up some of the fine details because Hale tends to leave those out and I don't want to make him dredge up the memories that are the most simple and the most painful.

"Would have never happened. We were destined to meet or the rest of your life would have been just a puff of nothing."

Hale told me he wrapped his arms around Ruth then and held her tightly. She wore a white cotton skirt and black tank top. I know because I have seen the picture on Hale's bookshelf. It is a perfect moment stopped in time. They sit on a picnic blanket with the Langdon Bay in the background. The frozen waves behind them are a serene dusky blue. The sun is mellow and gentle, golden with the color of late afternoon. Ruth wears her new engagement ring that Hale designed. She has said yes.

Hale told me after we became friends that he was supposed to spend the summer he met Ruth on his cousin Frank's boat. Frank wanted to set some sort of record for barhopping from his sailboat up and down the Atlantic. After considering his survival options of careening from coastal city to city at the hands of a half-drunk captain, Hale declined. The trip fell apart anyway because Frank ended up losing his boat in a poker game.

So Hale stayed on in Langdon and rejoined the summer crew of a bunch of pool maintenance workers. They opened pools for the season on the big oceanfront homes and serviced all the rest of the pools on the island. Being a rabid lover of nature, Hale hated dumping chemicals into artificial bodies of water steps from the real ocean, but it paid the rent. He was one year out of art school and a real career was the furthest thing on his mind.

Ruth's family owned one of those big houses and the first official day of summer, Hale looked up from tinkering with the valve on an automatic vacuum to see Ruth standing in front of him. She wore a T-shirt and shorts. The pink tie of a bikini poked out from her neckline. On top of her head sat a wide-brimmed straw hat.

"Did you break it?" she asked. Ruth, whom Hale guessed was about his age, smelled like something he would later place as grapefruit.

Hale blinked twice, not sure if this Daddy's girl was being serious or just flirting with him. You could never tell with these rich women. Some of them had zero personalities but loads of bitchy attitude. He waited to see what camp Ruth fell into.

Ruth waited on Hale, too, walking past him, trailing her grapefruit scent behind her. "Guess you did. That makes you a vacuum killer." Her mouth opened and she laughed.

Smiling back at her, Hale deadpanned, "I'm wanted in six states. It really sucks."

"Oh, that's a seriously lame joke." Ruth winced. She took a step toward Hale. He remembers she wore three or four jangly bracelets on her left arm. Her skin was pale, which meant her family had just arrived for the summer. It was a Friday afternoon and the streets of the island were thick with cars with out-of-state plates and SUVs hailing from Columbia and Greenville. On either side of Ruth's beachfront home, families unpacked minivans. Coolers were unloaded, grills cranked up for the celebratory first hamburger. Hale told me he sometimes got lonesome working on the pools when so much revelry was swirling around him, and he was somewhere in the background. You don't exactly invite the pool boy for a hamburger.

Hale made an excuse to go back to Ruth's house that week and then another. He brought unneeded chemicals or duplicate hoses. Both times, Ruth was out by the pool, sunning herself under the big hat and an even larger umbrella. "What's the point?" he would ask her. "Why the cover-up?"

"A woman's skin is her first and most important wardrobe," Ruth said, shifting the brim of her hat slightly. "If I don't take care of my skin, I'll look all saggy and baggy one day."

A few feet away, Ruth's two older sisters just rolled their eyes and greased on more Baby Tan Oil, a product Ruth liked to say had a negative SPF rating. Tamara turned over onto her stomach, reached around, and deftly flipped off her bikini strap. Cameron reclined in her chair, delicately misting her body with a small pump bottle.

"Vain women." Ruth stuck out her tongue at her sisters.

"Vain? Look at Miss Victoria 1887. Pale skin went out like in the last century, Ruthie," Cameron said.

Ruth's mood darkened. "I told you to stop calling me that. It's Ruth."

"Ruthie, Ruthie," the two sisters chanted.

"Want to get out of here?" Ruth stood up suddenly and linked her arm through Hale's.

He swallowed quickly and thought of his work truck strewn with fast-food wrappers and one or two sweaty, dying T-shirts. He was due at the Millers' pool two houses down the street. It could wait. "Sure. Lead the way."

Ruth was quiet as they drove to the tip of the island. Hale could sense her sisters had really gotten to her. Or maybe it was something else. Either way, he was happy to squire Ruth around for the afternoon. Her grapefruity scent filled the truck. Her hat lay on the seat between them.

"I've never seen your head," Hale said, throwing a quick glance at Ruth before looking back at the narrow ribbon of oceanfront road.

"It's an okay head." Ruth stared straight ahead.

The road turned gently toward the tip, which was called for no apparent reason Tip's Tip. Hale had lived on Langdon his whole life. There was no Tip. It wasn't even a good place to make out. Barely ten feet wide with a sagging pier, Tip's Tip was definitely one of Langdon's more down-market locales.

"So this is Tip's Tip? It's the stuff of island legend, someplace you locals keep to yourselves," Ruth said when they had pulled the truck off the road and walked up to the decaying pier. She stepped up to the weathered boards, but Hale pulled her back gently. "I wouldn't trust these old planks with my life."

"I would," Ruth said, batting away his hand. "Let me go. They look plenty strong enough."

"Ruth, please? I don't like the looks of it. Okay?" Hale felt self-conscious reprimanding this woman he barely knew.

Ruth, who had returned the straw hat to her head, smiled at him. "Look, I have one foot on the ground and one on the pier. Happy?"

Nodding, Hale watched Ruth turn and face the sun that was starting its afternoon arc toward the horizon. Plenty of the day was still to come, but this small reminder of summer's ebb and flow gave Hale pause. The summer season was his favorite. Sure, it brought crowds and noise but it was also a season to live outside from the earliest rays of orange and pink sun to the misty gray dusk of evening. Sometimes, driving home from a late pool job, Hale would be a little sad thinking he had only two months left of summer, then six weeks, then four, then just days.

Ruth told him about her job as a costume assistant on a traveling Broadway musical. She had studied costume design up north in college and then joined the production staff of *Fanny's Time Away,* a musical Ruth declared "dreadful," "expensive," and "heavy on the frills."

"But, I get to learn the business and hopefully do a good job, and that will lead to more jobs." Ruth stepped down from the pier and faced Hale. "Eventually, I'll design my own show and go from there."

"Do you like being on the road?"

"Not really. It's good to be home for a few weeks and stop living out of a suitcase."

Hale laughed. "You called Langdon home."

"Yeah, I guess I did. I mean, it's good to be with my family even though they drive me crazy." Ruth peered at Hale. "Why so many questions? What about you? Are pools all there is to your life?"

Hale dragged one sneaker-covered foot through the dusting of sand at the start of the pier. "Nah, it's just a way to pay the rent while I pursue my exotic art career."

"So, is your art exotic or is your art career exotic?" Ruth turned from the ocean to peer into Hale's eyes.

"Ah, you would have to be the judge of that."

Stepping down from the pier, Ruth twirled around, her long skirt unfurling around her shins. "Okay, what's your art about?"

"I paint. I'm a painter," Hale said.

"Now, that's no way to promote yourself, Mr. Hale. Tell me a little bit about your work. Don't be skimpy."

Hale considered telling her he had a pile of art-school loans and he had mounted exactly two one-man exhibitions, and the second was at the Java Hut over in Charleston. Not exactly the New York art scene. Maybe this rich, tan adverse girl would laugh at him. After all, she was making it in her art field. Hale didn't know too much about the theater world, but landing a gig on a touring show right out of school seemed fairly accomplished to him.

"Well, right now I'm working on a series of drawings. Pencil and conte crayon."

"And? Pretend I'm an influential art critic and you have my ear for two seconds." Ruth pursed her lips and slipped on her sunglasses. "Get ready, go."

Laughing, Hale tucked a piece of hair behind his ear. "Okay, Ms. Ruth the Art Critic, I am currently creating a series of drawings examining what floats up under the old bridge each Friday."

Ruth stared at him, dropping her art critic facade. "Really? That's cool. I go there when I want to be alone or when my sisters are just too loony to bear. I spent more time under the bridge last summer than I did on the beach."

"Well, I just started drawing there a few months ago. I like the way the sun sets over the bay. Of course, when the new bridge construction starts, it's really going to change."

"New bridge?" Ruth's mouth turned down. "What's wrong with the old one? I love the wide arches and the old-fashioned light posts. You can actually walk across it, you know?"

"Yeah, I know. I used to ride my bike across to the mainland to play in soccer tournaments when I was a kid. But now, there're so many people coming to Langdon, a big, shiny new bridge is going to go up. I think they start this fall. But you wouldn't know about our island business way up there in Greenville, now would you?"

Ruth continued to frown, ignoring Hale's teasing. He touched her arm briefly, his fingers barely brushing the surface of the skin. "Hey? Are you in there?"

She walked back toward the truck, rubbing at her eyes. "I don't know why people just can't leave anything alone. There's nothing that stays the same, nothing."

Hale opened Ruth's door and then silently climbed into the driver's side of the truck. He could tell Ruth was upset about something, not just the new bridge, but he was clueless as to what to say. He already felt as if he was breaking the rules by having a customer's daughter in the front seat of the pool truck. And then there were the two pools he had blown off to spend more time with Ruth. Maybe it was time to get back to work.

The truck rumbled over the narrow boulevard that followed the coastline. "I think I like being under the bridge so much because I feel protected," Ruth said, her hands tucked under her knees like a little girl. "The huge concrete spans arch over me and the water laps along at my feet. I sit on one of the benches and look over the park and then the bay. All the cars thunder over my head and whoosh on and off the island, but I'm down there, anonymous and small." She turned her head away from him to the open window. Strands of dark hair slipped out from under the straw brim of her hat.

Hale thought of his drawings of the underside of the bridge.

He had sketched empty bottles, broken fishing poles, white trash bags—whatever the waters washed up along the banks of the park. His charcoal and conte crayon could capture the mesh of fishing nets or the floating tin of abandoned soda cans. But Hale knew if he saw Ruth at the water's edge, among the foamy sea trash, it would be beyond him to get her down on paper. His hands would not be enough.

NINE

Hale never says she jumped. When he talks of that day, the day Ruth died, he mentions the bridge and the water. He might speak of tides and passing boats, and the way salt water covered your skin like a caul, but of the actual act of Ruth's passing, he was silent.

Officially, she was dead now. There was a death certificate, signed by the county coroner from the mainland. A memorial service was held, heavy on the hymns, and loaded with overpriced flowers. A local journalist or two followed the story with interest for a while, but Hale said they got bored when suicide was bandied about. Newspapers loathe suicide. It kills the story. A woman depressed, ending it all, where's the story there? Far better the predator in the night or the faked-death-by-sea narrative for the six o'clock newscast.

Hale was standing under the bridge when I got there, my ears still ringing with Vince's parting words. I imagined Vince roaring over the new Cooper River Bridge, eager to sever the last concrete tie that stretched between us. Two policemen stood on either side of Hale, almost as if they were protecting him. As I got closer, I realized they were waiting for Hale to do something. I wasn't sure what they had in mind. He was under the bridge—he couldn't jump off of it. Hale wasn't the type to carry a gun. And then I saw his face more clearly, and I could see why the officers were concerned.

"Mae Wallace," Hale said and then his arms were around me. I held on to him, my dear friend whose face showed a wide swath of pain, not unlike my parents' faces these past months. The officers drifted a few feet away.

"Hey, Hale," I said into his chest. He wore a plaid shirt, something I had never seen before. Then I noticed he was kind of dressed up, for Hale. I was used to seeing him in flip-flops and all sorts of ripped T-shirts spotted with paint. The Hale that was holding on to me was combed, neat, and orderly. I knew better than to ask him about his attire. Instead, I pulled back and looked into his eyes.

Hale looked away, toward the island, not the water. He held out his hand to me, almost as an afterthought. I opened my hand like a child expecting a treat.

The ring dropped into my palm. It was a hollow type of heavy,

the metal warming to my skin as it had Hale's. The band was plat-
inum and formed a perfect circle, the circle meant to follow the
wearer forever. I closed my fingers around the band, almost as if I
could rub out Ruth's story with my fingerprints. I wanted this dead
girl in front of me so badly. I yearned for her. I wanted to grab her
skinny arms, press my hands into her pale skin, and shove her toward Hale. "Here he is, he misses you," I would scream at her. "Take
your ring back."

Hale stood near me, his eyes darting back and forth to the
growing crowd gathering beyond a thin strip of police caution tape.
One man with a sagging belly sighed and turned off his camcorder.
There was no story here, just a man and a lost ring.

"It turned up this morning. A little girl found it at the water's
edge with her big toe," Hale said simply. "A little girl wearing a
yellow bathing suit with ruffles. She thought it was pretty and
asked her father if she could keep it. The father turned it into the
cop patrolling the beach who knew who it belonged to."

"You're kind of like a local celebrity, huh?"

"Unfortunately. For the way Ruth died and the signs I painted
on the bridge."

"Yeah, I noticed them the first time I came to Langdon. They're
kind of hard to miss." I pictured the purple and red signs with the
words *Miss Your Lips Ruth* attached to railings of the old bridge.
"How did you get up there?"

"The same way Ruth did. I climbed the bridge pilings with a
drill, screws, and the painted signs. I did it a few weeks after her
memorial service. It seems so long ago now, but at the time, it was

the only way I could think of to honor her in a very public way. She died so publicly, I don't know, it seemed the right thing."

"And now?"

"Now, I just wish they would get on with tearing the thing down. I don't like seeing the signs anymore. They're faded and worn. It's time for the bridge to go." Hale sighed.

I turned the ring over in my hand. I knew there must be an inscription, but to read it seemed rude. I waited, my ears catching for the first time the echoes of the bridge overhead as traffic passed steadily. The water echoed its own sounds, too. Here and there, a plastic bag or piece of Styrofoam twirled in the water.

"You know, I put this on her hand when we got married and she never took it off. Even when she slept or showered. She wore it always. So, it either slipped off her hand, you know, when she was in the water for a time," Hale said, blinking over his words.

Or she took it off herself before she jumped, I completed his thought in my head, running over the possibilities. Ruth's body was never recovered so it was hard to think of her wasting away to nothing but bones. It was even harder for me to take the black-and-white-picture Ruth, Ruth of the happy times and memories, and place her on the edge of a bridge and the long way down. I put a hand to my forehead, wiping away a speck of sand. My head hurt, and I hurt for Hale.

"I, Ruth, take you, Hale," Hale said the words from a few feet away. He looked toward the water and up to the bridge. In the distance, a crane was silhouetted against the old bridge. A handful of hulking pieces still remained to be taken down and carted away. Somewhere up there, Ruth had left her final mark.

"She had the jeweler engrave those words. She said she wanted a reminder of her vows. Simple, plain. Ruth could be flamboyant, but when it came to our wedding, she was old-fashioned, down to the gardenia in her hair. She made me wear a tux. She had the big dress. It was what she wanted."

I handed the band back to him. Holding someone's wedding ring is a strange thing. It's a piece of jewelry invested with so much meaning, that you want to admire it for a moment and then return it to its owner. Ruth's ring seemed sacred, like everything about her. She was frozen in time and a mystery to boot. That's some heavy baggage to wrap around a simple band.

Hale absentmindedly shoved the ring in his pocket. The police officers tipped their caps to him respectfully and then returned to their squad cars. The younger of the two officers pulled down the yellow tape. Hale did not seem to notice them leaving. With a sigh, he turned to me.

"What were you up to tonight? I hope I didn't disturb you too much."

"Nah, I wasn't doing anything." My lie didn't sound convincing. I thought of Vince and his real sadness. I missed him, but I knew I should have treated him better all along. I should have tried to explain things to him. But between March and Hale and Ruth, I had more than enough hard thoughts running through my heart. It seemed I didn't know how to make room for anyone else.

It was almost as if there was something wrong with me. Maybe all my problems could be traced back to some sort of larger failing. I needed therapy, perhaps, or medication. March wasn't the only one who needed the ear of a therapist. I felt a tightening in my chest. Or maybe it was more simple: I had given up trying to have a normal life, the kind where you try to move about the world and find some happiness. Something like a laugh slipped out of my mouth.

"What's funny?" Hale didn't look surprised, just worn out.

I shoved my hands through my hair, now sticky with salt and wind. "I can't believe myself, Hale. Please just forget that. I am the worst friend in the world."

To my relief, Hale smiled. "It's okay, it's a serious moment here. You're just cracking under the strain."

"Leave it to you to try to make me feel better. Are you trying to be heroic, or stoic, or just perfect?"

Walking over to a palmetto tree log, Hale sat down gingerly, taking his time. It seemed as if every bone in his body hurt. "I just know that some people respond differently to grief, and stress, and whatnot. You laughed. It's all right."

I sat down beside him. We looked at the space under the bridge, the traffic overhead constant and rhythmic. "I guess I was just thinking about the people in my life: March, you, Ruth. And it struck me that Ruth was as much a live person to me as she was a dead person. It seemed so absurd and then I laughed."

Hale clasped his hands together and closed his eyes. "I sometimes think of her as two people: the Ruth who lived with me and who I thought I was going to know forever, and the Ruth who stepped out for a minute but forgot to tell me where she was going."

And then we sat there like that, Hale with his eyes closed and me perched beside him quietly on the palmetto log. The sun was starting to set, but for the first time, I took no pleasure in its descent. I could tell it was a beauty—streaks of cream, purple, magenta. But I turned my mind off to the glory of nature as I sat beside my friend. I also knew that down the beach, March could look at the same sunset. We could almost make out the Sea Villas from where we sat. March was probably going to gripe at me because I didn't stop by for dinner or dessert, which I did almost every day unless we had more specific plans. I usually ate a plate of hospital food like lasagna or roast beef, and rambled on about whatever came to my mind. March had taken to nodding and asking a few questions. She didn't eat much, but preferred to sip on a glass of iced tea until it got cloudy and pale from the melted ice.

We both avoided looking down at her legs.

"March will wonder where I am, but I think that's all right. I can't be there every day, right?"

Hale nodded and smoothed the creases of his pants. "I, I actually wanted to tell you something. Tonight, before I got the call about Ruth's ring, I was going to visit your sister."

"March?"

"You have just one sister, right?"

"March?"

Hale laughed, the first real laugh I had heard from him in a while. "I hope it's okay. You know how I did some art therapy classes at the Sea Villas last month?"

"Yeah, they paid really well, I remember. You bought extra shrimp that week."

Hale nodded, recalling one of our dinners. We had invited the OFDs from our street. Most of them came and Hale charmed away all their grumpiness for one golden evening. "And remember how I told you March came to the class even though you said she probably wouldn't."

I remembered. I had told Hale not to take it personally. They had met once or twice, with me awkwardly doing the introductions. Devoid of her flirtatious ways, March had acted only marginally interested that I had a new friend. I wondered if she cared. Even Vince never came up in conversation because I wasn't particularly interested in retreading that ground, and honestly, there wasn't much to say about our lukewarm relationship. So, Hale's visit to my sister was definitely a surprise.

Hale continued. "Each week we talked a bit after each class, and I could see that she was really hurting—"

"You think?"

Smiling, Hale crossed his arms. "I know, I know. None of this is news to you. Anyway, there was something to her anger. Maybe I saw a little of me in there."

There was truth in what Hale was saying. Both he and March had lost something and they were living on this tiny island trying to scrape out the next thing in life. I was, too. But it seemed like there were no road signs, no "exit now" billboards pointing the way. I had even driven one day to a large chain bookstore over on Mount Pleasant hoping to find some concise self-help. Scanning the shelves in Grief and Healing, I looked for clues to guide whatever it was that I was doing. It was a waste of time. What did I expect to find: *Helping Widowers Mourn Their Missing Wives? Rebuilding Your Relationship with Your Paralyzed Sister?*

"Tonight, I was going to take her on a walk on the beach," Hale said.

"A walk? On the beach?"

"Don't look so shocked. Wheelchairs can make it up on the boardwalk and then down to the packed sand."

"But March hasn't left the hospital in months! She refuses to. I tried to get her to go shopping, to a movie in Charleston, you name it. I eventually gave up."

"Maybe she didn't want to run through the excuses with me. Maybe it was easier to say yes to someone she didn't know as well."

I stood up. "More like it, she just wanted to stick it to me. 'See, Mae Wallace, I would rather go out with a complete stranger than my detested big sister.'"

Hale got to his feet and stood beside me. "Maybe, but more likely, she was just bored and I asked at a good time."

We started walking back toward our cars. The night air was balmy as usual and infused with the salty smell of the coast. I thought briefly of Goss, and how this coastal smell came to be a version of home, in a similar way that our barn in Henderson could conjure up memories with its infusion of hay, oats, and the warm bodies of horses.

Hale and I parted, after I made sure he didn't want to have some company. He left to take his ring home, and I sat in my car for a moment. I didn't feel like facing my worn little house. Tapping the steering wheel, I got a wild hair and thought about driving to Charlotte to try to win back Vince. But even as the thought was formed, my body grew tired. Long road trips were romantic and fun years ago. Tonight, I was weary and filled with a sadness I had trouble identifying. It was Ruth and it wasn't Ruth. It was Hale and not Hale. Mostly, I think I just missed one person, dear to me forever. I missed my sister, March.

TEN

The year they married, Hale and Ruth moved into the rental where I would eventually meet only Hale. Their new home sat on the eastern end of the island and was a scruffy departure from Ruth's family's pristine beach house. But even so, their bungalow was in far better repair than my future home, sided with neat red clapboards and subtly landscaped with false indigo, Virginia Sweetspire, banana shrub, and native azaleas. To get to the beach, all they had to do was walk down a sandy path past a stand of granddaddy gray-beard and magnolia trees. The path gradually petered out to bright, splashy sun. Ruth, as usual, wore a wide-brimmed hat when emerging from the cooler, darker path.

Hale has told me he liked the short walk to the beach, his arm intertwined with Ruth's (they were close to the same height), the other arm toting a small plastic cooler. Ruth carried a collapsible chair and a beach bag. The air was more pleasant as they closed in on the beach. Chased away by the wind, the bugs and humidity seemed less, or at least, they wished it to be so. It was ten or eleven in the morning. The day had started with chocolate ricotta muffins and coffee on the side porch off of their bedroom. Walking to the beach seemed a natural continuation of the day.

Once on the beach, Hale told me that they always picked the same spot near an abandoned dinghy to set up camp for the day. The vessel is gone now, but for years, it sat in the same spot, over-turned and immobile, paint flaking. Ruth liked old things, and the dinghy was like a dear friend. One day, it disappeared, prob-ably a victim of Langdon's beautification program. Already, as Hale and Ruth sunbathed, the new bridge was beginning its rise; two cranes dotted the horizon to the west, if either Hale or Ruth had bothered to look. Busy with the sunscreen and the divvying up of iced coffee, they probably weren't inclined to notice much.

"Six months today," Hale said once they were settled. He sat on a towel and Ruth sat in the chair.

"Still glad you did it?" Ruth asked. She shaded her eyes and looked down the beach to the east. Two tall condo towers were being constructed toward the new bridge, to the west. Ruth pre-ferred to look the other way.

"Yes, I am glad we got hitched. What says my bride?"

Ruth leaned down toward Hale. Tipping her hat back, she placed a gentle kiss on his lips. "I would do it again, in a heartbeat."

Then they were both silent, because the truth was, Hale later ex-plained to me almost apologetically, it had been a hard first six months of marriage. Hale was used to living alone. Ruth had become accustomed to life on the road, away from Hale. When she left the tour to get married and took a job with a theater in Charleston, she was overjoyed. Hale, on the other hand, was more comfortable with his space. Ruth, for her turn, could be moody and Hale did not know how to handle that. For Hale, life was up or down—there was little gray. Some days, Ruth seemed to live in the gray.

Their spats weren't anything too serious, Hale acknowledged. But sometimes, he and Ruth each wondered if they had made the right choice. Ruth had grown up with her mother's words in her head: "Marriage is better if you marry the right person." *Have I married the right person?* Ruth wrote in the margin of her sketchbook in the first few months after the wedding. Hale showed me the entry one day, almost as an afterthought. It was one of the ways he explained things to me about his missing wife.

On most fronts, the casual observer would guess that the marriage of Hale Brock and Ruth Camden Hollis would be a successful one. The most obvious connection, the arts, was an easy story to tell. She would design costumes for the theater in Charleston and he would paint his paintings, offering them up for the more advanced art patrons in Charleston who had grown tired of Rainbow Row watercolors. His bridge paintings were edgy and cool; her costume designs were stellar and lauded. Their professional life would soar.

Family life would include Hale's parents, who lived in Anderson, a little Upstate town famous for its early electricity, and Ruth's parents, who were happily ensconced in Greenville. Not that either Ruth or Hale cared, but there were dinners in downtown Greenville at Sobe's if they were up for the weekend and Clemson games on Saturday if they felt like it. But both sets of parents seemed to be happy to let the couple make their way in the Lowcountry with little interference. On the surface, everything was fine.

And it was, Hale told me. He really believed they would make it. The first summer, they planted a container garden at the rental house. They grew herbs: basil, thyme, and lemon mint, and then searched cookbooks they had received as wedding presents for recipes. In fact, presents were everywhere in their new home. The professional grade cookware was used each day and then lovingly washed with gentle strokes and put away for the next meal. Sheets with sky-high thread counts settled over their antique double bed, and supersoft towels were stacked up in a stainless-steel shelf unit in the bathroom.

Hale told me he remembered a sour note in their first few months of marriage when Ruth's sisters stopped by for an unannounced visit. It was March, and the sisters had come down to the Lowcountry for a long weekend. Hale said Cameron, who was always the ringleader, walked up on their porch and settled into the hammock while Tamara perched on the front-porch steps. Hale and Ruth found them there when they returned from the beach, bags and coolers in hand.

"Hey lovebirds," Cameron called from the hammock. She held up a glass of lemonade she had helped herself to from their earlier breakfast on the porch. "This tastes good. Did you make it?"

Ruth looked shocked to see her sisters. There was no love lost between them, and they weren't the type to visit each other. Also,

Cameron was sore that Ruth had received a rather generous check from their father as a wedding present. In Cameron's mind, no one should celebrate until she walked down the aisle, certainly not her father and not her kid sister who had the nerve to get married first.

"Hey, Ruthie." Tamara blocked the stairs. She scratched at an espadrille-clad heel.

Hale returned the greetings, setting the cooler down into the crushed shell driveway. "What a surprise to see you both."

Ruth said, "Yeah, what a surprise." Her words were edgy, not that Hale could blame her. The sisters courted meanness, and trouble.

Cameron rolled her eyes toward her sister. "What, not holding hands? Guess the bloom's off the rose. And after only a few months of wedded bliss. What a pity."

Giggling, Tamara looked back to her older sister. She had majored in hotel management only to find that she would rather be a guest of the establishment than work in one. Now she was selling moisturizer at Belk, and trying to keep up with Cameron. Hale tended to feel slightly bad for Tamara. He thought there might be a good heart in there somewhere.

Ruth was under no such illusions. She told Hale more than once she felt as if she were born into the wrong family. Perhaps abandoned at birth. Lost by a traveling band of gypsies. Anything but a daughter of her tennis-racquet-toting mother and gin-swilling father. Once, when she was twelve, Ruth dug up her birth certificate from her mother's hope chest, fully expecting to see someone else's name for Father and Mother. That was not to be.

Where she expected to find truth, she simply saw the familiar names of her parents and the place of the great event: Greenville General.

"Well, Ruthie, we just stopped by to see how you two were getting on. It's been, what, three months since the wedding?" Cameron pulled out a tube of lip gloss and used the wand to expertly dab sticky color on her lips.

"Things are great, aren't they, Hale?" Ruth put her arm fiercely around Hale's lower back. Ruth wasn't the most demonstrative person, and Hale told me he was surprised at first but tried not to let it show.

"Got a bun in the oven yet?" Tamara asked, looking to see if Cameron thought she was clever.

"That's rude, Tam," Cameron said sweetly. "Everyone knows you have to do it to have a baby. Little Ruth is still a little wittle virgin, I'm sure."

Hale stepped toward the sisters. "Listen, it was really nice of you to stop by, but Ruth and I have a prior engagement and we can't be late. Come on, honey, these old maids were just leaving." Grabbing Ruth's hand, Hale climbed over Tamara on the steps, past the shocked Cameron, and into the house. Inside, Ruth blinked back tears, while Hale turned the deadbolt, a smirk on his face.

Hale is a perfectly gentle and gracious person. I have seen him speak for almost an hour to the nearly blind man who bags our groceries at the Shop All. He holds the door for every woman or girl who crosses our path. Hale hauls the trash cans to the curb for his elderly neighbors. His manners are innately Southern, which is to say, he looks out for his fellow man while he goes about his daily business. So to think of Hale telling off Cameron and Tamara in such a forward fashion gives me an idea of how nasty they were to Ruth.

Then one day when Hale was having more good days than bad, I saw the sisters in the runty grocer that supplied our end of the island. I knew that Ruth's family's beach house had been sold a while ago, and the family decamped to Hilton Head for vacations, so there was no reason that Hale would ever see her family again. Hale didn't talk poorly of his in-laws, but it didn't seem likely that they would have Hale around for clambakes. Maybe it was hard to see him, or maybe they blamed him, Hale shrugged. His eyes were flat when he said it. I didn't pry for more.

It was late morning when I rounded the corner in the Shop All and spied Cameron and Tamara giggling over the dusty wine selection. I recognized them immediately from Hale and Ruth's wedding album. Cameron, the oldest, had almost leonine features. Her tawny skin and perfectly applied highlights gave her an expensive, glowing appearance. Tamara was nearly as pretty, but with a slightly larger nose.

Neither woman looked anything like Ruth. In pictures, Ruth resembled a dancer from the 1930s or a silent-film star. Her dark hair fell in a self-conscious wave over her forehead and her limbs seemed almost doll-like. She favored vintage styles, wide plastic bangles, and the occasional silver antique hair clip. Flipping through their wedding album and the scrapbooks she made of the first years of their marriage, I am struck how Ruth looks as if she came from another era. Of course, in a way, she did. Ruth lived and breathed in another time, apart from March and me, and like a great-great-grandmother we only recognize from crumbling black-and-white photos, we will never know her.

When I figured out who the sisters were, I felt my breathing start to quicken. They wouldn't know me, of course. But even though I was blatantly staring, they didn't seem to notice.

"Do you think we should spring for the fifteen-dollar bottle? Looks like it's the top-shelf choice," Cameron remarked to her sister.

Laughing, Tamara bent down to take a look at the wines near the bottom shelf. I couldn't help but notice a nice ring of cellulite peeking out of her baby blue surf shorts. "Look! Wine coolers. From like 1985."

"Trip and Will will love the wine coolers. We're totally getting them."

"Good, can we go now?" Tamara stood up and brushed her black hair off of her face. "This island gives me the creeps, and you know why."

Cameron rolled her eyes. "Don't be a drama queen. You think too much." They turned and walked over the dingy linoleum toward checkout. I followed, feeling like a novice private investigator. "Trip wanted to come here for the weekend, and you need to just suck it up. I am this close to getting that ring, so zip it."

Pouting, Tamara pulled out her wallet. The women paid for their wine and walked out to a waiting Jeep. I stopped short of going outside. But I replayed their conversation over in my head.

They were on the island for the weekend at least. Hale should know—it might be hard for him to run into his deceased wife's sisters on some random trip to the store or the island coffee shop. When I found him at his studio, breathless with the news but oddly unsure of how to tell him, he didn't seem too bothered.

"Her two sisters are on Langdon, huh?" Hale put down the bottle of gesso he was absentmindedly shaking in one hand. His latest canvas was on the easel. It was a painting of the island bridge with various household items piled underneath. It was a large, noisy painting with dark gray colors. Pretending not to notice, I turned away. Looking at the bridge painting seemed like reading Hale's diary. He had painted many like this: the island bridge with junk heaped under it. Sometimes there was a four-poster bed smashed in the water. Other times, I could make out toasters and lawn furniture.

"Yeah, they were buying wine and talking about meeting up with a Will and a Trip. Apparently, there's an engagement ring in it for Cameron."

"That sounds like her. Always on the make." Hale put down the gesso and stretched. "It always burned her up that Ruth got married before her. And it especially bothered her that her little sister married for love and not for money."

"I thought Ruth's family had plenty of cash."

"Oh, they did. But Cameron wanted the big payout. She was going for some hedge-fund manager when Ruth and I were dating. He turned out to have a wife and a passel of kids he never mentioned."

"Well, here's hoping she's found her match," I said. "Do you worry about running into her?"

"Not really. We'll have a nice, fake conversation in which she subtly insults me and I pretend not to remember how mean she and Tamara were to their sensitive, artistic sister." Gripping his paintbrush, Hale moved his head to the side. I saw his profile and the slip of one brief tear beside his nose.

"Oh, Hale, I'm sorry. I shouldn't even have mentioned I saw them. You didn't need to know. You most likely wouldn't have even bumped into them. They're probably on their way to Charleston or Kiawah to some stupid party."

Hale motioned to his painting. "Like it?"

Swallowing, I nodded. "It's like a lot of the others?"

"Yeah. I have a whole bin full of them. I'll never show them. It's just good for me to paint what I see when I look under that bridge."

A few minutes later, Hale asked me if I wanted to get some pizza. I agreed, but with the caveat that we include March. It was early enough that dinner wouldn't have been served at the Sea Villas. I reached her on her room phone and she actually sounded eager to get out. It had been a recent development that we could take March off campus for short excursions, and an even more recent development that she actually wanted to go. I gave Hale all the credit. The day after Ruth's ring washed up on the beach, he took a deep breath and invited March out on their walk that had been interrupted. Since then, she has ventured out with us a couple of times. It's a huge job—there's the chair, her catheter, medications.

I felt so responsible, the weight of it was crushing. Luckily Hale was barely fazed by the arrangements. He handled March like she was hardly any trouble at all.

While Hale put up his brushes and covered his paints, I wandered outside to the beach. My thoughts returned to this woman I had never met, and her sisters, as wicked as the warty stepsisters in a fairy tale. I could see Ruth with Hale on the beach, iced coffee in hand. They were steps from the old dinghy and marriage, although tough, had brought them down the road another six months. They walked time and time again to the old dinghy, hands intertwined, mugs of coffee in hand. When winter came, they walked quickly dressed in sweaters and fleece hats. The water was gray and choppy. They had now been married almost a year. Ruth asked him if he was still glad they wed.

"Happy to call you my wife."

"Happy to call you my husband."

That was all they had to say, and all that Hale remembered. I stood at the water's edge, dragging my bare foot in the seawater-soaked sand and waiting for Hale to close up his studio. There was an emptiness inside my body. Although I would never meet this girl, this woman who loved my friend, I desperately wanted to find her on the beach near the old dinghy and warn her away from the place she was going.

March met us in the lobby of her villa, the Sea Oat, which was a first for me. I usually had to dart past the busybody receptionist

Alice, take the stairs to March's room, sign her out with the nurses, and hear a mini-lecture about March's fragility. As if I could forget it, when I leaned over to put her legs side by side and orderly in the backseat of the hospital van I borrowed for her outings. It was equipped with tons of supplies and the necessary electric lift for getting my sister up and around.

"Hey, March." I bent to kiss the side of her face. Her skin did not have the sourness I had come to expect. I smelled her favorite lotion, ginger and milk. It's from a small boutique in Henderson. Mom must have brought some on her visit last week. I mentally chastised myself; I should have thought of getting March this small indulgence.

"Mae Wallace, thanks for coming to get me."

"Glad to. We wanted your company."

If Hale looked surprised by all the sisterly niceness, he hid it. "So, did you ditch your minders?"

"Yeah, something like that. Nurse Crazy is a few hours from beginning a week's vacation to Orlando, so she barely noticed when I asked for permission to come down alone."

"I think maybe they're trusting us to do these little outings," I said, trying to sound jovial.

"Maybe." March's voice was flat. I noticed for the first time that her friendliness was like a faucet and the spigot was turned directly to Hale.

"Did you get through that biography?" Hale asked March, naming a famous Pop artist.

I could hear the smile in March's voice, touched with a bit of pride. "Well, I had to wade through the latest fascinating issue of

Celeb Now but then I picked it up. Not bad. My mind hasn't totally rotted yet at the Villas."

"That's next week and then the Villas' evil master plan will be complete."

"My brain is two quick steps from actual Jell-O. Thanks for the book loan. You may be saving my life."

"It's what I do." Hale looked over at March with a grin. "May I escort you to the van?"

I stopped gawking at my suddenly flirtatious sister and went into autopilot, getting March into the van and fussing with the collapsible wheelchair.

We were headed for Louis Pizza, which made delicious garlic knots and stuffed shells in addition to amazing slices. As we drove away from the Sea Villas, I felt an ache in my heart for the beautiful pink sun setting over the water. I wished Vince were here to see it. I pictured his schedule: home from work by now in Charlotte, heating up a can of soup before reading or watching a Netflix movie. Or maybe, I thought with a sharp intake of breath, a date with someone who would pay more attention to him.

"So, March, what's the latest with your painting?" Hale looked over his shoulder from where he was sitting in the van's passenger seat.

If March was still painting after Hale's art classes at the Sea Villas, it was news to me. I pretended to pay very serious attention to the twenty-mile-per-hour street sign two blocks away from Louis Pizza.

March laughed a little. "Well, I'm still working on that wig series we talked about. It's a bit pathetic, me and the paintbrushes. I'm killing all sorts of canvases. I should be stopped."

It had been months since I heard March sound remotely like herself. And here she was, gamely strapped into her seat, on a pass from the rehab center, basically being March—funny, interesting March.

"What's the wig series?" I pulled carefully into a parking space about a block down from the pizza place. The last thing March would want was a big production with the ramp, chair, and her smack in front of the diners eating outside.

From the back of the van, I heard March sigh. "It's nothing—just a bunch of rough sketches of the wigs down in the salon. They have them there for the head-injury patients who have their heads shaved. I guess some people worry about being bald."

"Your paintings sound really neat. I would love to see them." I turned in my seat, looking back toward my sister. My eagerness was palatable. I suddenly felt like the desperately uncool older sister.

"Ah, they're pretty crappy. Just something to do to pass the time."

Hale said, "I disagree. March shows a deep grasp of the inner artistic torture known to wearers of the wig."

March threw back her head and laughed. Her long, dark hair, which was freshly washed, swung over her shoulders. My sister looked pretty, and I felt a quickening in my heart for her. Even though things were bad between us, I still remembered the girl she was—the maker of s'mores on camping trips, the sister who knitted me a magenta sweater one summer that was hopelessly tiny. March and I shared so much history. I didn't know how to get around it.

Inside Louis's, a small line had formed near the front. "I'll get us a table," Hale said. "Do you ladies mind eating outside? It looks pretty crowded. We might have a better chance of actually sitting down."

"Whatever you can find, Hale," March said with a smile. "I'll be sitting down regardless."

I froze, thinking the night was ruined because of Hale's careless remark. But he just looked into March's eyes and winked. "If I can't find a table, I'm on your lap."

March almost snorted with laughter. I wheeled her up the wooden ramp to the restaurant, bumping over the occasional warped board. I never noticed how many obstacles could get in the way of a chair until I had to push March in one. People act so weird when they see a wheelchair, too. They look over March's head and greet me. It's like she's not even there.

While we stood in line, I noticed with an ache the dozens of couples eating, clinking wineglasses, and laughing in the restaurant. Of course, I knew I was probably more aware of the romance on display because Vince was no longer speaking to me. I missed him often with a fierce longing, and then sometimes I didn't. It was strange—caring for March and tending to Hale took so much out of me, I didn't have much energy to take care of the most basic things. The oil light in my car had been on for two weeks. I couldn't remember the last time I tweezed my eyebrows or painted my fingernails. Call it hanging on by a thread, but that was me.

"Talked to Mom today," March said as we inched toward the counter.

"What's she up to?"

"Oh, you know, those new dancing lessons she dragged Dad to last month. They're learning the rumba this week."

Smiling, I thought of my parents. They never stayed in one place for long. "Dad complains, but I think he secretly likes dancing."

"Yeah," March said, her brow furrowed. "I wonder if they aren't doing too much, you know, so they don't have to come down here."

"March! That's ridiculous and you know it. Mom and Dad visit you all the time."

"I know she was just here," March said, looking down at her gauzy, flowing skirt. I picked it up for her at a little boutique in Charleston last week. "But before that, it was two weeks between visits."

It was true our parents didn't visit a lot. I think it was really hard on them to see their daughter so different—angry, sad, bitter. I know my father blamed himself for letting March ride Butter when she was so out of shape. Just like I blamed myself for pro- voking March the day before she rode Butter, my father held some sadness inside regarding March's accident. Mom, on the other hand, was a whirling dervish of activity; she was never home and never stopped taking classes, starting hobbies, and lunching with friends. So their visits to March were a bit fewer than I would have imagined. Besides, I took pride in the fact that I was just a few miles from my sister. I could handle anything that came up, right?

Hale waved to us from across the restaurant, beside the door to the outside porch. Wheeling March through the crowed place, I could feel the stares at the sight of a young woman in a chair. "Mommy, is she broken?" a little girl with a white bow in her hair said in a loud voice. March stared straight ahead, her hands folded together tightly. My face was a mirror of hers: *Let's just eat and go back, okay?*

Hale and I drank draft beers, while March sipped on a diet lemonade. I noticed she hardly touched her pizza. The old March would have thrown down a whole pie and a pitcher of beer. There was no denying the fact that March continued to lose weight. I always was surprised when I stopped and really looked at my sister lately. The person who was emerging from under her extra pounds was different and the same to me: the familiar brown eyes, but a sharper jaw. Her arms were skinnier, the muscles becoming defined by physical therapy. Her collarbones, too, were starting to surface.

"So, how's the house search going, Hale?" March wiped her mouth and looked across the table.

Hale glanced over at me and then looked away. "That was kind of a secret, March. I hadn't told Mae Wallace my plan yet."

Clapping her hand over her mouth, March looked as pleased as she could be. "Oh, sorry. Guess I thought it was public knowledge."

I was instantly irritated at both of them. Didn't Hale tell me everything? And what did March know that I didn't? "You're looking for a house?" I squeaked. I couldn't imagine living on Langdon without Hale as a neighbor.

Hale reached for the last slice of pizza. "Yeah, I figured I couldn't stay in that rental forever. It's so big and the street gets busy in the summer. You know," he finished lamely.

We three were silent as a busboy came by to remove our empty pizza pan. Hale looked at me, his eyes soft and friendly. I figured there was more to the story, and I knew to be patient.

"Where are you looking these days?" March asked.

"Charleston, Mount Pleasant, you know. Around the area."

My mind flipped back to the time Hale had spent in the house he once shared with his bride. It had been almost two years. Was he now ready to move on? Hale told me once he never left the house after Ruth disappeared because he wanted to be there if she came back. He said the word "if" deliberately with a careful slowness. He and I both knew she was not coming back, but staying in the house made it slightly easier for him to bear, Hale said. "It was space she moved in, space she inhabited," he said. That made sense to me.

In the months after her death, a smoothie stand opened up near the strip and Hale told me he felt funny going there. It was a new place, with no history of Ruth and Hale. To the smoothie employees, overly tanned high schoolers, he was just an older guy who was an artist in flip-flops and cut-off jeans. No wife clung to him or asked for a ten to pay for smoothies. He ordered one, not two.

"Well, good luck looking for a house," I said. "Just remember—you can't find the number or quality of OFDs that we have up on our end of the island."

"OFDs?" March asked, biting the tip of her straw.

Hale explained, "Old Fuddy-duddies. We have a bumper crop of irascible seniors living on our street. Play your music too loud or leave your laundry on the line too long, and they'll let you know."

"Gosh, you wish some people would get a life and stay out of your business, don't you?" March said the words idly but looked over at me.

My face felt hot and I looked down, confused.

In his laid-back way, Hale didn't seem to notice any new tension. Instead, he stretched his arms overhead and asked, "Who wants to go swimming?"

"What?" March and I both said the word at once.

"Summer's not going to last forever, you know. Come on, the water awaits." Hale stood up and turned March's chair toward the door.

March smiled wickedly. "I don't think Nurse Crazy would approve."

"Then, that's one more reason to do it, don't you think?"

For an answer, March smiled again and looked straight ahead as Hale pushed her through the dining room. But this time, there was a look on her face not of resignation but of expectation.

The Atlantic Ocean was as warm as a bathtub in July. Swimming in its waters under a full moon could make you feel amazing and peaceful, both at the same time. Since I was little, I loved floating on my back with the inky night sky above me, hearing the waves tumble into the wet sand on shore. We had spent so many vacations as children, even when we were penniless, at the beach. Somehow, my parents found ways to take us places. They were resourceful, borrowing friends' beachside condos or finding coupons and free offers. Of course, as a kid, I never knew what they had to do to give us a good time. I didn't know the sacrifice.

We drove back to our end of the island, parked, and wheeled March down to the beach using the old boardwalk that crested a sand dune dotted with sea oats. The moon gave the boardwalk a yellowish hue, while wispy clouds stretched over the black sky. As usual, the sea breezes were sharp and warm, carrying just the slightest hint of summer rushing past us on her way out. What was it Ruth once said to Hale? "There is a point at which each day of summer can be matched by another yet to come." Hale told me she meant that there was this perfect point in the summer when there were as many days of sun and sand ahead of you as behind you. Once you crossed that perfect day, it was all downhill from there.

As we approached the end of the boardwalk, the wooden planks gave way to a thick, stiff matting covering the sand. The wheelchair bumped along until we came to the open sand. The water rolled and crashed ahead of us.

"You still want to do this, March?" I gripped the wheelchair handles tightly. Hale was pulling off his shirt and scanning the beach.

"Tide's coming in," he said.

"What are you waiting for, sister?" March turned her shoulders slightly, addressing me.

Hale walked down the beach to give us privacy. I pulled out a navy blue bag and squirted some antiseptic cleaner on my hands. I then rolled down the waistband of March's skirt to expose her supra-pubic catheter bag. Tugging gently, I separated the rubber tubing that led from her abdomen to the bag. I wiped the end of the tube clean with antimicrobic cleaner and then reached into the blue bag for a catheter cap. Once that was on, I gently stored the catheter bag inside the blue bag and gathered up the used wipes.

March tugged off her tank top, exposing a pretty lacy bra I had never seen before. "And the skirt, too," she said, looking past me to the waves sounding in the distance.

I did as she asked, reaching down to gently roll the skirt off her body, lifting her a bit as I edged the fabric off, carefully trying not to nudge the capped catheter tube. We would have to swab the opening carefully before we took March back to the Sea Villas.

I felt a tenderness for my sister I had never known before. Her body showed the results of her weight loss, of course, but it was more than that. Her legs had a thin sallowness to them that did not match her robust upper arms. Seeing her legs, useless, and un-apologetic, made me accept March's condition more at that moment than any of the speeches I had heard by her doctors.

I waved to Hale, and he returned quickly, offering to carry March down to the water. I watched as he picked her up in his arms as if she were a two-year-old. I left the wheelchair, stripped off my T-shirt as March had done, and joined them. As opposed to March, I wore the most basic navy bra known to woman. Sexy it was not, but it doubled as a bathing-suit top in a pinch.

"It feels great!" March screamed as the first warm waves washed over her in Hale's arms. I strode through the little breakers beside them, nervously casting a glance at Hale's grip on my sister. As usual, he seemed perfectly safe and irreverent at the same time.

We moved out into calmer water that came to my shoulders. Hale squatted a bit, allowing March to remain covered in the seawater so that she wouldn't become chilled. Finally satisfied that my sister wouldn't drown tragically, I allowed myself to flip on my back and drift a few feet from Hale and March.

The black sky looked like a dark cup of coffee with a generous dollop of cream. Thin strips of clouds arched over the sky, making me wonder if I were looking at the Milky Way or just simply clouds. I was lousy at weather, clouds, and all sorts of meteorological stuff in school. Cumulus, nimbus, it was jumbled up in my head.

March had always gotten into all things heavenly. When she was ten, she could rattle off the weather forecast for the week, and recite the mythological origins of twenty or more constellations. Dad had joked half seriously that one day she would be on TV as a meteorologist. Mom said she would be an astronomer. They agreed to both be right as the parents of a future genius broadcaster. But then when March was twelve, she discovered boys and her hobbies morphed into collecting adolescent hearts. Of this, she was the undisputed champion. Dad often remarked that if college scholarships were handed out for crushes and admirers, he would be a lucky man.

I backstroked for a few feet to stay close to Hale and March. They talked in low tones, Hale's strong arms wrapped around my sister. It was nice to let my mind wander.

"And once or twice a year, you can actually see the South Atlantic whale venture up the coastline," March said. "I've swam just a few hundred feet from one. It was like I could almost reach out and touch it." She pointed lazily over the water.

Hale gazed out toward the open sea. "That's crazy. Weren't you scared?"

March's reply was soft and slow. "Scared? No, no, South Atlantic whales are such gentle giants of the deep. They're known for their kindness. You could keep them as pets, if it weren't for their size."

Hale looked impressed. I rolled over on my belly and paddled toward them. The water felt heavy and warm under my hands. "Tell me you are not believing this crap."

March smirked. "You're just jealous because animals flock to me."

"Oh, please."

Hale looked confused. "What are you talking about?"

I laughed. "Come on, South Atlantic whales, the 'gentle giants of the deep'? Doesn't that sound a little made up?"

Hale looked down at March, who was quietly laughing. "Is this true? Are you shamelessly lying to an eager pupil?"

Flipping her hair over Hale's shoulder, March rolled her eyes. "Swimming with whales? You fell for that? Please."

"I'll show you a gentle giant," Hale said, laughing. He lifted March up and out of the water and then smoothly ducked her under.

March emerged from her brief dunk, water pouring down her face. The smirk gone, she looked shocked. "I can't believe you did that! My health is fragile. I'm a patient, for God's sake. I have health problems—"

"You have two seconds to hold your breath."

"What?" March grasped Hale's neck. "Then you're coming down with me."

"You said so." Hale tightened his grasp on March and dunked under while I watched. After a second, they both surfaced, laughing.

"Truce! Truce!" March wiped the water from her eyes.

"Okay, I've exacted my revenge."

I reached over to flick a piece of seaweed off March's face. "Nurse Crazy would have arrested us all for that. But she never has to know."

"I know. They treat me like I'm freakin' going to die any minute." March squeezed water from her hair. A warm breeze blew across the ocean. I barely dared to hope; we were acting like sisters. Even out under the moon, with the water gently bumping our bodies up and down, I kept track of our sisterhood. I watched over it, guarding it with hope and fear.

We left the water shortly after that. It was time to get March back and into her sterile rehab room. After cleaning her catheter entry site and the bag end, we reattached it, giggling that no one was the wiser.

"I think I'll barely make curfew," March said. "Not that I care. What are they going to do? Take away my wheelchair?"

"Nah, they'd probably suspend your Jell-O privileges," Hale said as he lifted March into the borrowed van. "Or worse, lock up the pipe cleaners and dried macaroni in the art room. How would you live?"

"I would persevere, somehow." March made a stoic face.

Hale climbed into the van and double-checked March's seat-belt harness. "Seriously, how are you doing there? It can't be easy with people hurting all around you."

Looking down at her hands in the darkened van, March twisted the ceramic ring I gave her for her birthday last year. "The worst are the teenage girls, with their shaved heads and thin little necks stuffed full of tubes. They look like tiny, shorn chicks. I think of how I was at their age. Carefree and crazy for boys. They are, too. Or were. They're the ones who bother me the most. I feel sad for them, or pity them, or get mad at them for being in that place. My therapist says I am transferring my anger from my situation to theirs."

"What do you think?" Hale said.

March made a face. "Now you sound like her."

"Sorry."

"What do I think? I think I've spent too much time talking about stupid things. Take me back. I'm getting pretty tired."

Nodding, Hale joined me up in the front seat. The easy-going March of a few minutes ago was gone. The normal March, or what I had accepted as normal, was back in her full glory. I swallowed, my throat dry. Suddenly, I fiercely wanted a tall glass of water.

I cranked up the van and backed slowly away from our end of the island. Of course, before long, Hale would be gone and I would be living here along with a bunch of crusty old men and women who fussed when the shaggy grass grew tall in my front yard. How long Hale would last as my neighbor was anyone's guess. All I knew was at that moment, I needed him to stay more than ever. Even though the memories he had to sleep with at night must have been half comforting and half terrifying, and even though he was sending signals it was time to move on, suddenly I wanted him to stay. I needed Hale for March.

ELEVEN

My cell rang the next morning, startling me with its tinny sound. I didn't get many calls. Hale usually just yelled over the porch, and March or her nurses called only once or twice a week. Vince had moved on. My parents checked in on both of us about once a week. My phone wasn't exactly hopping.

"Hello, Mae Wallace?"

I inhaled sharply. The voice was accented and dripping with sophistication. It was my old boss from World Matters in Atlanta. "Andreas?"

"Yes, Mae Wallace. How are you?"

I couldn't imagine why Andreas was calling me. I pictured her, sleek and composed, with a tiny phone in her hand as she surveyed the highways tangled beneath World Matters' headquarters building. "I'm good, March is good. We're still here on Langdon."

"That's the reason I am calling, Mae Wallace. My old friend and colleague Hans Macher is pulling together a World Matters marketing campaign for the southeast. He's working as a consultant out of his home in Charleston. When he called me looking for people for his team, I immediately thought of you."

"Me?" My face flushed with heat. World Matters was my old life, the Atlanta life where I shopped for furniture at IKEA and tried out new sushi restaurants. Langdon was the opposite of that world. Here, I changed the sheets on March's bed, washed her long hair, consulted with doctors and occupational therapists, made sure she had taken her meds. I wore flip-flops all the time. My T-shirts were faded from the sun. I had a permanent collection of sand between my toes.

"Yes, don't be so bashful. You know I would give anything for you to come back to World Matters. This is my way of keeping you close."

"I don't know, Andreas. March takes up so much of my time. There are appointments, doctors—"

"I know you are taking very good care of your sister," Andreas said quietly. "You are being a model big sister. But you also have to think of your future. You can't stay on that little island forever."

Wanna bet? There were a million chores to do each day. I had March, of course. There was Hale with all that he was going through. "And there's Ruth," I blurted into phone.

"Who's Ruth? Is she a patient at the hospital?" Andreas sounded confused.

I rubbed my eyes, wishing for a loss of the crystal-clear cell-phone connection.

Andreas continued firmly, "Okay, so just take his name and give him a call. Okay? The beauty of this position is that you can take as many hours as you want. Spend some time at the hospital, spend some time helping people get decent housing."

I took Hans's information, thinking it would be a waste of time to contact the poor guy. After I hung up, I looked at my shaky handwriting. *Hans Macher. World Matters.* I wondered if there was room on his planner for all of us: Hale, March, Vince, and Ruth. Sighing, I shoved the piece of paper under a magazine on the kitchen counter.

The afternoon was spent at the Sea Villas in our family-counseling session, meeting with March and Moon Fairy. Actually, her name was Melinda, and she had a master's in social work but March had given her a little private pet name. Melinda dressed in long, flowing skirts with tiny mirrors sewn onto the hem. She painted elaborate henna tattoos on her hands and feet, and talked frequently of meeting up with her aura so that she could take it out for coffee. I cannot emphasize how much March despised meeting with Moon Fairy.

We three sat down in Room A in the counseling center on the ground floor. The room held comfortable chairs upholstered in expensive-looking fabrics. A few potted trees huddled in each corner.

"Okay, so March," Moon Fairy began, "have you given thought to your General Life Plan since last we talked?"

My sister looked up from the spot on the floor she had been staring at intently. "Well, I have been journaling daily, as you suggested—"

"You have?" Moon Fairy practically knocked her granny-glasses off her nose, her head snapped up so quickly. "This pleases me to no end, March. I just think you have so much *potential*." Moon emphasized this last word as if March were hard of hearing. "Potential. I believe it."

"I know, I feel it." March nodded earnestly. I stifled a laugh. March no more journaled than she cartwheeled down the halls around the nurses' station. She spent her afternoons surfing the Web in the computer lab or sitting outside under the jasmine-covered gazebo.

"Mae Wallace, isn't this wonderful news that March has been so introspective?"

"Yeah, it's great." As the required family member for the sessions, I was supposed to bring up my feelings of inadequacy or resentment or whatever, but of course I didn't say a thing. I didn't want to feed March's anger or sadness. She had enough problems of her own. March, on the other hand, volunteered lots of fabulous emotions complete with stories and subplots, but they were someone else's stories and subplots. Today's journaling segment was no doubt ripped off from an online support group for wheelchair-bound young women.

As if on cue, Moon Fairy asked, "Did you visit Wheeled Babes this week?"

"I sure did. Good stuff happened to our interior lives. I told

Carrie—that's my friend from Pasadena—that she had the paint palette and she was the only one who could color her world."

Shifting in my chair, I tried to give March a look. She was pushing it with Moon. March regarded online support groups with a high degree of disdain. The idea of strangers writing back and forth about their meds, infections, and sexual problems made her want to gag. So she trolled them just often enough to steal the good stuff and recycle them for Moon Fairy sessions.

"That's an interesting analogy, March. Let's unpack that. Mae Wallace, what do you think March means: 'She is the only one who could color her world'?"

I could sense the mirth in March's eyes, so I avoided looking over at her. Moon nodded earnestly, urging me on. She nudged a tissue box closer on the table.

"I guess what March was telling that girl—"

"Carrie. From Pasadena," March piped up.

"Ah . . . Carrie . . . is that even though she was in a wheelchair, she could choose how to view her world. And if she wanted to be bitter or happy or determined, it was her choice."

"Splendid, Mae Wallace. Splendid," Moon closed her eyes and murmured to herself.

I sneaked a glance over to March. She was trying not to laugh. All of a sudden, I felt sorry for Moon Fairy. She was an honest, if slightly wacky professional, trying to help my sister. March was playing with her mind, like she did with most everyone who crossed her path since the accident. The only person she didn't seem to push around was Hale. I thought about the two of them and wondered what Moon would say to that. Did a still-grieving widower figure into March's General Life Plan?

"So, Mae Wallace," Moon turned to me with a hopeful smile. "What is going on in your world sphere these days?"

Taken off guard, I was tempted to toss off a few platitudes, but resisted. March was barely paying attention. She might not even hear what I said. "Well, I got a call from my old boss this week. She wanted to see if I was interested in some freelance work."

"Splendid. What did you say?"

"I didn't commit to anything. I just took down the information. Maybe I'll call, probably not."

Out of the corner of my eye, I could see March stop doodling on her journal cover. Some part of me wanted to tell her what that call meant to me. I felt the pull of my old life, even down here on sandy Langdon. I could hear and smell the heat of Atlanta, the rush of the interstates wrapped around downtown. In my mind, I could see the art galleries, women trotting off to work in high heels, coffee shops on every corner. It was a world I remembered and, I was coming to realize, missed dearly.

"You worked in the nonprofit sector, correct?" Moon opened her notebook for reference. "In Atlanta?"

"Mae Wallace was gonna save the world," March said in her snarkiest voice.

"Something like that." So much for family revelations. I decided to shut up and let Moon take the conversation somewhere else.

Moon rushed on, oblivious to any tension floating about in the room. "What I am hearing, Mae Wallace, is that you had a career you enjoyed that you gave up to help your sister. That's love." She reached for a tissue, the mirrors on her skirt rustling softly.

"It wasn't exactly—" I tried to stop Moon. March hated any display of pity. "March could have taken care of herself, we all know that, but my parents and I thought I was the best person to do it. And I wanted to. I did."

"Sure you did," Moon said, her voice swimming in sympathy.

I thought back to the time when March was being transferred to Langdon, after she had stabilized and the next step was rehab. At first, we were hopeful when we toured the Villas, like this could be the place where she miraculously healed. This is where the latest clinical trials would make March a cord-injury miracle baby. There would be interviews. *The New York Times* would send a reporter. CNN would camp out on the doorstep of the hospital.

But now, I see where our hope was misguided and probably harmful. I was sure that March could see the flimsily veiled dreams in our eyes. My mother, in particular, kept reading statistics she had gleaned off the Internet and the hospital brochures. " 'Eighty percent of patients at the Sea Villas go on to resume careers, have families, and cultivate rich lives in the private and public sector.' Why, did you hear that, March? Eighty percent!"

"Does it say what the other twenty percent are doing? Probably drooling in a corner somewhere."

My mother looked confused, her hopeful face softening into the sadness I had come to understand and expect. My mother and I were similar in that we tended to hide our disappointments. She grabbed a hold of activities and classes and other distractions. I ran toward the problem, masking my depression in an effort to help. In college, that had worked well. All of my causes and drives had given me a sense of accomplishment. If I didn't want to think about how Ellis wasn't exactly the perfect boyfriend, all I had to do was schedule a meeting or dive into the event details for a fund-raiser.

Now that I was in the adult world, that place where every teenager longs to be, I could see a life of masking hurt made more problems. The big dilemma, of course, was how to stop doing it. Old patterns were comfy, and I climbed headfirst into the soft chair they made.

Back in our family-therapy session, Moon had turned to March. "What do you think of Mae Wallace's phone call from her old boss?"

"She didn't tell me about it, so I really don't know."

"I didn't mention it, because it's nothing, March. I probably won't even call. It's no big deal."

Moon scribbled a few notes. "I, for one, think you should at least consider it. You have to remember that you are in transition, and this life of being on Langdon is not meant to be forever."

"It's not forever," March parroted.

I nodded, eager to get the spotlight off of me. Moon assigned some journaling to March and then we were dismissed. As March wheeled herself down the hall toward the elevator, I walked beside her without saying anything. I liked for her to drive the conversation. That way I couldn't make her mad or say the wrong thing.

At the elevator bank, March turned toward me. "So, do you think that you're going to go back to work?"

"It's not back to work, March. It's some freelance. Just a free-lance thing."

My sister swept back her long hair over her shoulder and looked up at me. For the first time in a long while, she looked straight into my eyes. "Well, I think it would be a good idea. You can't hang around me all the time."

I was not expecting her words. I didn't know what to say, so I tried a joke. "I like the smell of disinfectant, March. Why would I stop coming here?"

"Whatever. Just giving you my poor, crippled opinion. Sorry you can't deal with it." The elevator opened and March angrily thrust herself onto it with a rapid wheel turn. I stood there, un-sure of what to do. My last glance of March was her back and her wheelchair, with its black leather seat and shining chrome wheels.

I knew I needed to find Hale, to vent and get some perspective. I drove back to our end of the island. Hale's car was parked in the crushed seashell drive, but his bike was missing from the side of the one-car garage where he always propped it against the weath-ered clapboards. I drove on, figuring he could be anywhere—the smoothie stand, the Shop All. I don't know what made me think about the bridge. I wasn't even sure if he would be there, but I turned down State Street and made my way over to Ocean Drive and followed it to the turn in the island. The new bridge arched up and over, blocking the sun with its massive piers.

I pulled up under the bridge and killed the engine. A few feet away, Hale's bike stood alone near an overflowing trash can. Two seagulls picked at the gray, sandy soil, scrapping over the remains of a candy bar. I got out of the car, my problems with March forgotten as I walked toward the water. I wasn't sure what I would find.

Hale once told me he felt at home near water because it wasn't as confining as land. He had tried to live in various inland places before, he said, but ultimately found his way back to the water. Langdon was home with its slip of sand and dirt and then the wide, wide sea. For Hale, that was the way to live. Up in Henderson, I never felt that way. I was surrounded by acres and acres of pine, oak, and honeysuckle, and I liked it. Being Southern people, Hale and I both thought about land a lot; we just looked at it in different ways.

A wide opening in the scrub brush under the bridge had been formed into a down-at-the-heels park. I picked my way past the derelict picnic tables with their rusted bolts and tired-looking planks. A couple making out on a sagging table paused to take a breath as I skirted the park. I didn't see Hale anywhere, and I started to have a mild bit of concern. Of course, my every day was filled with more than mild bouts of panic for March and her condition, so being alarmed seemed to be my new way of approaching life. In fact, I was starting to become at home with the teensy tightening that had taken up residence in my chest.

After I cleared the park area, there were just a few yards more of sand and shells. The bay water struck the sand, echoing under the bridge with wet-sounding slaps. Plastic bottles, empty cups, and Styrofoam bobbed up against each other, jostling for position as cars roared overhead. I couldn't help but think of Ruth. Did she see this trash before she made her way out to the pier she would eventually climb? Was the trash a dull omen or did she blithely walk right past it, black skirt swinging with impatience as she set her sights on the bridge that was slowly being dismantled?

"I don't know why she decided to climb the old bridge," Hale told me not too long ago. "It's not like she had a thing for climbing or was a thrill seeker. Actually, she was more of a homebody. She knitted. I mean, how does someone like that decide to climb a hundred feet into the air?"

I didn't have an answer for Hale then, just like I didn't have one now. For as I gazed across the water, with the new bridge high above me, I saw the last three piers of the old bridge rising out of the bay, and on top of them, a short, pointless stretch of highway. Each still had its long-dark lampposts. The first one out had company, though. The pier stood proudly, almost defiantly in the bay with white-capped waves brushing up against its blunt base. On top, on that abbreviated ribbon of asphalt and concrete, stood my dear friend Hale.

TWELVE

When Ruth died, Hale was left with his wife's collection of costume notebooks and fabric scraps. As a professional costume designer for the theater, Ruth would have been expected to be the owner of quite an elaborate and extensive fabric collection. That would be the wrong assumption. Hale said she was always deliberate. She didn't buy endless reams of fabric. No, she was careful, even choosy, about the fabric she let into her life.

"If I fill up room after room with bolts of cloth, how am I ever going to find the right fabric?" she asked Hale when he first questioned her about her methods. "I would rather have one project in mind and then go look for fabric in the stores rather than have whole rooms crammed with stacks of stuff."

When Hale told me this story, he explained that Ruth was

exacting about her work. There were no late-night sketching sessions, no last-minute dashes to churn out thirty-eight pirate costumes for the next week's opening. Ruth was organized, meticulous, and disciplined. "She could be dramatic, moody, you know, an *artiste*," Hale said, shrugging. "But the larger sum of Ruth was that she kept a detailed day planner, she got regular eye checkups, she clipped coupons—she was in charge of her life, you know?"

Especially after they got married, Hale said, and her meddling sisters were out of the way. Ruth also became more independent once she was out from under the thumb of her parents who, though caring, had never really known how to handle their youngest, most sensitive daughter. It was then that Ruth really started to shine.

Being involved in the Charleston theater scene was a good fit for Ruth. After the demands of living on the road with touring shows, Hale said she enjoyed the more mundane aspects of a smaller theater. Often, it was just she, the director, the lighting designer, and the set designer sitting down to work up a show. There were no nosy producers, bus drivers' unions, or set construction crews running amok. Sometimes, with the theater bay doors open to the sounds of Charleston street life going by, Ruth would sit and sketch in a red velvet chair and thank her lucky stars she had the job.

The designs for her last show were in a moss-green notebook. It was the kind of book art students or English majors carry around—serious, with thick, creamy, unlined paper. Hale placed it on the coffee table between us one night when I stopped by after dinner. We drank hard apple cider. The ocean was a muffled soundtrack outside. It was a few weeks after I had discovered Hale on top of the first section of the old bridge. I had started screaming for him from my spot in the park, but he was oblivious to my calls. He finally saw me when he started swimming for shore. I paced in the sand frantically. But Hale took it all in stride. He told me nonchalantly that he liked climbing the old bridge pier from time to time to sit where Ruth last stood.

"The show was a good one, her last design." Hale took a long sip from the cider bottle, nodding toward the notebook.

"What was it?"

"It was a premiere. A young playwright in residence at the College of Charleston. The story was about three siblings and their parents' estate. There was land—an old plantation. The land meant different things to each sibling. And, there was this unscrupulous developer and the ghost of the plantation's soul or something like that."

"It sounds interesting."

"I'm not making it come out right, but it really was very good. It was very theatrical, which sounds like I'm being condescending, but I'm not. You know how some plays just sound like they're supposed to be heard on stage? Like you know they couldn't make the transition to the small screen or to movies very well?"

I took a sip of cider. "I actually don't know too much about the theater. I mean, I would love to go, it's just something I haven't done very much. March dragged me to some experimental plays in high school and one performance-art piece when we were in college, but I'm kind of out of the play scene."

"What are you doing next Friday?"

Washing March's hair, I think to myself. "Nothing, I guess."

Looking pleased with himself, Hale smiled. "Then it's settled. We're going to Charleston. Ruth's theater is doing a production of the show I was telling you about, *The Zee Bee*. It's an encore performance, which means they produced it recently, and to save money, they're presenting it again because audiences sold it out the first time. It's a sure way to make some cash without investing in a new script, costumes, and sets."

"That sounds pretty calculating. I thought it was all about the art," I said, propping my feet up on the glass coffee table.

"Yeah, right. These small, regional theaters have to struggle for every dollar they get. Most are in the red year after year. Ruth's theater had a great reputation because they premiered a lot of work by hot new talents, but even still, they had trouble paying the bills."

"Well, sign me up. I would love to see the show."

"Cool. I'll get us two tickets unless you think March would like to come."

I paused. "She's pretty ticked off at me right now. Let's just go without her. I'm not sure she wants to spend any time with me. Although you seem to cheer her up."

Letting my comment pass, Hale set down his empty bottle on the hardwood floor. "Surely you can work it out by next week?"

Suddenly, I felt tired and worn out. Even getting to next Friday seemed like too much to think about. "Maybe, who knows? She gets angry with me and then I tiptoe around and then it all gradually gets back to normal. Or what seems to be normal these days."

Walking into the kitchen, Hale called over his shoulder, "So, do you ever get mad at March?"

"What do you mean?" I heard the clink of glass and the refrigerator door closing.

Hale reappeared, carrying two more bottles of apple cider. He held one out to me. "I mean, you are always walking around, afraid of what March will say, and then backing down when she does get pissed off."

"So?"

"So, that's no way to be in a relationship with someone."

The cider was cold in my mouth. I had a little buzz, probably because I drank so little these days. I was a total lightweight. "What are you, Mr. Relationship Expert now?"

Hale held up his hands. "Okay, okay. Forget I said something."

"I mean, really, are you saying you know all about sisters and their complicated, tangled web of emotions?"

Hale looked contrite. "Look, Mae Wallace, I apologize. I shouldn't have said anything."

I swung my beer in the air, and climbed onto my soapbox. "'Cause the last time I checked, you aren't a sister who has a sister who is in a wheelchair." The blood rushed to my head. I knew I was speaking words that were not what I meant. "And another thing, if you're so perfect, why don't you have any other friends? Why hang out with me all day and dispense relationship advice?"

"Don't say that, Mae Wallace." Hale gave me a warning look.

"Yeah, me, who has a penchant for getting people hurt. I'd watch out if I were you."

"Mae Wallace, you had nothing to do with that accident, and you know it. March decided to ride that obstinate horse. She chose those actions. Not you."

I pressed the cold bottle to my forehead. "If you just could have been there, you would have felt the tension. She was still mad at me because I took Vince away. She had something to prove."

Sitting quietly for a moment, Hale looked over at me. "Mae Wallace, I'm no expert in any of this, but one thing I know is that you have to forgive yourself. You have to realize that sometimes you go through life and the wrong thing happens. You might not necessarily know why or how it all goes down, but it does. And then you have to learn to keep living."

Even with my buzzed little brain, I knew we weren't talking about my sister anymore. I could see the hurting part of Hale. But I could also see the part that made him stronger, strong enough to offer help.

"How do you do it? I mean, how do you get up and go on knowing that someone you loved is not there anymore?" My eyes filled with tears.

Taking a deep breath, Hale closed his eyes. "Because I have learned to see what is left. What Ruth left behind." He nodded toward the green notebook. "Ruth left behind beauty, like the costume designs in there. She left behind her tiny stitches in hundreds of costumes in three or four theaters around the country. She left behind the painted walls in the bedroom we shared. Cappuccino. Ruth always said she liked looking at them because it reminded her of cappuccino.

"Sometimes, it's not enough that all I have of my wife is what she left to remind me of her presence. But sometimes, it is." Hale opened his eyes and looked at me.

"It's not fair, Hale, it isn't." I was crying now.

"You're absolutely right. It isn't. And it's not fair what happened to March, either. She could have done a million things that day besides ride a fat horse. But she didn't and now you are stuck here."

I thought of his choice of words. "Stuck" seemed to describe me pretty well. I was stuck, mired, running in place—whatever you wanted to call it—and I wasn't sure how to move on. "Can I ask you a question?"

"Of course, you know you can."

"Why do you do those paintings of the bridge and what floats up under it? You know I think they're great, I just wonder why you go back to that place."

"You mean the place where Ruth died?"

I nodded. It seemed hard to say the words out loud.

"Well, when Ruth was on that bridge, hundreds of people saw her. She was an oddity—a woman climbing up onto a dismantled bridge. One chunk of concrete and steel with a very real and living woman on top. Most blew past on the new bridge without doing anything. Others picked up their cell phones and called 911. One man even stopped his car and yelled over to her to see if she needed help."

I pictured the slim Ruth up on top of the bridge, buffeted by sea winds. Did she look over the edge to see the whitecaps below? Did she smell the salty air and maybe wonder what Hale was doing at that moment?

"So when I got the call from the police chief that there had been an accident, everyone knew about it. There were a hundred people at the command post under the bridge. Divers, emergency crews, the TV newspeople. It seemed so impersonal—this drive to recover her body once they knew there would be no rescue.

"After the memorial service, which we had in Ruth's family's church up in Greenville, I came back to the bridge and stood there, noticing the junk that floated up underneath. That's when I knew what I would paint. All of the crap. Because it's out there; it was in the water when she went in, and it keeps coming. It's still there. I have just learned to deal with it."

I felt very close to Hale. We talked about Ruth a lot, but I had never seen him open up like that to the events surrounding her death. I wasn't sure how much I could ask. And then I remembered what he said about me being afraid to talk to March. He was right—some things you couldn't tiptoe around. Sometimes you had to take the risk.

"Hale, what do you think happened?"

Sighing, Hale looked toward the ocean, visible through the tall windows in the room. "Take your pick: she jumped or she fell. We know she wasn't pushed. No one reported seeing another person up there."

"But what do you think?"

"Of course, I wanted to believe she fell. That's the best and cleanest answer. You never want to think someone would remove themselves from your life on purpose with such finality. But as the weeks after her death went on, I wondered if, in a small flash of time, Ruth had wanted out of everything."

I paused, not sure if I should pry. "Why do you say that?"

Hale stood up abruptly. "Hey, this isn't supposed to be all about me, right? I'm supposed to be helping you. Instead, we're talking about my sorrows. I get sick of that sometimes, you know?"

We walked out on the porch, the sea breezes still warm with a hint of a cooler wind rolling through the skies. Hale pushed back a chunk of hair falling over his forehead. "Thanks for talking to me about Ruth. I want you to know it helps to put it into words. Sometimes I can only stand it for so long, though. I get tired of hearing my own voice."

"I'm probably the opposite. I don't talk enough about March. Not to my parents, or to March, and not when I was with Vince. I keep a lot of stuff inside. And then it comes out all weird."

"That's why we're a good team," he said, putting his arm around my shoulders. "We should set up an illegal, nonlicensed therapy center. I'll take the grieving-widower segment of the population, and you could go after the equestrian-accident market."

Laughing, I smiled up at him. "I'm glad I moved into that dump next door and met you."

"Likewise."

And then we both turned back to the ocean. The sun was a perfect ball of pink, hanging low in the sky. Summer was ending, and taking with it balmier days. I hoped for a moment, a hidden, secret hope, that our sad days were falling behind us, too.

The next morning, I picked up my cell and dialed the World Matters guy, Hans Macher. My hands were shaking as I punched in the numbers. *Please go to voice mail,* I thought to myself. That way, I made the call but didn't have to really do anything.

Seeing Hale pick up the pieces made me want to do the same thing. And even though March seemed hostile to my idea of working—or was she hostile because I hadn't told her my plans?—I felt a surge of something expectant in my heart. I had a feeling, probably true, that I was afraid to move past March's injury and back into something like a real life.

"Hello?" Hans answered. His English was touched with a slight accent, probably German.

"Hi, Hans, this is Mae Wallace Anders. I worked with Andreas at World Matters." My voice was a tad squeaky, not at all the polished professional I was striving for when I picked up the phone.

"Oh, yes, Mae Wallace. I was hoping you would call. Andreas told me all about you. She said I had to have you on the team for the campaign."

"I would love to hear about the campaign if you have time."

"Better yet, let me take you to lunch and tell you all about it. I have a vision and I tend to go on and on. A plate of crab cakes might make me focus a little better. What about today?"

Hans talked a mile a minute, without seeming to take a breath. That was typical of a World Matters staffer, though. Out to save the world, right this second. The funny thing was, I was becoming intrigued. I wanted to know all about this campaign he was running. To be honest, I was also flattered that Andreas had tracked me down and recommended me for the team.

We decided to meet downtown at noon at a bistro I had never

heard of called Sandy Lane. "They have the best peach cobbler of any I have had in the U.S.," Hans said. "I will order some for you when we get there. If it is not the best you have had, I will give you five dollars."

Hans seemed to love his food. I hung up, smiling that this would be an interesting lunch, even if I didn't end up working with Hans.

Since I had two hours before lunch, I decided to go outside and pull a few weeds that had sprung up in the planters out front. I pulled on an old T-shirt and shorts, and shoved my feet into a pair of battered sneakers. Luckily, there was cloud cover so the mugginess would be more bearable.

Pulling steadily, I made a tidy little pile of the flowering weeds next to the shell-packed driveway. Weeding was like dusting or washing windows—you received instant gratification with a bit of exertion. I liked being outside and working with my hands, feeling the cool, sandy soil between my fingers. After I had been weeding about fifteen minutes, a car pulled up next door at Hale's.

I recognized Hale's landlord, Mr. Forrester. He was an older man who showed up once a month to inspect the property. Hale said when Ruth died he sent a large basket of cookies, cakes, and other treats. It was the most practical condolence gift he received, Hale said, because there were all sorts of people in the house and having something sweet lying around gave people an unexpected lift.

Mr. Forrester carried a camera in one hand. He waved and then disappeared into the house. I continued weeding, and when he returned, he went to the trunk of his sedan and pulled out a "For Rent" sign. Grunting and swearing a bit, Mr. Forrester shoved the metal sign into the sandy soil. Going back to the car, he opened the driver's side door and sat sideways in the seat with his feet on the driveway. Taking a sip from a silver flask, Mr. Forrester wiped his brow and rested. Then he waved again, swung his legs inside the car, and drove away.

I left my growing pile of weeds and walked over to the sign. It read, "Charming 2/1 cottage. Available Oct. 1," followed by Mr. Forrester's number. A fleeting sense of loneliness flashed over me. I couldn't imagine Langdon without Hale as my neighbor. He said he might move into Charleston. Would we still be friends when we didn't watch almost every sunset together from the wooden decks of our two cottages? Or would we become friends that were only close because of proximity and then gradually cool when there were more miles between us?

I had been afraid to bring up the subject of Hale's moving since we last talked about it. I had hoped that Hale was just going through a phase and if I didn't mention it, he would forget all about it. Clearly, there were flaws in my plan.

October 1. That was a little less than a month from now. I wondered where Hale would end up living. My guess was that he would leave Langdon. It wasn't like he needed to stay here to paint, and his memories were the stuff of nightmares. No, he was probably off to the city. Maybe to one of the hip, little up-and-coming areas near Park Circle. I resolved to ask him when I saw him next, no matter how painful it was to hear his response.

I grabbed big handfuls of the pulled weeds and hauled them to the dented metal trash cans near the street. My back was soaked with sweat. It was time to grab a shower and get ready for lunch with Hans.

Sandy Lane Bistro was near the College of Charleston, so there were plenty of earnest art students and slouching theater majors on the sidewalks. Did I look that angst-ridden when I was in school? I hoped not. But I knew I probably did—rushing from event to event, with "Save the Something" buttons on my cardigan sweater and sheaves of flyers stuffed under my arm.

It was good to be in the real world, I realized with a start. I used to fantasize about ducking back into the Goss cocoon, but it struck me quite forcefully that I was older now and ready to make my mark on the world in whatever way that I could figure out. Maybe that meant helping March. Maybe it meant helping out my parents by staying near March while she rehabbed. I just knew it didn't mean slinking back into the safety net of college.

I scanned Sandy Lane's outdoor terrace. Hans told me to look for him there. I pictured a tall, serious European World Matters employee, probably wearing a canvas vest with a lot of pockets and a satellite phone within arm's reach.

In the flesh, Hans was nothing of the sort. He was about my height, with a shocking head of corkscrew curls of the most perfect honey-blond color. I knew women in Atlanta who spent hundreds of dollars a month to get that shade of blond. I almost couldn't take my eyes off his hair as we shook hands.

"The hair?" Hans said, shaking his head and making hundreds of tiny curls dance a little jig. "I know, I know. My mother says it was wasted on a boy."

"Sorry, you just have sort of really interesting—"

"Pretty? You can say it. I have pretty hair."

I nodded. It was true. He had probably the most amazing hair I had ever seen. "If the humanitarian thing doesn't work out, you could always take your hair on tour," I said.

Hans laughed and nodded. "We're booked at Carnegie Hall next month."

I laughed, too, and sat down at a small patio table Hans had staked out. I liked him instantly. And a long-deferred competitive drive in me wanted the job. I decided to go for it. Maybe I could do the World Matters campaign and still tend to March. It could work out, couldn't it? I pictured the windowless cubicle I had to give up in downtown Atlanta. The oatmeal-colored space contained a hip metal desk and matching swivel chair. Even my trash can was a cool, wire mesh basket.

After ordering crab cakes and sweet tea, Hans waved to the stack of papers he had placed in the center of the table. "World Matters has hired me to develop a grassroots awareness campaign in twenty cities around the country. Charleston is one of the first places, not because it's the biggest, but because we just happen to have a tremendous donor presence already. Three or four of the top World Matters donors in the country live within twenty miles of this very spot." Hans nodded at me very seriously. "My mission is to launch the campaign 'My World Matters' by the end of the year. Our thinking is that if we engage the local community, we will not only increase our brand presence of course, but also increase the buy-in and loyalty of our existing base of donors."

"Sounds great," I said. "One of the issues we faced in Atlanta was that a lot of people barely knew who World Matters was and fewer understood our mission. There was only a vague awareness, you know?"

"Do I. Our research shows that name recognition of World Matters is fairly anemic. This campaign aims to change that. Our plan is to host two events this fall—one VIP dinner at a major donor's estate and another event at the College where we invite a leading humanitarian to speak. Beyond that, there are numerous small events at high schools and presentations to local corporations."

My mind was swirling with ideas about the dinner event—what to serve, decorations, white tents—when I felt Hans staring at me. "Yes?"

"You looked kind of far away. Don't tell me you're not interested. I need some fast thinkers on this one. Andreas tells me I won't be disappointed in your work."

Was I interested? It would mean half days or full days away from March, plus even more hours spent driving in from Langdon. But yet, I was intrigued. Could March handle me not being around as much? Sure, it wasn't like we were the closest of sisters anymore—well, not at all, really—but I felt a connection and a responsibility to her and to her care.

Hans paused, and took a sip of tea. "Andreas told me there is a sister—"

"Her name is March."

"March. Well, I wanted to let you know that this job assumes you have family responsibilities that are more important. You can set your own hours, work around your sister's appointments, whatever. It is a completely flexible position and you can start when you are ready."

My eyes filled with tears as I looked over at Hans and his ridiculously beautiful head of blond curls. The crab cakes arrived, steaming and fragrant. The waiter quietly refilled our sweet tea glasses. March never liked sweet tea; our entire family drank it like water, but she was never a fan. I thought of her now and wondered what she was doing. When we were kids, she was always so excited about whatever "big sister" privilege I was allowed to do first, whether it was driving or going off to middle school. She would look at me with excited, wide eyes and I knew she was dreaming of the day she could get her ears pierced or stay at the mall until 8 P.M. Now, as I thought about leaving her once again to do something she could not yet do, my heart swam with misgivings.

"If you take the job, your biggest project will be arranging the event at the home of Lucie and Richard Trayham on the Ashley River. They are generously opening up their estate for a fall harvest feast. It's not a fund-raiser, per se, but a chance to have all of their circle and invited guests learn about World Matters. We'll have the president of World Matters and some board members attend, also probably our celebrity spokeswoman, Baker Land."

Again, my mind clicked into planning mode. I would need to get a laptop and probably upgrade my cell phone. I had dropped my current one in the sand at the beach one too many times. Plus,

I would need to get a decent wardrobe. Meeting with the Trayhams in flip-flops was a definite no-no. I looked across the table at Hans, who was contentedly munching on his second crab cake.

"Sign me up. What do we need to do first?"

"That's what I like to hear, excellent. We'll hit the ground running, with some pre-meetings before we visit the Trayhams. How's your ballroom dancing? The Trayhams are amateur champions, I understand."

"Uhm, I think I can waltz a little," I said. "I took a few forgettable years of tap and ballet."

"Excellent. We'll suggest a dinner-and-dancing theme for the event. They'll go crazy for it. And hopefully foot a lot of the bill. Alcohol for this set is not cheap. If you get what I mean." Hans signaled the waiter. "Now, are you ready for that peach cobbler?"

The next Friday, Hale stopped by to drop off Ruth's last notebook. He held out the mossy-green book to me, smiling almost apologetically. I reached out to take the book, unsure of what to do next.

"I meant to drop it off earlier in the week, sorry."

"Oh, okay," I said, not sure what he was getting at or if I had missed something. It was entirely possible. The week had been hectic. March had had more therapy and life-skills appointments than usual, and I tried to attend each one. Hans and I talked at least once a day about the campaign. I was supposed to start officially on Monday, but he already had me researching and making lists. Was I supposed to do something with Ruth's book?

"I just thought if you looked over her designs before you saw *The Zee Bee* tonight, it would give a sense of her idea for the show. You might feel more of a connection, you know?"

Nodding, I ran one hand over the front of the book. It felt strange to touch the property of someone you never knew but knew so much about. I imagined her hands on this book, and I longed to be alone so I could page through it. But Hale waited expectantly, looking at me. "You don't mind—reading it, that is?"

"No, of course. Like you said, it will help make the show tonight more meaningful. I do have a question, though. It might sound strange."

"Shoot."

"Well, you know how you told me that this play had been performed before? Well, will all the costumes be the same ones Ruth worked on? I mean, what if a different actor joined the cast and he was thirty pounds heavier or something?"

"Ruth designed the costumes, which means they exist not only on hangers, but in notebooks, DVDs, and sketches the director has access to. So, while many of the costumes probably will be the ones she stitched—or her staff—some might be reproductions, so to speak, for newer cast members."

I laughed, cradling the notebook carefully in my arms. "Told you I didn't know anything about the theater. March was always the ham, onstage or in front of the camera. I was more shy, as if you couldn't tell."

"Want to head into town at six? I'll drive." Hale turned to go.

"See you in an hour. I'll take good care of this."

"I never had a doubt."

Once Hale was gone, I poured myself a glass of wine and sank down into the comfy pillows on the sofa. I carefully set the wineglass down on the coffee table and placed the green notebook on my lap. Taking a shallow breath, I opened the book to the first page. "Ruth Hollis Brock" was written in a curling script and the name of the theater, Indigo. I paused for a moment, taking in her last name, which was the same as Hale's.

I turned the page, taking care not to bend the corners of the thick paper. The first two pages were a jumble of inspiration: a dried flower, brittle and brown. A matchbook, faded and gray. Two movie theater tickets. A few lines of colored pencil drawn here and there. In the margins, Ruth had written in her rounded, curling hand, *A land that no one cares about?* It looked like a bit of sand had been glued to the page at one time, but was now mostly gone. A few grains remained, frozen in glue in the bottom-right corner of the page.

In the next six pages, Ruth had begun to imagine the characters. There were lines of dialogue written out longhand, along with names such as Cary, Helene, and Dell. She had included sketches of the men and women, and in one delicate pen-and-ink drawing, a plantation house. Along the way, Ruth made notes to herself: "Linae is fond of the past and carries vintage purses. Her fortunes, however, are not the best. She wears cheap shoes."

For another character, Cary, Ruth wrote: "Cary is drowning in debt. The old land means nothing to him, which makes him the most dangerous character. He dresses very well, but everything he touches (wears, tastes, enjoys) reminds him of his crushing burden. He is owned by others."

I was intrigued. The play sounded complex and heavy, but altogether interesting. I was eager to see what the three siblings would do with their land and what toll it would exact on the characters.

The next page in the notebook concerned the plantation's character, or what Hale had called its soul. Of course, Ruth did not have to design a costume for the plantation, but she seemed to enjoy the idea of the ghostly land having a say in the futures of the siblings. "Zee Bee," Ruth wrote. "Rumored to be a 'haint' or ghost, probably a former slave named Zediah who was parted from his wife and his children. Zediah vowed revenge on all members of the future owners of the plantation." Then, in a colored pencil, Ruth had written, "Find the real Zediah."

Ruth had immersed herself in the play and its characters. I turned the page and began to see the costumes take shape. Helene's page had several rough sketches. She looked like something out of a 1950s issue of *Vogue,* but Ruth had imagined her slightly flawed. There was a knot of off-center hair on top of her head. The cheap shoes adorned her feet. Ruth had chosen a color palette that was sort of cool for Helene. She was dressed almost totally in a pale blue.

I ran my fingers lightly over the fabric swatches stapled to the page. Ruth had found a mousy blue polyester. "Morning suit?" she had written in the margins. Another fabric, a chunky bouclé, was marked with the words, "On sale, this week at Richard's."

Other pages held more finished drawings. A man's handwriting was scrawled across some of them, commenting on the cut of a suit or a color theme. Most of the comments were positive. On the last page, a colored pencil sketch of Helene in an evening dress with a drooping hem, the man's hand wrote: "Excellent. You've done it again."

I took a sip of wine and closed the book. I felt as if I were prying into Ruth's world. True, I did that all the time, with each detail Hale offered up. But holding something of hers seemed as if I was crossing an imaginary line. It was like the time Hale gave me a bag of Ruth's vintage purses and scarves. I took the bag—it seemed rude not to—but when I dumped it out onto my bed later that day, I could only stare at the neatly folded scarves with their crisp creases. I did not touch the patent leather clutches or the silver basket-weave purse. To do so seemed like it would make Ruth more real to me than photos or secondhand memories.

I stood, carefully carrying the notebook over to the kitchen counter. I worried briefly about Hale. How would he handle seeing Ruth's name in the theater program tonight? Would there be sympathetic glances from the cast or would life go on, with sequined and beaded costumes prancing across the stage? As I often did, I felt anxiety for my friend, mixed with unease. After all, I arrived on Langdon after Ruth died. I was a part of Hale's "after" and I wasn't sure how far my protectiveness and sympathy should extend.

I suddenly thought of Vince. My heart revved up its musings. He would be home from work, or close to it by now, in Charlotte. His condo would be bathed in a late-afternoon glow, and a scattered assortment of early fall leaves would decorate his tiny balcony. For a brief moment, I wished to be inside, lolling on the sofa while wearing one of his worn fleece tops, the sleeves rolled up to make it fit better. I could smell his special doctored marinara sauce simmering on the stove. Vince could take a jar of pasta sauce and make it into something amazing with a few spices and a pinch of cinnamon. I saw, and felt, almost as if I were there, his soft lips and gentle, careful kisses. A sadness came over me, knowing how far apart we had become. I almost didn't know how to even think of him anymore.

A knock on the door made me jump. It was Hale, picking me up for the play. A whole hour had gone by while I was stuck in the past. I shook away the thoughts of Vince. I was sure he had moved on by now while I was down here in Langdon. There was no use moping over him or dreaming about pasta sauce. I turned to open the door and my elbow caught the edge of my wineglass on the counter, knocking it over. I yelped out loud as a wave of liquid rolled toward Ruth's notebook.

Without thinking, I flailed at the green notebook, pushing it off the counter and onto the floor with a solid thud. Throwing a towel over the wine, I glanced down to see the notebook's contents spilled out onto the kitchen floor. Swatches and scraps of cardboard were scattered about and the spine of the book was cracked open to reveal bent and broken pages.

"Mae Wallace? Are you there? It's me." Hale rapped at the porch door.

I scooped up the notebook, wincing as another page detached and floated to the floor. I opened a low cabinet and carefully placed the notebook inside. Gathering up the scraps of fabrics and other pieces of the notebook, I put them all inside the cabinet, crunching a bit of sand underfoot. I could not believe my clumsiness at destroying one of Hale's prized possessions from his late wife. I was such an idiot.

"Mae Wallace? Everything okay?"

"Yeah, just getting my shoes on."

I tore back to the bedroom and pulled on a black skirt and gray shirt with a ruffled neckline that made me look a tad sophisticated. Shoving my feet into my dressiest black leather slides, I grabbed my bag and ran breathlessly to the door.

Stepping outside, I noticed Hale had shaved and was wearing a pressed shirt. "You look nice," I said.

Hale leaned forward and kissed me on the cheek. "Thanks. I think I am more nervous about this than I should be."

"Why are you nervous?"

Hale ran one hand through his hair, messing it up slightly. "I don't know, maybe it's all the people who will be there who knew Ruth, worked with her—you know, our friends. I don't really see them anymore. She was the glue there." Hale sighed. "I should get out more, I guess. But Ruth was the one I think people were really drawn to. Not me."

We walked outside. The overcast sky was shedding some fat raindrops.

The drive into Charleston would be slow. I was looking forward to just being in the car with Hale. His presence was comforting. I realized with a smile that he had become my best friend.

"Did I say something funny?" Hale asked, opening the car door for me.

"I was just thinking that you are my best friend. Hope that's not too high school—it's just something I came to all of a sudden."

"Well, duh," Hale said, closing the door. I could see him smiling as he walked around to the driver's side. "I hope you know that only a precious few are admitted into my exclusive inner circle."

"I am truly honored."

"As am I, my friend. Are you ready to see some theater in the big town?"

"I am. Let's go get some culture."

Theatre Indigo was as I had pictured it with old Charleston brick walls and worn carpeting. The lobby held a velvet chaise lounge and dusty framed pictures of past performances. A dozen people milled about, sipping wine and champagne. A couple spotted Hale immediately and walked over.

"Hale, so good to see you. We're glad you came," the man said. He wore a black suit. A tiny diamond earring nestled in one earlobe. His wife had big hair and a silver palmetto pin on her jacket lapel.

"Yes, Harmond was thinking you might be put off by all the publicity, you know. But I told him that wouldn't deter you," the woman said.

"What are you talking about?" Hale said, looking at them.

They exchanged glances and Harmond took a quick sip of wine. "Surely you're joking. You mean, you didn't see it?"

Hale looked uncomfortable. I was beginning to wish we hadn't come. The lights dimmed once and then again, signaling the final minutes before the start of the show. A woman with a sequined top veered over to us and pointed to Hale. "There's that poor artist,

Hal or something." She stood a mere five feet away and stared at Hale like he was a circus animal.

I felt Hale's hand slip into mine in a fierce grip. "Harmond, tell me what you mean. Just tell me." His words were terse.

Harmond looked over at the gawking woman. She got the hint finally and moved away from us. "The story in today's *Post and Courier*. It's all about your painting, your bridge series. And Ruth's death. Everything." His companion nodded and looked down at her feet.

Hale moved suddenly and forcefully for the exit. My hand still gripped in his, I was dragged along for a few feet. I heard Harmond say, "If it's any consolation, I really like your work!"

Not slowing until we were two or three blocks away from the theater, Hale suddenly stopped and turned to me. His eyes were wet with tears and his chest heaved. "Sometimes I miss her so much, and sometimes, I wish I had never met her. If I hadn't, I wouldn't be walking around with this deadness inside of me."

I put my arms around Hale, feeling him shake and sob into my shoulder. I wished I were taller and larger so that I could cover him with my body. I felt protective and sad for him, both at the same time. It was a sensation I knew from being March's keeper all these months.

Hale squeezed me tightly and then pulled away, wiping his eyes. We had stopped down the block from the bright lights of Joe Joe Coffee. I knew they had a newsstand, and I figured we would go in there and take a look at the *Post and Courier*. As if he could read my thoughts, Hale turned from me and walked through the front doors of Joe Joe. He grabbed a tattered copy of the newspaper from a pile by the door and stalked over to a table. I made my way to the counter and paid for two cups of regular house coffee. It was going to be a long night.

When I got to the battered wooden table Hale had selected near the front windows of Joe Joe, I found him staring at the front of the Arts section. I set the coffee down and slipped into the chair across from him. The coffee shop was fairly empty; a few people sat here and there.

"Is it bad?"

Hale shoved the paper across the table to me. I picked it up and read the headline: "Ghost Bride Captures Artist's Soul." Unbelievably, there was a picture of two of the bridge series paintings. A portrait of Ruth on her wedding day. A shot of the outside of Hale's beach bungalow. A picture of one of the "Miss Your Lips Ruth" signs on the old bridge. But the most jarring item on the page was a huge, gray image of the bridge where Ruth died, stretching across the story and serving as a grim backdrop for the text.

"Oh, Hale. I am so sorry." A million tattered thoughts raced through my head. Who did this? How could they?

"Unbelievable. It's not enough to lose your wife on the six o'clock news; now I have complete strangers watching me grieve over and over again." Hale looked down at his coffee and then out to the street. His face was pained, his eyes red and swollen.

I picked up the story, reading phrases like "Hale ponders his lost love's demise and picks up a paintbrush to capture the lost things under the bridge. The bridge that claimed Ruth's life." A few paragraphs down: "Even though no one knows her reasons for climbing the bridge, in the end, it would be Hale who tried to figure it out, painting after painting."

"I was out most of the day and didn't answer the phone. I don't subscribe to the paper. So I find out about this stupid story on a night when I want to honor my wife's memory at her theater."

"Maybe we can catch tomorrow's performance." I try to be helpful and smile over at Hale.

"Yeah, maybe. Not if it's like tonight."

I turned the Arts section over, so I wouldn't have to look at the story. "So, how did the reporter get access to your paintings? I thought you never showed them." I read the byline: *Story by Ansley Whiddon.*

"Never." Hale's eyes were intense.

"So, did you lose any? Did someone break in?"

A group of students from the college burst through the front door of the coffee shop, laughing and hanging on to each other. One girl with striped leg warmers threw her arms around a guy and shrieked. "Come on, Tater. Give me a kiss!" Suddenly, their youth and exuberance made me feel tired and impossibly old. What did Tater know of broken sisters and missing wives?

We sat in silence for a while, drinking coffee. Hale stared out into the darkening street at passersby, mostly young couples holding hands on their way to something else. One or two women wore the pout of changed plans or evenings gone slightly awry. I thought of how Ruth's play was on stage a few blocks away, and how Helene's blue gown was being worn by a thin, graceful actress. She would be nervous, backstage, before her entrance. The slight sting of perspiration hitting the delicate material of the ball gown with the drooping hem sewn by the lost Ruth.

"She wouldn't want this attention, Ruth wouldn't," Hale said. "She was elegant and gentle. Being plastered on some piece of newsprint would have made her ill."

"You know I like these paintings, but I know you didn't want to show them. Should you go to the police? Someone has been in your house. It's creepy."

Hale threw back the last of his coffee. "The only people who have keys to my house are you and Mr. Forrester."

Our eyes met across the table. "I saw him at your house last week. I was working in the front yard. I thought he was there to put up a 'For Rent' sign."

Hale swore quietly, but with enough volume that a grad-student type at the next table reading a Proust title gave him a quick, nasty look.

"I'll bet he had something to do with this." Hale looked through the plate glass windows toward the street.

"That nice man? No, he couldn't do that, could he?" I tried to picture sweet Mr. Forrester with his black socks and brown sandals sneaking around Hale's house snapping pictures of paintings. It sounded like a bad art film.

"He's always been nice to me, but when I called him to tell him I was moving, he acted really strange."

"How so?"

Hale leaned back in his chair and shoved his hands in his pants' pockets. "It was creepy. He asked me a lot of questions about Ruth. Like if she would want me to move on from the house we shared together. And would I still work on my art if I moved into the city, stuff like that. I didn't think anything at the time because he's always been so nice, really kind."

"Is there anyone else who would know about the paintings?"

"Well, there's you, and March, of course. Other than that, no one else. It's been a private thing. Not anymore, I guess."

We were quiet then, thinking. My mind could not even grasp the thought of March doing this to Hale. And the pictures? There was no way she could have gotten into Hale's house and taken them. It had to be Mr. Forrester. All of a sudden, I remembered the camera in the landlord's hand when he went into Hale's house last week.

I told Hale what I saw that day. "I would change your locks. What a nut job."

Hale smiled over at me. "I'm the nut job. It's just me going back to that bridge time after time to visit Ruth, no one else."

Looking down into my coffee cup, I asked, "Is that what you are doing?" I thought of Hale's painting. Even though he didn't paint Ruth per se in his images, there were always the bridge girders and columns somewhere in the frame.

"I guess I am trying to go with her to the last place she touched on Earth. I want to let her know she's not alone. Sounds crazy, huh?"

I reached over to grab his hand. "Not at all. Why do you think I live on Langdon? To let March know she's not alone. I don't know that I've ever thought of it like that, but it's true. When my family had our big meeting to discuss March's care, I was the one who stepped forward to go. My parents would have, of course, but

I think now that this was their way of making March and me confront our past and try to work on our relationship."

"Yeah, how's that working out?" Hale gave me a wry smile. He squeezed my hand and released it.

"Very funny, Mr. Gloomy Artist. I'm working on it piece by piece."

"Yeah, well maybe you should work on it with another person. Oh, I don't know, how about your sister?" Hale stretched his arms over his head and grinned.

"Okay, enough about me. What are you going to do about this?" I said, nodding my head toward the newspaper.

"First, I am going to have a little talk with Mr. Forrester. And then the reporter, Ms. Whiddon, and her editor. After that, who knows? Maybe I'll go climb a bridge."

I looked over at Hale's dark eyes. "Don't say that, Hale. Please."

"I'm sorry, that was a mistake. I shouldn't have said that."

We were quiet, and I drank the last of my coffee. The irritated grad student stood up and tucked her Proust neatly into a gingham sack. Tater and company sat across the room, devouring slices of Joe Joe's infamous chocolate cake.

"You know, I was really looking forward to seeing Ruth's work on stage tonight."

"Really?"

"Yeah. I went through her notebook this afternoon." I paused, thinking of the damage I had inflicted on the special book. "And I kind of, I don't know, got lost in the characters or something. Their costumes were spectacular and special. It made me want to know Ruth more, too."

"She was really talented, you know. Ruth had a gift for seeing the story and making it come alive. I try to do that with my paintings, but it doesn't always translate."

We stood up and walked outside onto the street. The September air was cool and leaves curled up like little animals at our feet. "Want to walk a little?" I asked.

"No, I think I want to go home and pretend tonight didn't happen. After that article, I am going to have to deal with a lot more garbage, no pun intended. I can't wait to move away from that house."

We walked in silence for a few minutes. "I've been totally chicken about asking you this, but where are you moving? I haven't wanted to talk about it because then it would make it too real."

"Well, I found a loft condo near the Ship Yard that would give me room to paint. It's a new loft conversion building. The place was an old mattress factory."

"It sounds so cool, but I am going to miss you like crazy."

"I know, I know. But I think I'm overdue for a fresh start. I met Ruth on Langdon, we courted there, were newlyweds there, and then she was gone. I see her everywhere. Like it's not obvious to everyone now, thanks to the newspaper."

"And the nefarious Mr. Forrester."

"What a jerk," Hale said.

"I can think of a few more choice words, actually."

"Believe me, I've thought of them. What I can't figure out is what he expected to gain from this. Here's a man who owns dozens of rentals, so you know he's not hurting for money. And he's old—what's he doing sneaking around taking pictures of art?"

"Didn't you say he asked you about your art and if you would keep painting?"

"He did. I still don't know why."

"Maybe he wants to be your patron," I said, laughing.

We walked back toward Hale's car. "Well, our professional relationship is off to a rocky start, wouldn't you say?"

I stopped walking and touched Hale's arm. "You have such an amazing attitude. Most people would be talking about suing or whatever, and you can joke about it already."

Hale started walking again, fishing the car keys out of his pocket. "I think you have a choice in life—go around perpetually pissed off or take what you get and stumble on." He sighed. "It's taken me a while to get to that Zen garden, but there you are. All of life distilled down to a greeting-card phrase."

We walked the last block to the car and climbed in for the drive back to Langdon. As the city lights faded behind and the Cooper River Bridge loomed ahead with the shining lights of the shipping lanes below us, I glanced over at Hale. He seemed lost in thought, both hands carefully on the steering wheel. A corner of his shirt collar turned up against his neck. His hair ruffled slightly in the wind created by the half-open driver's side window. His profile was so familiar to me by now. I knew Ruth had looked over at her husband, as I did now. Of course, while I looked at him with a friend's love, she would have gazed at him with a wife's adoring eye.

With a start, I realized that if she had lived, if Ruth had never climbed the bridge, I would not be sitting in this car right now. Ruth and Hale would be at home, making popcorn or love, or whatever other diversion existed. Maybe *The Zee Bee* would have been staged as it was tonight, so Ruth would have been there, watching her creations before her pleased and proud eyes. We would never know. I closed my eyes as the tires of Hale's car took us up and over the gray concrete of the bridge carrying us back to Langdon Island.

THIRTEEN

The day after the play debacle, I was up early, determined to get a jump on some housecleaning. My side of the bungalow was a mess. Clothes choked the hamper, the tub wore a nasty grime ring, and my dishes moldered in the sink. It seemed as if I was never in a mood to clean things up.

I bounced out of bed with a to-do list in my head. I would officially begin working for World Matters on Monday, and I wanted to start with a clean slate at home. No more messy rooms and dirty floors. I also needed to get over to see March today as well. We didn't have an appointment with anyone since it was Saturday, but I thought I should check on her and see if she wanted to get out, maybe take a ride somewhere.

Before I began, I carefully bagged up the pieces of Ruth's broken notebook and took it out to the car. Gently setting it down behind the driver's seat, I glanced guiltily over at Hale's house. My plan was to take the ailing notebook to the Sea Villas and get the resident craft goddess there, a cheerful, clog-wearing woman named Merry, to rebuild it. I didn't care what it cost; I was planning to beg her to fix it, and fix it fast.

A few minutes later, Hale knocked on my door and then let himself inside. I crouched over the stuffed laundry basket on the living room floor, sorting colors. "Good, you're just in time to do my laundry. Use the delicate cycle, please," I said, throwing a dirty towel at Hale's head.

"Sorry, you're on your own. This place is starting to look a little seedy, you know."

"Yeah, appreciate that. I'm working on it," I said in my huffiest voice. "Besides, I've seen your place at its worst. This mess doesn't come close."

Hale eyed the dirty counter and laundry strewn at my feet. "I wouldn't count on it." He sat down on the couch, moving a pair of shoes and two magazines for more room. Sighing, he rubbed his face and blankly looked around the room.

I stopped sorting dark T-shirts from white ones. "I've been thinking of you ever since I woke up. I still can't believe the paper published that story about you and Ruth. How are you doing?"

"Oh, I turned my phone back on and found more than twenty messages. Mostly family who read the stupid newspaper story online after Aunt Greta forwarded it to her zillion-person distribution

THE WIDE SMILES OF GIRLS

list. She's eighty-one and online all the time. A few calls were from crackpots, looking for a little love. A male stripper left a sweet message, and there was a short call from a New York art dealer."

"Hale! What did he say?"

"The stripper? Well, you know, he was pretty straightforward."

"You know I'm talking about the art dealer. What did he want?"

"It was a she, and she wanted to talk to me about 'my art.' And yes, she said it about as snooty as you think a New York dealer would say those two words."

"So, did you call back?"

"Right. And I have a one-man exhibition in Chelsea next week. They love me up there."

Standing up, I looked at my friend. "Okay, Mr. Art Star. I'm just asking—did you call her?"

"No, of course not."

"Why on Earth didn't you?"

"Let me count the ways. First of all, Ms. Feauto is probably the owner of a lame, six-floor co-op walk-up gallery on a shabbier Chelsea block. Two, my bridge paintings aren't for sale, and even if they were, I don't think they are all that good; and three, I am not inclined to share them with the world at this moment." Hale stood up and made a little bow.

I returned to my laundry pile. "Excuse me for taking an interest in your art career. Won't happen again."

Hale sat back down on the couch and picked up a magazine. He flipped through a few pages.

"But if you *were* to call, what would be the harm?"

Glaring, Hale closed the magazine. "I thought you weren't going to mention it again."

"I lied."

Leaning back on the couch, Hale picked up a half-eaten apple core and tossed it toward the kitchen trash can, missing by about five feet. "You've really let this place go, Mae Wallace."

"Nice try, changing the subject."

"No, I just know that if the dealer is legit and if she is really interested in my work and if I decide to let some of these paintings go, it will be a huge headache. I've known artists who have gotten themselves into tough positions. I'll pass."

"Well, just because some friends of yours had that experience doesn't mean you will. I mean, all art dealers aren't the same, right?"

From his lounging position on the couch, Hale shrugged. "I don't know about Ms. Feauto and The Divide Gallery, but I would say that—"

"What did you say her name was again?"

"Lark Feauto. Ms. Lark Feauto," Hale said, stretching out her name in what I guessed was an imitation of her New York accent. "She's probably not even a dealer. She probably runs a little tiny gallery from the back of her beat-up Subaru in New Jersey. Lark probably isn't even her real name. It's Betsy or Glenda."

"Wait, 'Lark'? Did you say 'The Divide Gallery'?" I dove over to the couch and reached for the magazine Hale had tossed onto the floor. It was a battered copy of *Time* from earlier in the summer. Flipping through the saltwater-curled pages, I found the story that grabbed my attention a few weeks ago. I read from the first paragraph: "Among the rabid New York art scene, there is hardly a more influential or more sought-after dealer than Lark Feauto. Her eye for what's new and what can be new next week is unequalled. At least this year." I tossed the magazine into Hale's lap and settled onto the couch. "Now, what do you say to that?"

His response was unusual. Total and complete silence.

"You can use my phone."

I had a little laugh to myself as Hale stared at the magazine in his lap. He seemed stunned. I finished sorting and dragged one of the laundry baskets to the mudroom where the washer and half-broken dryer lived along with way too many plastic milk jugs that begged to be recycled. From the mudroom, my ears strained for the telltale sounds of Hale pushing buttons on the cordless phone, calling information for the gallery number. I didn't hear anything, so I loaded the washer with whites and dumped in some blue detergent. I planned to march back out to the living room and dial the number for him. Geez, it wasn't like the New York art world came calling every day. Hale was just freaked out, that was all. Every starving artist dreamed of being noticed by someone huge like Ms. Lark Feauto. Hale could be poised to make it, big time.

I stalked back out to the living room, hands on my hips. The couch was empty. Hale was gone. He left my *Time* magazine, the one with the article about Ms. Lark Feauto and her glamorous gallery, upside down on the floor.

Peering out the porch window, I saw Hale walking determinedly down the boardwalk to the ocean. His T-shirt rippled in the sea breeze. I watched him go, unable to think of any words that would make him stay.

After I cleaned the house, down to its warped and uneven hard-wood floors, I headed out to the Sea Villas to have lunch with March. I called to let her know I was coming, and she didn't stop me, so I took it as a good sign. She had been frosty of late, even more chilly than usual. Everything I did seemed to irritate her. With my job starting Monday, I was even more anxious that my sister would think I was abandoning her. There had to be a way to make her see I would still be there for her.

March met me in the garden near the lot where I always parked. For a moment, I was shocked. I was used to seeing March in a cer-tain way, and something about the light or the early autumn colors of the garden made her look, well, different. Maybe it was her hair swept up on top of her head or the new skirt she wore. A thin dust-ing of face powder and lip gloss gave March a polished look. She glanced up at me. "What have you been doing?"

I suddenly felt self-conscious in my faded capris and T-shirt, the same clothes I wore to clean the house. I hadn't even thought to shower or try to look a little nice. After so long without a rea-son to get dressed up, I was really starting to slip. "Getting the house in order. You know, cleaning and stuff."

"Well, you're lucky the Sea Villas doesn't have a dress code." Turning sharply, March wheeled into the main entrance. I followed, desperately trying to smooth my hair back with a stray hair elastic band I found in my purse.

Lunch at the Sea Villas was festive, with fresh flowers on the table and servers wearing crisp green polo shirts and khaki pants waiting on the guests. I slipped into a chair at our table and tried to look completely at ease with my casual attire. I was so focused on Hale—I had been replaying the events of that morning in my head over and over—that I had forgotten about everything else.

"So, I read the story in the newspaper," March said as she eyed the one-page menu. As usual, there were three entrées and salads to choose from, plus a dessert cart that was wheeled around after the meal.

"And?"

"How's he doing?" March asked the question casually, her eyes still on the menu.

"Well, we went to the theater yesterday to see a performance of the last show Ruth designed costumes for, and it wasn't pretty."

Putting down her menu, March took a sip of iced water. "Why in the world did ya'll go there? I mean, the story was all over everywhere. Alice, that crazy, nosy woman at the front desk tried to get me to talk about Hale since she knows we see each other. Even the nurses were blabbing about 'that poor, sweet artist.' Made me sick. I hated how they talked about him. They do the same thing to the patients, too. And we can hear what they say." March looked down at the table. "Well, most of us, anyway."

"If we had known, we wouldn't have gone to the theater. It was awful, March. People staring and whispering. And we're pretty sure his landlord is the one who took the pictures. What a total creep."

The waitress took our order. I ordered the fried chicken salad with chunks of apple and blue cheese. March, I noticed, ordered the chilled melon soup and a house salad. I looked at her again. Maybe it was the weight loss she was undergoing that made her appearance so different. March's heaviness had become such a part of her growing up that I had almost ceased to notice it until she started to lose the weight. It was like her body was hers but not hers.

"Why are you staring at me?" March asked, not unkindly.

"Sorry."

"No, tell me why, Mae Wallace."

Without time to think of a fib, I blurted out, "You've lost weight. You don't look like you."

To my surprise, March laughed out loud. "I know, I have! It's funny, isn't it? I can't run or take a yoga class, but the pounds keep dropping off. I can tell the most when I'm in the chair. It's easier to wheel myself around the halls."

I laid a cloth napkin in my lap, happy that March was talking to me again like a sister. She even smiled at me. "Are you trying to lose weight? Or are you just not hungry?" I wasn't sure how much to pry.

To my relief, March waved her hand in the air dismissively. "Oh, I guess I really just don't eat as much now. It used to be I never felt full, and I was always rushing around from place to place, doing so much. Eating was like one more thing." March rubbed her nose. "Moon Fairy says my eating was emotional and now my center must be filled and I don't have to eat anymore."

I wanted to take a roll out of the breadbasket on the table, but it seemed like an inappropriate time. To make matters worse, the aromas wafting off the table beside us—roasted chicken and potatoes—were killing me. All that cleaning had really made me hungry. "Do you miss food?" I asked her. "You always seemed to like eating so much."

A waiter dropped off sweet tea even though we hadn't ordered any. It was like that growing up in Henderson—sweet tea came with your meal whether you wanted it or not. March ignored the tea and sipped her ice water with lemon.

"I don't really miss the food because now I am so cut off from that life. I used to tear from boyfriend to boyfriend, to club meeting, to film-school storyboarding without ever taking a break and asking myself what I wanted or what I needed. Somehow, I pushed me down and let this desire for food well up." In a rare moment of vulnerability, March ducked her head. "Or at least, that's what Moon Fairy thinks."

"Are you getting sucked into Moon Fairy's evil psychological web?"

Rolling her eyes, March shook her head from side to side. "It was a weak moment, but I plan to be strong from now on." She took a sip of water. "Actually, she can be pretty enlightening sometimes, when she's not having me do all that feeling crap and journaling mess. Everyone wants to talk about my emotions. I just want them to shut up."

"Well, I think I made Hale mad today." I told March briefly about my helpful art world suggestions and how Hale left my house.

"Yeah, that wasn't too slick, what you did," she said as our entrées arrived.

March's comment stung. I didn't want to confront her because we were getting along so well, so I made elaborate salad preparations, dousing my salad with balsamic vinaigrette and cutting up the apple pieces.

"Are you done massacring your salad yet?"

"What do you mean?"

"Mae Wallace, look at me." March clipped her words.

"I am looking at you."

"No, you aren't. You never look at me. You look above my head and at the wall, but you don't look at me. Not anymore."

The diners at the next table paused their roasted chicken feast as March raised her voice. Giving them a testy glance, my sister continued, her fork clenched in one hand.

"Ever since that moronic horse threw me off, you have acted like the long-suffering sister, groveling and penitent. You even moved down here to keep up the self-flagellation routine. I don't know why. But now your act is seeping over to Hale and I have to say something about it. And what do you do? You sit there, afraid to tick me off by having a real conversation. Mae Wallace, I am dying to have someone tell me the truth and not sugarcoat my spinal cord. You can't do it and Mom and Dad can't do it. Who can I go to if I can't go to my family?"

"There's hope, March, I don't know why you can't—"

"Look on the asinine bright side? Search for the deeper meaning of my broken back? Close a door and open the ever-loving window?" March dropped her fork, and the echo off the china drew more stares. "Sorry, sister of mine. You can't fix Hale's life with art dealers until he wants to, and you can't make me jump for joy because I ended up like this until I decide that's what I want to do."

Pushing away from the table, March wheeled off and left me sitting alone. My stomach growled once and then again. The other diners offered a few pitying glances. I didn't for a second think I deserved them.

The waiter rounded back to our table, his lips turned down in a frown. "Will you be taking the salad to go?" I nodded, sure that it was not a question but in fact, a request.

I drove back to the bungalow, hoping to find Hale sitting on my porch, waiting for me to come home. I checked and rechecked my cell. March had not called, begging me to return and apologizing for everything she had said. I laughed to myself in spite of the great sadness I had at running off two people I loved in one brief morning and early afternoon. I knew I had erred in dealing with the two most important people in my life, first by pushing Hale to do something he did not want to do on the heels of his invasive exposure; secondly, I had acted condescendingly toward March. I was so afraid of making her even more mad at me I had ceased to act like any type of sister at all. The long-suffering sister role was wearing thin, and she called me on it.

I decided to go for a walk on the beach. Dropping my flip-flops off on the boardwalk, I headed for the hard-packed sand near the ocean's edge. As I walked west, I reached for my cell. But who to call? Hale needed some space, thanks to me, and March probably wouldn't take my calls. I wished I had a good girlfriend to call, but I had been horrible about keeping up with old friends since the accident.

So I thought about Ruth. It wasn't in a creepy, dead-girl kind of way. But I thought of her face and her voice from the video Hale had shown me of the two of them, and I pictured walking with her. What kind of advice would she give? Especially since one of the people I had harmed was her beloved husband.

Hale had told me before that Ruth felt things very deeply and that others' pain bothered her to distraction. I thought of her now, walking beside me, her brunette bob swinging slightly in the wind. I hoped she would understand what I was going through; I had a feeling she would have even more empathy for my sister, as she should.

I stepped into slightly deeper sand, feeling the effort on my calves and thighs. Ruth walked with me like a whisper, like a ghost. Her elegant face was turned gently toward mine, and as we walked, I could almost feel the soft pressure of her footsteps slapping the dry sand. We might walk like this, talking or not talking, for miles.

Hale once told me he never felt lonely in Ruth's presence. "I craved her, honestly. If she was in one room of the house, my ears always perked up to hear what she was doing. Sounds funny, I guess."

We were on the beach after dark when Hale told me that, our toes cradled in the still warm sand. Nearby, some college kids had started a bonfire. They danced around the flames, arms flailing. A cooler of beer stood at the ready. The kids would drink out in front of our houses for a good part of the night. It was probably Mrs. Chester's grandson. He was a notorious partier and ended up at her empty beach house most warm fall weekends.

Hale shook his head, his profile outlined by the orange bonfire.

"I was a fool, I guess, like anyone else in love. You think you have all the time. All the time you'll ever need or could possibly want."

It was cool the night Hale talked to me of missing his wife. As he spoke, I wrapped my arms around my legs and tried to imagine their life together. She loved fresh basil. She waterskied and spoke passable French. Her friends received letters in longhand, penned in Ruth's neat, flowing script written across fancy stationery.

"As happy as I was, sometimes I think Ruth was a bit restless. I mean, she was settling into married life, Langdon, and her job over in Charleston, but sometimes she seemed a little distracted."

The bonfire ebbed on the beach and the partiers began drifting toward Mrs. Chester's darkened house. I looked over at Hale, his strong features etched against the dark night. The waves rumbled nearby. The tide was coming in. Soon, the sand where we were sitting would be underwater. I listened. It seemed like Hale had a lot to say and the darkness helped.

"I just wonder if she climbed that bridge thinking of me, you know? It sounds so maudlin, like this is all about the tragic surviving husband, or something. But I really want, I really need to know sometimes."

The water swirled up to our feet. We stood, giving the ocean another look before walking back toward the houses. Hale dipped his toes into water that was pressing up toward the sand dunes. He paused and looked over at me. "You know, I lost her but she's always here. Sometimes, it's like she's walking right beside me."

I listened, quiet and still, that night by the ocean.

We left the dying bonfire on the beach and walked slowly back to our houses that night. Hale kissed me on the cheek and started toward his back porch. Our lights were off and the moon was cloudy, hidden by wavy and rolling clouds.

I felt a deep closeness to him, not unlike the friendship I used to share with March. Now, a week later, I walked again on the beach and replayed Hale's words. As Hale talked, I knew it comforted and probably embarrassed him to reveal how much he needed Ruth.

I turned to retrace my steps back to the beach house. I had a lot of work to do. As Ruth's image faded from my mind, I thought of the beach ahead with its millions of grains of sand and all the many erased footprints. All of us—Ruth, Hale, and March—had spent time on this beach at some point not too long ago. I silently thanked Ruth, and then I headed home. There was someone I needed to see, someone who once meant more than everything to me.

FOURTEEN

At first, the bridge to the island is in the distance. Ruth walks along the beach, her black cotton skirt twisting in the stiff sea air. She carries her journal. A white plastic bangle encircles one wrist. Her bare feet pad over the hard sand, her steps lighter than usual. Today is the day she will do something daring. Today is the day she will surprise Hale.

The ocean sky carries low clouds. A storm could pop up at sea, or just as likely, not, depending on the air currents. Ruth has always loved the water, considers herself lucky to live so close to the ocean. The day unrolls before her—take a walk, draw in her sketchbook, and delight Hale. Her heart feels full, as if there is nothing that can stop her.

The old bridge is off to Ruth's left, hovering in shambles over the gray bay. Ruth still thinks darkly of the city fathers who allowed it to be broken apart in order for the high speeds and flashing traffic of the new bridge. If she could have her way, Hale has kidded her, horses would once again draw carriages in Charleston for everyone, not just the tourists. Cars would be banned, cast out of the Lowcountry. She agrees, of course. If only she could have her way.

The air is balmy, warm with humidity and infinitely familiar to Ruth. This is the air she has breathed since she was an infant. From her tiniest self, she has only known a heavy, wet air that presses at the small of your back and leaves you panting for relief in the summer.

Now, on a day like most others, Ruth walked along the beach on her way to give Hale a surprise for their anniversary. She carried in her pocket a new digital camera her husband did not know about yet. Ruth was a fan of all things old-fashioned, and had resisted converting from film to digital. But she wanted to create a photo book of the old bridge before it was totally dismantled. She was planning to use an online photo book Web site. She had researched and learned all about the bridge's debut back in 1932, and how mule carts and kids on bicycles had all shared its concrete span. A 1950s update had erased the mule lanes and only the most unsupervised children still biked across.

The bridge was closer now, and Ruth could hear the steady whir of cars and trucks bearing down on the asphalt lanes. Sometimes, Hale said living on an island made him feel trapped. Even the smallish bay felt like a barrier to him. "Why, you could swim it if you really needed to get to the mainland," Ruth told him, laughing. "You're not trapped."

But Hale persisted in his thinking, Ruth mused, as she walked toward the bridge. To him, the island had its own mysteries, perched off the coast of the rest of the country, isolated by water and sand. Ruth rather liked living on an island—the wind, the surf, the old bridge, they were all elements that made her home special.

As she walked, Ruth pulled her hair back into a short ponytail with a stray elastic band she found in her skirt pocket. Her hair was salty and stiff to the touch. She wore tiny pearl earrings, an Easter gift from her parents. A hot pink Band-Aid covered a scratch on her knee.

Ruth thought of the angles she wanted in her pictures of the bridge. She had already collected old archival photos that she would scan in for Hale's photo book. And she had stumbled upon a Web site of a Low-country history buff who had a fondness for the old bridge.

After contacting him, the man mailed Ruth several more archival pictures of the bridge, the mule carts, and some Langdon beach scenes from seventy years ago. She gave him her work address so the package would not pique Hale's curiosity. The new pictures she took today of the bridge would join the old ones, and the book would be truly magical. It would be kind of like creating one of her costume scrapbooks, Ruth thought, smiling. She and Hale always tried to make gifts for each other, and this one would be a favorite, she was sure. Last year, she knitted a brown scarf for him, and he gave her a small painting of a tiny lemon tree.

Arriving at the first large piling, Ruth stopped to catch her breath. She had been walking quickly for more than thirty minutes. The stained concrete piling beside her was pitted with bird droppings and tagged by graffiti enthusiasts. A sagging picnic table and several plastic bags took up residence in the clearing. The sand was ground down to a packed hardness littered with cigarette butts and a few broken wine-cooler bottles.

Ruth surveyed the bay and the bridge, considering the angles. Should she shoot down low, her camera propped on the sand? Or what about standing on the picnic table to get a few more feet of height? Remembering that she now had a digital camera, Ruth laughed out loud. She would do it all—there was no film to hoard. She started snapping photos, almost with abandon. Glancing into the screen, Ruth could see some of her attempts were clumsy, hollow. It didn't matter—she would just delete them.

After a few minutes, she walked down to the shoreline, noticing the Styrofoam chunks, plastic bottles, and plastic bags that washed up under the old piling, bobbing in place. The traffic noises on the new bridge off to her right became more rushed as workers from Charleston streamed home after the day's work.

The light was perfect, tinted with the coming sunset. It was pink and yellow with undertones of bluish purple. Ruth's fingers itched for her colored pencils and sketchbook. She envisioned fabric made to this color, maybe a dyed silk, and the characters from a fantasy, maybe Midsummer or something Tolkien. Ruth held the camera aloft and looked through the viewfinder across the bay. She counted the pilings that made up the fallen bridge and then stopped, her eyes narrowing. With the zoom on, Ruth noticed something for the first time. Each piling came complete with an iron ladder fashioned to its side. The iron rungs started about twenty feet above the waterline, too tall for thrill seekers trolling by on boats or rafts in the bay. The closest piling to Ruth, however, had a longer iron ladder, one that extended down to the water. If one was imaginative, Ruth thought, her excitement rising, one could swim out to the piling, climb the ladder, and take some amazing shots of the bay from the top. She thought of the cracked concrete and the weeds *sprouting in the asphalt. The old iron light posts, each one the owner of a starfish design crafted on the upper brackets holding the dome-shaped light. A little whimsy from the 1930s, back when even a humble island bridge could be lovingly tailored. The new bridge had none of these charms.*

Ruth paced the hard, packed sand beside the water. She guessed the distance to the first piling, the one with the long ladder, was about the length of two swimming pools from her parent's country club in Greenville. Ruth swam in that pool almost every day of her childhood summers. It would take her maybe ten minutes if she swam slowly and carefully, the camera above her head and wrapped in some discarded plastic. It would be a total adventure, and one all the more exciting be-cause she would have a great story to tell Hale.

Eyeing the iron ladder again, Ruth weighed its worthiness. She walked around to the piling beside her on dry land and looked up at the ladder high above her head. The iron was flaky with weathered rust, but the bolts held firmly to the concrete. Examining the ladder at this close distance, Ruth could see now that the ladder actually was designed to extend down to the water, but that a hook secured it higher for safety. Someone must have worked pretty hard to get the ladder down on the first piling in the bay. Teenagers, probably. Ruth grinned, thinking of their low-rent vandalism.

Two seagulls swooped in and danced up to Ruth, their gray-white beaks opening and closing. She had nothing for them, so they skittered away, but not before attracting others of their kind. The little beggars soon gave up and took back to the sky, flying low to the water under the pilings and out to the bay. Ruth envied them briefly for their freedom and ease. Her mind made up, she searched for a clean plastic bag for the camera. She pulled off her skirt and tank top, glad she was still wearing her bathing suit from a quick morning swim. Wrapping the camera in her clothes and then putting them all into a dry Piggly Wiggly sack, Ruth walked back down to the water. She put one foot in the grimy-looking water. It was time to swim.

FIFTEEN

I climbed out of the car, my limbs stiff from driving through the night. I was never a great driver past ten or eleven o'clock. I had a habit of getting a little too sleepy for others' comfort. If I had to get somewhere that late at night, I generally depended on someone else. I blamed it on my internal clock. My body seemed to much prefer curling up on a lumpy sofa with a chenille throw and a good book to piloting a car swiftly through the ink-black night.

But for this journey, it was up to me to get down the road. After my beach walk, I returned home and threw some clothes, flip-flops, and a makeup bag into a canvas tote. I scrawled a note to Hale and taped it to his front door. The lights were off, so I didn't bother to knock. I don't know if he would have opened it anyway. Then, I took a deep breath and called the Sea Villas and asked to speak to March.

"Mae Wallace?" It was the receptionist, Alice.

"It's me."

"Oh, I thought you knew. March's friend picked her up tonight. That poor artist, Hale. The one who lost his wife on the bridge, the one going up to the island?"

"I know Hale, Alice," I sighed into the phone.

"Well, bless his heart, it's just the saddest thing. You know, I'm glad he's taking an interest in your sister. Maybe he's getting over his wife, rest her soul."

"Did you say March is with Hale?" I said, feeling a little slow.

"Oh, yes. This is the third time they've gone out for a stroll or dinner, or whatnot. Poor man, I don't know how he bears it."

I mumbled a good-bye and then hung up. Sure, the three of us had done things together plenty of times. But Hale and March? It seemed odd, like a match that didn't quite fit. Maybe Alice had it wrong. Maybe they were just friends. Or they were angry at me and plotting a gentle revenge, one that would teach me a valuable lesson but still allow for some sisterly dignity. That had to be it. I had overstepped my bounds by giving Hale orders and by slinking around March every time I saw her. I could straighten this out.

First, I had to drive half of the night to see Vince. Although Hale's silent reproach stung and March's anger hit me hard, their emotions were dead-on. I had run from everything in my life— my family, my relationship with my sister, my job, and the man I had fallen in and then out of love with.

I backed out of the driveway, and took a last glance at our two darkened houses. Hale was set to move out soon. I made a quiet vow to make things up to him by then. I needed his friendship. I also knew that deep down, Hale needed mine as well. I had been a companion to him in the space after his wife was carried away by water and wind. I knew he depended on me, like I depended on him, not just for pizza dates and walks along the beach, but for someone to reach out to when the cloying, wool cloak of hopelessness was pulled over his head.

I drove and drove, stopping only for a cup of truck-stop coffee and then, thirty minutes later, a bathroom break. The first two hours were easy. I was pumped up on caffeine and the thought of seeing Vince's face. It had been hard, and then easy, to walk away from him when I moved to Langdon. Maybe I had used Hale and Ruth as a crutch. I know I had probably used March as well. It just seemed easier to devote my time to her and the accident than to face anything else in the real world.

The last hour, I rolled down the windows and sang along to cheesy country songs to stay awake. I chewed a bunch of breath mints, hoping to prop up my furry teeth. On the outskirts of Charlotte, as I buzzed up Interstate 26, I imagined Vince's reaction to my unannounced arrival. I pictured it all—a dim but attractive new girlfriend standing behind him in the doorway, visibly annoyed; a lonely Vince holding a dusty engagement ring box; Vince, sweaty and disheveled, coming back from a run in his neighborhood, his flushed face happy and loving as I pulled to a stop in front of his condo. How would he take what I had to say?

The reality was something different. I took 77 into town and then exited on Woodlawn Road. I drove quickly and carefully through

Myers Park, passing Park Road Books, our favorite bistro, and the dozens of stately historic homes sitting neatly back from the street on yards stuffed with ivy.

Pulling into Vince's condo complex, I coasted up to his building and then turned off the car. It was just after four in the morning. The streetlights cast a yellow glow over the condominiums. I thought of the occupants asleep inside, children snoring lightly in their beds, dogs curled around their tails. I wished I could creep to Vince's side and watch him sleep. When he woke, I would talk to him and try to explain what it was that I was thinking—or not thinking. I leaned the car seat back to rest my eyes.

"Mae Wallace? Mae Wallace?" Vince yelled. I was in a dreamland where all heartfelt speeches were delivered to sympathetic audiences.

I opened both eyes but lay in the car seat without moving a muscle. I saw the fabric of the armrest, the visor, and the rearview mirror. Lots of green landscaping, so different than the island. And Vince, standing outside my car, dressed in his weekend office clothes: a light blue polo and khaki pants. I squinted and then grimaced. My teeth were beyond furry now.

"Mae Wallace? Are you okay? What are you doing here?"

From my position in the seat, I closed my eyes and considered the question. I suddenly felt stupid coming all this way to see a man whom I had treated so poorly. For all I knew, Vince only had contempt for me and would order me off his property. I opened one eye, a trick I picked up in summer camp when I was twelve, and then closed it again.

"Mae Wallace, I have to go to work. Open the door."

There was definitely a tone in his voice. Actually, it was more like the voice of the man who yells out the window of the car behind you when your car breaks down at a tollbooth. Not caring. A little mean.

I pressed the little lever to bring the seat upright and then opened the door. My arms and neck felt stiff, as if I had passed out. I guess in a way, I had. I barely remembered parking in front of Vince's. Thank goodness I had the presence of mind to lock the doors before I crashed.

I stepped out of the car gingerly, blinking in the early morning light. A few sprinklers bleat out a *chug-chug-chug* sound on the strip of lawn between the road and the condo building. A red awning fluttered slightly over Vince's door.

"Is that awning new?"

Looking back at his building, Vince nodded. "Yeah, we did an overhaul to the property this summer."

I stared at Vince. He had used the word "we." Was that a "we" as in "My new girlfriend and I replaced the awning together, while we held hands"? Or a "We, the owners of the condos here, we collectively spruced things up"?

Vince cleared his throat and looked down at his keys, which if I remembered correctly, were attached to a pair of miniature flip-flops. Most people would think Vince was being ironic with such a totem of kitsch, but he told me long ago that he really liked the little rubber shoes with their tiny, nubbed soles. That was Vince—he sometimes surprised you when you least expected it.

"Why are you here, Mae Wallace? Just passing through?"

I scratched the back of one bare leg with my big toe, temporarily freed from a flip-flop. I had an irrational urge to reach over to Vince and take his little flip-flop key chain and see if the tiny pair could fit my feet. A headache flared in the front of my skull. It had been hours since I drank a glass of water. "I'm thirsty," I said.

"What?"

"Do you think I could have a glass of water?" I felt light-headed. The street tilted off to the right farther than it had just a few minutes ago. The sprinklers abruptly stopped and then started again. *Chug-chug-chug.* I grabbed for the reassuring metal of the car and felt myself missing the fender and going down, down, down.

Vince looked at first startled and then panicked as he reached for me. I was already gone, though, and closed my eyes, waiting for the green grass underfoot. The cool, recently sprinkled carpet would be a relief—what did they call it? A sweet relief. It never came.

When I woke up, I was stretched out on Vince's sofa. I recognized the pattern immediately. I had always called it bachelor brown. Tiny circles encased little triangles, all floating in a sea of brown. It was altogether terrible.

"Hey." I looked over at Vince, who was holding a cup of coffee.

"Hey. How do you feel?" He rubbed a spot over his left eye, concentrating. He was probably wondering how to get my crazed person out of his house and back down to the Lowcountry.

"Why in the world do you still have this awful couch?" I winced as my head throbbed.

Smiling, Vince looked at me with more warmth than before.

There was an uncertainty in his face. "I do need to replace it. I don't know, shopping for a couch just seems like too much hassle. I would rather some couch elves show up and pick one out for me."

"My mother redecorates every few years. I've picked up some tips. You start with eliminating the kinds of couches you don't like." I tried to sit up.

Vince leaned forward and gently pushed me back onto the couch. "Take it easy, Mae Wallace. You fainted outside. You've only been out for a few minutes, but you can't push it. If you want, I can take you to the urgent care around the corner. Even though it's a Sunday, they'll be open." The businesslike Vince was back.

"Oh, Vince, I've ruined your day. I'm sorry."

Taking a sip of coffee, Vince didn't argue with me. Instead, he went over to the kitchen and poured a glass of water. "I think you wanted some water?"

"I feel so silly. People don't just faint, do they?"

"They do when they have driven all night, eaten nothing, and hopped themselves up on caffeine."

"Don't forget 'pissed off everyone they love,' too. That counts for double fainting points, I'm pretty sure." If I was laying on the sad-sack routine a little thick, that was okay with me. I actually hung my head, something that was fairly easy to do since my headache was raging like a series of little battles in my head.

Settling onto the other end of the couch, Vince looked over at me. "So, are you going to tell me why you are here? I'm guessing it can't be good news."

I took a deep breath, knowing that things with Vince were as broken as they were with March. The scary thing, the thing that kept me driving during those ink-black hours between Langdon and Charlotte, was that I knew I could cling to Vince through it all. Through the doctors' appointments, the horrible diagnosis, the sadness I felt over leaving my job, the fake front I kept up in front of my loving parents—every threadbare piece of my life. And he would be there for me, faithful and true as a Hallmark card.

I *could* have clung to him, but I didn't. In fact, I shut him up and out of my life like he was a summer-camp boyfriend in September, forgotten and old news. I had treated Vince terribly. He wanted to help me, he wanted to get me through the last six months with my sister, but I didn't know how to let him.

"Vince, I know we've been out of touch for months, and it's all my fault."

"Yeah, I guess you could say that," he said sadly.

"The reason I'm here is to tell you that I know I screwed us up. I think we had a chance, but I didn't let you help me. I guess I thought carrying every one of March's burdens was a good idea. I can't explain it, and I'm not expecting pity from you, but I've lost everything—you, March, my parents, my job—and I wanted to let you know that I can't do it anymore." I paused, feeling as if two cement blocks had been lifted from my shoulders.

Back when things with Vince were rosy, and March still walked around like she owned the world, I remembered playing that girl's game of imagining my own wedding. I planned the church, right down to the orchids on the altar, and the calla lilies in my perfectly manicured hand. There was a beautiful, full-skirted dress, and March in her place as maid of honor. Everyone was there—Mom, Dad, my best friends from Goss, coworkers—everyone, it seemed, but Vince. For when I tried to imagine him standing at the end of the aisle, I only saw a fuzzy groom, face blurred amid the violins, flowers, and attendants. It was a detail that bothered me, sure, but one that I tried to gloss over. But sooner or later, I had to face it, my future with Vince seemed less clear the longer I was with him.

"I don't know why I couldn't let you in. I don't know why I thought I had to save March all by myself. Do you know how many of her infections I kept from my parents? How many dismal doctors' meetings I attended and never breathed a word of bad news?"

Vince leaned forward from his spot on the couch and rested his elbows on his thighs. He lowered his head and rubbed his face. "At first, I was understanding when you shut me out. And then I was angry. I tried being supportive, detached—everything. I even tried going on a few dates. Those were disasters because my heart wasn't in them. It was somewhere, down off the coast of South Carolina."

I nodded, tears forming in my eyes. I really loved Vince at one time, I knew that all the more painfully now.

Vince continued, "And then, one day, I realized I wasn't a part of your life anymore. I could pretend we were on hold or going through a rough patch. But that wasn't being true to myself or what we used to be. You had given up on us, on me. And I had to learn to do the same."

I sat up and leaned back on the couch pillows, also untastefully done in bachelor brown. "I'm so sorry, Vince. I loved being with you. I loved you. I don't know what happened to me."

"From my perspective, it seemed like ever since you went down to live on that piece of sand, you kind of lost your mind. I mean, it's one thing to care for your sister, but it's another when you let it take over your life."

I cried a little, thinking of what I could have done differently.

Vince wasn't finished. "You could have moved there for a few months, taken a leave of absence from World Matters, and then come back. Or you could have volunteered to help March for the first two months and then asked your parents to move there, something like that."

"My parents had a hard time with March's accident."

"Of course they did. But letting you take the brunt of March's care was your idea, not theirs."

He had a point. Once March stabilized and was moved to Langdon, I made sure my parents heard peppy, upbeat reports. I didn't cry on their shoulders. I saved that for Hale. March was in her own angry fog—I sure didn't share my feelings with her.

I tried to rally to my own weak defense. "Well, things happened so fast, there wasn't really time to figure it all out. I did what I could at the time. And March is really getting better now," I said, biting my lip. "At least, I think so. She's not exactly speaking to me."

Vince's face softened and he leaned forward, his voice lower and less strident. "You say things happened fast, but the truth is, I was there, trying to support you. I asked questions, remember? Like if moving down there was the best course for you to take? I tried to push you to think about it long and hard, Mae Wallace."

Taking a deep breath, I thought of Hale and wondered what

he was doing. Maybe he and March were together again today. I hoped so. Maybe they could help each other. I wasn't doing the best job of it. Not that I was looking for pity—I was starting to move past that—but I was at a loss as to how to make everything turn around and work out. I didn't know how to fix this.

"What are you thinking?" Vince asked.

"I'm thinking about how I hope my sister would be okay after all of my stupid mistakes. I really love her, Vince, I really do."

"I know you do," he said, his voice soft and caring. "But somewhere along the lines, you lost yourself in March's tragedy. I guess I stopped trying to reach you. Things between us seemed so unfinished, and she treated you horribly. It was hard to watch."

A small glimmer of understanding began to grow in my head. A big part of why things with Vince had gone so wrong was that I never stood up for myself with March. My refusal to defend myself from her attacks, criticisms, and barbs only made my distance from Vince seem more of a betrayal, because the person I was sacrificing everything for treated me with such contempt.

I thought of all the mean words, rolled eyes, and blunt statements March had generated in my direction in the past six months. And I just stood there, taking it. What did that say about me? Why couldn't I sit down and open up my heart to her? Tell her that I was sorry about a lot of things, but that the biggest regret I had was the day she rode a horse and was hurt, and there wasn't anything I could do to make it better.

Tears pooled in my eyes, and I stood up from the couch, mechanically folding the chenille throw. Vince stood, too. We had an air of formality to us, we two who had once been in love. All I had to do was walk out of his condo, cross the clipped grass to the car, and make the long drive back home. It seemed impossible to do.

Vince reached for me and I leaned in to his hug, feeling the warmth of his chest and arms. I could hardly remember the last time I touched him. A crashing wave of sadness rolled over my empty heart. One thought kept rattling through my head, *Fix this, Mae Wallace, don't leave this man.* But I had no answer, and no way to make things better.

A moment later, I walked back to the car. The sprinklers were silent, the early-morning artificial rain almost dry on the grass. My car was unlocked. I climbed in. Three stained coffee cups lolled on the floorboard, along with a chocolate-bar wrapper. The interior smelled damp and sweaty. I had only empty hours ahead of me, so I turned on the ignition, pulled the seat belt over my shoulder, and put the car in drive. It was time to go home.

SIXTEEN

The swimming is hard at first. The water is choppy, colder than expected, and smells sour. Some of it splashes into her mouth, which is open as she dog paddles, one arm pulling her through the water, the other one holding the camera aloft. Out in the gray bay, dented trawlers head for open water, their outrigger booms closed like bird wings. She thinks she must look ridiculous. She starts to reconsider.

But no, there is a plan here, and an artistic mission to accomplish. She had lost her nerve, perhaps. Is there more to their lives than they know? Maybe she and Hale should try to make it in the New York art and theater world. Maybe they should talk about having children. Ruth is confident in her artistic abilities. She is a professional with a résumé of several show designs under her belt. She has seen Topeka, Des

Moines, and Milwaukee. New York, London, and Florence. She has a house, and a husband. Her life is real.

The first rung on the ladder is something to shoot for as she swims. It's now a football field away. She pictures the yards and counts them off, thinks of firm grass beneath her feet. Grass like the kind found in well-tended subdivisions back in Greenville. Like the house she grew up in. Far beneath her feet, she knows, there is firm sand. It's back on the beach, too, but she doesn't allow herself to think of the beach. One glance back and she knows it could unnerve her, for if she admits it, she is not a terribly brave person. Her heart is brave and loving, and it beats fully formed in her chest. But a person who craves adventure, she is not.

The first rung of the ladder appears, wet with the sea, corroded and rusty and flecked with bird poo. She grabs for it and misses as a wave slams her back. Dog paddling in a circle to try again, she makes contact with the metal and hauls her wet body up its first two rungs. The plastic bag now swings freely from her wrist as she climbs.

She does not reconsider the plan at all now. The hardest part, the swimming, is half over. Now there is just climbing, something she did endlessly as a girl in the large trees in the front part of the estate. Oak, pine, sycamore—all perfect trees for climbing and daydreaming the day away from her two sisters who had other interests. She knew then not to climb too high. For this climb, she will have to break those childish, self-imposed ceilings. Climbing now is serious business.

As she mounts the ladder, the weight of her body pulling down, down, down and her palms pressing into the rough, cross-hatched metal rungs, she becomes aware of the traffic crossing the new bridge. Each rung takes her more into the passing traffic's view. A thin, worrisome thought begins to form. Can I get in trouble for this? After all, the ladders were all tied up, with the exception of this vandalized one. A maritime official probably had jurisdiction over the dismantled pilings and the rusting ladders. No doubt she is breaking some serious rule.

With about twenty rungs to go, a dryness falls across her mouth and her legs start to cramp up with a fear that feels at once paralyzing and exhilarating. She has never done this before. She is majestic—a cliff diver, a bear trainer, an icy-water kayaker. Does the passing traffic see her? Somebody in one of those cars is bound to be impressed. She decides to finish the climb strong, not looking down or up, but straight ahead. The pictures she will take for her husband fade from her mind. There is just the flaking metal under her fingernails, the whisper of traffic treading across asphalt. The top is in sight. The wind tears at her skin, no longer wet from swimming. The air feels heavier and saltier than on land. A boat engine whines on its way out to sea. The island retreats from the corner of her eye.

Two more ladder rungs are conquered and then she climbs on top, owner of a forty-foot-long section of bridge, tragically disconnected from its sisters. The pavement is soiled, old, cracked, and dotted with scrubby weeds. Langdon swings out in a slim crescent below. Far down the beach a cluster of homes fades into gray stands of palmettos and even grayer sand. One of those is her home, the one she shares with Hale. The sun has started to arc downward, toward the night at the end of the day. She takes it all in, and then seems to remember why she is up there so high. Digging out the camera, she raises it to her eye and begins.

SEVENTEEN

Ellen remembered little of her life before the accident. This was at once a problem and a curse because she knew enough to know she had been injured, but not enough to really understand what that meant. She did comprehend certain things used to work with her body, she was sure of that, but now they did not. She lived at a nice place called the Sea Villas, but was it really nice? She had little with which to compare it.

Ellen was aware she was about sixty years old and that she had little people that visited her, claiming to be her grandchildren. These little people visited once a month. Their mother dressed them in fancy jumpers with embroidered pockets. Their hair was fixed in curls and smelled like cherries. Ellen did not mind when they came.

From scattered bits of conversation, all overheard because Ellen no longer used words to communicate, she has figured out there was a horrible accident involving a tractor trailer that ran a stop sign near Beaufort, a little South Carolina town a short drive from Hilton Head Island. Beaufort sounded like a lovely place, Ellen mused, and she wondered if she lived there at one time. Perhaps there was still a house waiting on a neat and trim street for her to come home. Perhaps.

The little people's mother also came to visit. Her name Ellen can't recall, but she stroked Ellen's rough skin and placed the little well-dressed people on Ellen's bed and urged them to sing songs. The melodies of the songs were familiar, but not in a comforting way. It was irritating to have a song on the tip of your tongue but not remember a single verse. The little people sang anyway. They did not know how Ellen felt.

On one of the visits, a nurse made small talk with the mother.

"She seems to recognize you a little more each time," the nurse said, folding a blanket at the end of Ellen's bed.

"That's nice of you to say that, but really, the doctors say there is no change. It's still the same as it was last year and the year before." The woman speaking glanced over at the little people in their pretty dresses who were watching a cartoon on the room television. Ellen despised the television. She wished it would fall off the wall and be dashed into a million pieces. The staff turned it on each day for her, as if she wanted to watch it. She did not.

"Well, maybe," the nurse said, turning her attention to Ellen's feet. The toenails needed cutting. A nice pumice stone would be helpful, too, Ellen thought.

"I guess you get used to seeing people the same, day after day," the woman said to the nurse.

"Yes and no. Some make improvements very quickly. Others don't, but you see gradual changes. Like your mother here. When she first arrived, she stared out that window all the time, remember? Now she seems more tuned in to what's happening in the hospital. And she likes to go for strolls around the hall in her chair." The nurse paused in her clipping. "At least I think so, it's somewhat hard to tell."

The woman hugged her arms to her chest and turned away from the nurse. She walked over to the window, a large span that offered a beautiful view of the end of the island, the bay bridge, and the mainland in the distance. The water was a faded blue today, almost like a pair of prized blue jeans.

The view was one of the reasons she and Dad had selected the room for Mom. No one knew how much her mother understood, but surely she could see the natural beauty outside her room and receive some small comfort. Dad agreed, but he didn't make the trip anymore to see Mom. He paid the bills, which were considerable, and stayed in their old home in Beaufort. "She doesn't remember me, so what's the point?" he'd asked his daughter more than once.

A whirring in the hallway grabbed Ellen's attention. The dark-haired young woman who lived next door rolled by, her eyes focused on something at the end of the corridor. Ellen had seen this young patient many times before, and knew she wasn't the type to wave or make pleasantries. As usual, she wheeled past without a sideways glance.

"What's her name? I see her each month, but we've never spoken," the woman said to the nurse, who had switched to a nail file and was carefully attending to each of Ellen's toes. A bottle of apricot-scented lotion sat on the table nearby.

"That's March. She's been here, what, six months?"

"What happened to her?"

The nurse stopped filing and glanced at the open doorway. "We're not supposed to talk personal details, but that one, she was thrown off a horse."

"How terrible."

"Don't you know it. People are here for all sorts of reasons—shootings, car accidents, freak things, but then there are the horse people, the hang gliders, the race-car drivers."

"I guess I never thought of it that way," the woman said with a glance toward her mother. The older woman's eyes were closed, like she was dreaming.

"Yes, people get themselves in a whole heap of trouble. And it takes years to get it right again, if we can get it right at all." The nurse looked up to Ellen's daughter. "Not like with your mother, though. It wasn't her fault that truck driver blew through a stop sign. Nope, not her fault at all."

Ellen sighed as the apricot lotion was rubbed into each toe. It was nice, for once, to sit and just listen. Often, she felt panic that she could hear a lot of what was going on and was unable to respond. So she had invented a way to pass the time. Ellen would take each conversation and put it in a mental filing cabinet in her mind. Each cabinet would have the name of the person who was talking neatly typed on a white card and affixed to the front of the filing cabinet. If she didn't know the person's name and they were important, like the daughter who sat a few feet away, she simply put a star on the cabinet. Some people got red shiny stars or blue shiny stars. If Ellen ever regained the ability to talk, she would go to the filing cabinet and tell the person all the answers to the questions they had asked her over the last few years.

Another way Ellen passed the time was by staring out of the window. She mostly did that in the afternoon when the sun was starting to warm the bay with yellows, pinks, and soft blues. Ellen could see the strong, sharp bridge deliver streams of traffic from the mainland back to the island each afternoon. Depending on the season, she could view an endless parade of headlights or simply the flash of metal under a low sun as the commuters found their way home. Once, the daughter had brought a pair of binoculars for her bridge watching. They sat on the nightstand beside her.

One thing Ellen did not understand was the broken bridge. It was an odd sight—parts of a dilapidated bridge next to the nice, functional bridge. It made no sense to Ellen. Still, she watched as pieces of the bridge were removed. Men wrangled large cranes and huge barges to do the job. Sometimes she used her binoculars to watch. Other times, she just sat back in her bed, arms at her side, head turned slightly, and looked at the bridge traffic in the distance.

"I wonder what she's thinking about now," the woman mused, almost to herself. Her two little girls had tired of the television and were standing shoulder to shoulder at a low table that held potted plants. They stroked the same leaf of a fern in a brown basket.

Collecting her pedicure supplies, the nurse stood up and stretched. "No telling. Maybe she's thinking about that young, handsome Doctor Billings." She winked at the mother of the young girls.

Ellen's daughter smiled, distracted. It was time to go, but she never liked leaving her mother like this. She had long given up hope that something would happen, that there would be a miraculous recovery. Regardless, it still felt cruel to leave Mom. Her care was excellent, but it wasn't home. Mom should be back in Beaufort, making sugar cookies with the girls and stitching them little blankets for their dolls, like she used to before the accident. The daughter felt a familiar guilty twinge. She wanted her mommy back.

Ellen sensed the women and girls getting ready to leave her. She mentally placed the visit in her filing cabinets and then started to drift off to sleep. She closed her eyes and relaxed. Sometimes it was good to be alone again.

When she reopened her eyes, the room was dark. Shadows padded the walls of the room. The blinds to the window were still open, so she turned her head slightly to the left, toward the bay. It was all she could manage these days.

The bridge was lighted a cheery, blazing white. Traffic was lighter now—it must be after nine. Most everyone was home in bed or having dinner, bathing babies. It was night, Ellen thought. The binoculars were just out of reach, and Ellen could not be sure her arms would listen to her and pick them up if she asked. She decided not to chance it. No need making a scene if she was somehow unable to move like she wished. It was easier to rest.

The binoculars were a fine pair, brand-new and selected just for her. Ellen owned many nice things that her daughter brought to her. New robes, slippers, pants with elastic waists, even some beauty products that the staff dutifully applied. Her room was clean and comfortable. There was not much to complain about.

Beside the white glow of the bay bridge, the old, hulking bridge stood alone in the night. Ellen could barely make it out. There was a nagging feeling somewhere in her mind about that bridge. It was not right to have something so broken standing for so long. She closed her eyes, the night shadows of the room disappearing.

No, Ellen thought as she headed toward sleep, an eyesore like the bridge should be promptly dismantled and taken away. No one needed to see that and be reminded it was where someone died. No one wanted that in their head all the time. No, sir. Her binoculars had picked it up the day the pretty young girl with the long hair climbed to the top of the broken bridge. Was it yesterday? Or a year ago? Ellen could not much remember, but she could remember the girl on top of the bridge.

Why on earth a young thing like that wanted to be such a daredevil, Ellen did not know. Her own daughter—Stephanie? Sally? The name escaped her, but maybe it started with "S"—would never have done something so foolish. In any event, the girl did, and Ellen saw her smile with delight and pride as she looked around from her tall perch. She even took pictures and carefully stood at the edge of one of the broken edges of the bridge, with nothing between her and a steep fall.

Ellen couldn't look away. That day, from her room, Ellen pleaded with the girl to be careful. Traffic streamed by on the good bridge. No one seemed to notice the foolish young girl standing there, her skirt flapping in the breeze. Be careful, honey, Ellen begged from her room, behind the powerful lenses.

Mercifully, the girl was cautious and backed away from the abyss. The sun was lower now and Ellen wondered how she was going to get out of this pickle.

The girl was so small and so high in sky. Then, the girl slipped her skirt off, bundled it into a bag, and turned her back to Ellen. She gripped a ladder or some such item and began her descent. Remembering the girl's long, brown hair whipping out behind her, Ellen felt tears begin to slip from her eyes in the darkened room. She could recall the girl's strong arms, the iron ladder, and the wind blowing her hair about. It was too much, too much to think about so late and when she was so alone. The wind was strong, too strong. Ellen closed her eyes and went to sleep.

EIGHTEEN

As I approached the ramp for the bridge to Langdon, the nervousness in my stomach grew. I felt absolutely bereft, like I had no one in my life who cared at all if I crossed that bridge or not, if I came home or left forever. Of course, I was starting my World Matters contract work tomorrow, but that didn't really count. The main people in my life were missing.

Blinking back tears, I switched on my turn signal and moved over to the left lane. My tires hit the bridge with a smooth, drumming sound.

The old bridge, Ruth's bridge, stood out starkly as I drove. I was surprised to see more activity on it than usual. Two more cranes had joined the other two already in place. Workers swarmed over two of the abandoned pilings, while others labored far below on barges. I flashed past the bridge section where Ruth made her last climb. The largest of Hale's signs and the words *Miss Your Lips Ruth* were faded, the purple and red turned pale. A man in overalls strode past it, a cigarette hanging from the corner of his mouth.

It looked like the bridge was finally coming down, every piece of it. There had been angry letters to the editor of the island paper. The island council blamed the state, the state blamed the demolition company, but the bottom line was it was past time for it to go. Everyone had grown tired of the broken skyline and the broken bridge.

I turned down our street at the end of the island and felt my heart fall. I saw a distinct, white van from the Sea Villas in front of my house. Was it March? Had something happened? I was so stupid to have left her to drive to Charlotte. I glanced over at my cell phone in the passenger seat. Surely, the Sea Villas would have called if there had been an emergency? As I picked it up, I realized the battery had died.

Racing into the driveway, I parked the car, ripped off the seat belt, and opened the door. Two men got out of the van and walked toward me. I recognized one of them as a hospital administrator I had seen from time to time on March's hall. My skin felt cold; I was terrified.

"Ms. Anders?" The administrator looked grave.

"Yes, what's wrong with my sister? March Anders? My sister," I babbled, hardly able to stand. I needed food, water, and a place to lie down. I tried to imagine what might have happened to March. An infection, perhaps? One of those super bugs that were on the news all of the time—you could get one of those, develop sores, and there was nothing anyone could do about it. Just like that, you were a few lines in an obituary.

"Yes, well, that's why we're here," the other man said. He was shorter than the administrator, with kind brown eyes. "I'm Lawrence King, legal counsel for the Sea Villas and this is my colleague, Isaiah Parker, chief of staff. We want to tell you about a distressing situation concerning your sister, March. Is there a place we could talk privately?"

I thought of my house, steps away, and promptly forgot it. Whatever the men had to say, they could say it here, in my driveway. I was sure plenty of my old neighbors were watching us from behind their plaid café curtains, but I didn't care. "Just tell me what you've come here to tell me."

Lawrence cleared his throat and looked over at Isaiah. "March, it seems to appear, is missing."

"Missing?" I felt light-headed, like the time I drank eight diet colas on a dare freshman year at Goss. My mouth was dry and my right eye throbbed with an urgent pulse. I didn't know how much more I could take. March was mad at me, Hale wanted nothing to do with me, Vince was officially out of the picture, and now this. To top it all off, my parents were living in a beautiful home of denial about their daughter, built carefully by me.

"What?"

"Her whereabouts are unknown," Lawrence said, again clearing his throat.

"Do you need to sit down?" Isaiah asked with concern in his voice. "You look a bit under the weather."

"Forget about me," I said, ignoring their kindness. "Tell me where my sister is or where you think she is. And for heaven's sake, she's paralyzed! Where could she have gone? It's not like she can walk or drive."

Clearing his throat Lawrence said, "We're still trying to figure that out. Your sister is turning out to be incredibly resourceful. It seems she convinced one of our seasonal kitchen staff to take her to the beach. From there, we know she found a ride with a sympathetic Belgian family. We're interviewing them now with the help of a translator. Of course, we're sure she's fine."

I closed my eyes and pressed my fingertips lightly on my eyelids. "She's trying to leave the island," I said.

"What?" Isaiah dropped his serious demeanor for a moment.

"March is trying to get away from here. She just wants to get away."

"This is very troubling. Did you have any indication that she was plotting an escape from our facility?" Lawrence pulled out a small pad and pen.

"Let's not call it an 'escape' but rather an 'unauthorized leave,'" Isaiah said, turning his lips into a frown. A thin line of sweat broke out on his brow.

"Have either of you talked to March's friend, Hale? He might know where she is."

Flipping to a page in his notepad, Lawrence nodded. "Hale Brock. Yes, we're in touch by cell with him. He's promised to call us if she contacts him. In the meantime, he's driving the island in an unofficial capacity, looking for her. He seems quite fond of Ms. Anders."

I felt a pang of remorse for my fight with Hale. He was not fond of the other Ms. Anders. I needed him on my side, and I needed to be there for him. March's disappearance was no doubt stirring up all sorts of emotions for him. She was another missing woman in his life.

My heart thudded in my chest, thinking of March away from me forever. She used to be my best friend, the one person that brought joy to the every day and zaniness where it was least expected. Although we were a long way from that, she was still the girl to whom I long ago pledged that if I were given a space rocket ride to the moon and I could bring one person, it would be my sister.

My head was spinning. I thought of a bath, something to eat, and clean clothes. But no, March needed me. Maybe she was scared, confused, and lonely. We would need maps and more cell phones. I whirled around, ready to ask questions and give orders when I caught a delicate whiff of smoke in the air. It smelled kind of like barbecue, mixed with the salty ocean breeze.

Lawrence looked up from his cell phone toward the house. "Ms. Anders, I know it's a bad time right now, but it appears your bungalow is in a bit of trouble."

I turned slowly in time to see an orange ribbon of flame dance across the roofline of my poor, rundown rental. The sun was as cheery as ever, and the sky was a serene blue. But my home was burning. My mind took a second to digest that fact, including a thought that maybe, in my numb, sad, and depressed current life story, I was making up this cataclysmic scene. It was entirely possible. Missing sister, burning house. It made sense.

Isaiah whipped out his cell phone and called 911 while I took three awkward steps toward the building. Maybe the fire wasn't that bad, maybe I could unroll the garden hose and put it out. As I moved, Lawrence grabbed my arm.

"You can't go in there," he said, panting just a little.

"It doesn't look too terrible. I'll just put some water on it." I felt vaguely embarrassed, as if the fire reflected poorly on me.

In response, my little dump of a house spat glass at us as one of the front windows shattered into countless shards. Lawrence dragged me backwards to the street. A wall of flame shot out of my kitchen window as my ankle twisted and I lurched awkwardly into Lawrence's arms. He caught me as the battered deck burst into flames, aided by a sudden ocean breeze.

Slowly, it started to dawn on me that my house was being destroyed. That my lumpy bed frame was melting and my dingy flip-flop collection was on its way out. While it burned, March was missing. She wasn't here and no one knew where she had wheeled herself. My mind raged at stupid Belgian tourists and the inept Villas security who let her go, and all the worry she was causing. I then turned my rage on Vince for being such a nice guy, and then at Hale who was decidedly *not* there when I needed him the most. I ping-ponged back and forth, assigning blame to everyone. I even had a heated thought toward poor, dead Ruth. So *this* is how it started: one lost girl.

The smoke grew thicker, the island's vintage fire truck squealed onto the scene, and suddenly I felt myself being lifted onto a nice, white bed. I heard Lawrence telling them I was acting strangely. I tried to sit up and talk to a kind, burly paramedic, offering him just two words: "Garden hose." Then they gave me an oxygen mask. I really just wanted a drink of water, but no one seemed to be able to understand my thoughts.

That's the way it always was for me. I had a lot of things to tell the world, but somehow those feelings stayed inside. I wasn't able to form them into words. Poor Vince saw this firsthand. I wasn't able to tell him that I loved him and I loved March, and I couldn't understand how to fix it all. So I kept him frozen and distant in another state until it was far too late.

I loved Hale as a confidant and friend, but I failed him when he needed patience and support, the same gifts he had always given me. The rest of the world was pushy enough; I should have been the one to respect his slow advance through the process of mourning Ruth. Art shows could wait. It was more time Hale needed.

I knew I had disappointed my parents enough for two lifetimes. I couldn't repair my rift with March and I couldn't mend her problems now. No doubt the Sea Villas had called and informed them their daughter was missing. My carefully constructed sunny tale was crumbling. Mom and Dad were probably on a borrowed private plane winging their way to the small airport on the other end of the island. I closed my eyes, too tired and sad to think more.

The burly paramedic held my hand in the ambulance, saying, "Hey there, Mae Wallace, talk to me. We're going to get you feeling healthy again real soon. You just got a few buckets of smoke in those lungs of yours. Your friend says you wanted to go back in the house. I'm glad you didn't."

"Yeah, not so good. You could have cooked your goose," said a voice from the front seat. I figured it was the driver, but my eyes were closed and I couldn't see him. "We get those calls all the time: 'But I needed to save my collection of crystal seashells!' Nope, not too smart. Those peeps don't go home again, if you get my drift."

The paramedic squeezed my hand. "We're okay, right? You didn't go back in. You've made me a happy paramedic man."

"I thought I could put it out with the garden hose," I mumbled through the oxygen mask.

"What? I can't understand you," my paramedic said, lifting the mask.

"I said, I thought I could put it out. With the garden hose." I opened my eyes.

The ambulance lurched over a speed bump. We were probably close to the tiny island hospital. I'd been there a few times when March got really sick and the Sea Villas transferred her. I groaned, thinking of March for the first time in a while. She wasn't safe at the Villas—she was missing.

"What is it?"

"My sister, she's the one they're looking for," I said, tears forming in my eyes. "The one from the Sea Villas. That's March, my sister."

"Don't you worry about her," the driver called as he swung the ambulance into a sharp turn. "This island's a small place. If she's not in the water, they'll find her really fast. We got good guys on search and rescue here."

I must have looked scared because the paramedic beside me glared at his partner. "What he means is, your sister's probably just found a little place to hole up. People do that all the time, they want to get away for a time or two. Everyone usually has a happy ending."

"Usually," I said, closing my eyes again. The ambulance swayed and rocked, bouncing over the old asphalt island roads.

Once inside the hospital, I was triaged and assigned to a small emergency bay with beige curtains. A succession of nurses and doctors with drawn faces did blood tests, ordered X-rays, and administered more oxygen. It seemed that everyone made too big a fuss out of a little exhaustion and smoke inhalation, but in all honesty, it was sort of a relief to stop and not have to worry about anything. My head and chest hurt, but it was nothing compared to the soreness in my heart.

When one nurse found out I hadn't eaten in forever, she brought me a bowl of chicken noodle soup that I gulped down with a few crackers. Three hours later, I was finally discharged with instructions to go right home and relax. I found this incredibly amusing and waited for someone to look at my chart and realize the reason I inhaled too much smoke was that my house had burned down. No one did, so I hopped off the table and wandered toward the front entrance of the emergency room.

"Give a ring if you need something, honey," the receptionist called after me.

I muttered, "I need a new house." The receptionist smiled and waved as she reached for a ringing phone.

Somewhere, my crazy landlord, Mrs. Pelham, was getting the news her firetrap had been reduced to an insurance claim. The OFDs were probably resting after spending an exhausting day at their windows, bearing witness to my personal tragedy. I didn't have renter's insurance, but that didn't bother me too much. My possessions were minor; there wasn't much in the house that mattered. Thank goodness Ruth's broken notebook was still in my car, safe and sound. I did wonder idly where I would spend the night. Maybe I could get a room at one of the local beach hotels. I still had my purse and wallet. I made a mental note to call Hans Macher. I wasn't going to be up for starting my new World Matters job tomorrow. I was sure he would understand.

I walked stiffly outside, wondering what to do next. There was no one I could call. I didn't want to bother my parents or Hale who was probably busy chasing March. Outside, the sun was setting. I picked a bench to sit on, too tired to care where I was going or what would happen to me. A few pelicans flew low across the setting sun. The tall palmetto trees in the parking lot swayed slightly. The warmish night air was heavy with humidity.

A young couple walked across the parking lot toward the entrance. The woman's straining belly seemed to point the way. The husband rubbed her back, saying, "Visualize a flower opening, honey." They passed me without a glance, intent on their journey ahead. For the first time in hours, I smiled. Women go missing, houses burn down, but life goes on, turning its wheels over and over with each passing day.

Without a car or cell phone, I was completely cut off from the search for March. And for the minute, that was okay with me. I wasn't sure what had happened in the past few hours, but at some point in the emergency room, I realized that I couldn't join the search for my sister. For one, I was too weak, having inhaled smoke, eaten nothing for almost a day, and having had too little sleep. If I took stock of my life, almost all columns were coming up empty.

I shifted on the metal bench and pulled on my hoodie. It smelled of smoke, making me cough slightly. Maybe an hour passed, my bent frame pressed into the hospital bench. The night was cooler now, the sun almost spent. I hoped March was safe, wherever she was.

And just like that, I let go of my sister. Not forever, of course. I totally believed she was alive and just stubbornly somewhere out of sight. No, I let go of her almost like I was a child with a pretty, red balloon and a string that was snaking across my palm until it was just out of reach, whipping up into the sky. Crossing my legs, I leaned back on the bench. I released all the dreams I had for my relationship with March. If we were never best friends again, I would learn how to do that. If our friendship changed into two young adult women who had respect for each other, then that was great. If it didn't, then there was nothing I could do about it.

I vowed to take March as she was, not the miracle-healed paraplegic I wanted her to be. If she had to be in a chair the rest of her life, I was going to accept that. I was done trying to look at the bright side of everything. It was horrible that the accident happened, but it did. No one wanted it. But March rode that horse and she was thrown into a dew-soaked field one autumn day. I could accept that I had paid for the accident, too, and the price had been my close relationship with my sister, my beloved job in Atlanta, my house, my boyfriend, and my new best friend. I could not give anything else.

Two cars followed each other into the parking lot, their head-lights splashing over me and my faithful bench. For a moment, I wondered if they might be coming to my aid—someone realized that my house was a pile of ash—but then they passed the bench and parked. I watched as two middle-aged couples got out, each carrying brightly wrapped packages. One of the men held a bou-quet of flowers stiffly in his hands. The group swept by, nervously chatting. I imagined they were the parents of the young, pregnant couple I had seen earlier.

I sat there a little longer, trying on my new approach to all things March. It felt kind of like a lazy Saturday when you know you have a dozen hours all to yourself. After the better part of a year concerned with March's every diagnosis, test, and treatment, it was freeing just to be a woman on a bench at night, with no one to take care of, no one to worry over every hour of each day.

Standing up and stretching, I decided to go back inside and call a cab. Without thinking, I pictured walking inside my house, shutting the battered porch door, and then sinking onto the faded couch. Suddenly, I saw clouds of smoke, streaming water, and ash. My old couch was gone. I felt a huge sob start in my chest and heave itself up and out. The tears fell fast and I gasped for air. My home was gone—the physical structure, of course, but I no longer had a home inside myself. Where could I go? My parents' home was the place where March was changed forever. Hale's house was a memory box to Ruth, and March's home was temporary. She couldn't stay at the Sea Villas indefinitely. I cried and cried, standing there beside the bench until my smoke-stained hair was wet from falling over my face as I wept.

A car pulled up beside me, headlights bearing down, and I turned away, embarrassed to be in the middle of such a public breakdown.

"Mae Wallace? It's me, Hale."

I peered over at Hale through the open passenger window. I squinted, not sure what to do. Then the tears started again, and I sagged back down on the bench. He was beside me in a moment.

"Hey, there, there," Hale said, wrapping his arms around me. "I've been looking for you. The hospital said you were discharged to your home. When I tried to explain that was impossible, they transferred me repeatedly to a succession of unhelpful staff members."

I leaned into Hale, my nose runny and my stinky hair knotted together. "I can't go home." My words came in sobs.

"Yeah, I know. I'm so sorry. While I was combing the island for March, I heard over the local radio that your grand rental was in flames." Hale rubbed my back. "I have to ask, though. Did you start the fire yourself? You were always complaining about that place. I figured, you know, you took matters into your own hands."

I sat up. "You've got to be kidding."

Smiling, Hale grabbed one of my hands. "Yes, I am kidding. How else was I going to get you to laugh about easily the most tragic and stressful day of your life since the accident?"

Inhaling sharply, I pushed back my hair from my eyes and said, "Hale, I've been here all night thinking all these kinds of things about me and March, and I have to tell you that I figured out . . . well, I just stopped—"

"March is safe, Mae Wallace. She's back at the Sea Villas under lock and key, so to speak, but they're keeping a tight rein on her. Your parents are with her."

"She's safe?" It was colder now, and I hugged my arms to my chest. "She's okay?" My mind was having trouble keeping up with what Hale was saying.

"March is one-hundred percent alive and well. She was found at the island marina, signing a waiver to go paragliding when the staff at Bob's Paragliding noticed a hospital bracelet. They quietly called the police."

Although I felt like wringing March's neck, I was also secretly amused. "Paragliding, huh?"

Hale smiled. "I found it pretty funny, but I told her next time she wanted to worry everyone who loved her, she should take a moment and reconsider. I don't want any part of land and water searches again, thank you very much."

Tears came to my eyes. "Oh, Hale. Even in the midst of all of this, it was killing me that you had to be told my sister was missing, that you had to, you know, look for her. Like Ruth all over again."

Hale turned away from me and gazed down at the concrete pad under our feet. "I'll admit that today was really hard. Seeing the same people, the sheriff, the deputies, the search and rescue boat going out from the marina—a person shouldn't have to do that once, let alone twice. Luckily for me, your dad was on the scene pretty fast and he handled all of the tactical details. I was left to search on my own."

I winced. My parents. By now they had figured out that life wasn't a bowl of cherries between March and me. "How are they?"

"They're better now. A little confused. I don't think they realized how sad and depressed their youngest daughter was, or how trapped she felt. I don't think I did, either. Did you?"

Sighing, I knew I could dodge the question, lie, or talk my way around it. But the truth was, I knew deep down that something was very wrong with March. My sunny, let's-just-fix-this mood didn't help her, and neither did my insistence at trading in my old life for this new one. Now that I was ready to shed both, I felt stronger but also a tad afraid. What would my parents think of my decision?

"Are my parents mad? At me?"

"Nice smoke smell. It works with the whole disheveled, home-less thing you have going on." Hale slid his arm around my shoulders. "No, they're concerned about you. I was with them when they got word you were, uhm, displaced from your craptastic house. I volunteered to ferret you out and bring you back to the family fold again."

"Then, they're not upset that I let March go missing?"

Hale looked me in the eyes. "March is responsible for her own mistakes. Not you. It took me a long time to realize this one thing: people can do what they want and it has nothing to do with you."

If Hale knew anything, he knew that. I closed my eyes and

longed for a quiet, soft bed. "I've decided to let go of March, Hale. Everything that I've done has been wrong. Taking all of her attitude. Pretending that life was fine. Faking sisterly togetherness for my parents' benefit. All of it—giving up my old life in order to feel guilty all of the time—I'm done."

"Gee, and it only took helicopters, the local K9 unit, two earnest Charleston television reporters, plus a house fire thrown in to get you to see the light?"

"Don't forget fighting with your best friend and breaking up for good with your boyfriend, the one you thought a long time ago that you were going to marry."

"Ouch, I'm sorry. Stick a fork in it?"

"Yup, we're done." I leaned forward, elbows on my thighs. "I can't say it was easy. Admitting you were the world's worst girlfriend, with a side helping of reticence is never easy. I don't even know if I made the right decision." A cool breeze stirred a candy-bar wrapper near my feet. It turned over: brown, silver, brown, silver. "No, scratch that. It was the right thing to do. We were damaged and things weren't ever going to turn around. Vince knew it before I did, I'm pretty sure."

"Well, I'm sorry for you, all the same. I got your note that you went to Charlotte. Figured you would be stopping to see Vince."

"The midnight road trip is a thing best left to the dramatic college freshman, I think." I rubbed my greasy, smoky forehead. "It was awful, and I came back here."

Hale stood up and offered me a hand. "We're a little old for that drama, right?"

"You got it."

Opening up the passenger door, Hale helped me in with a steadying arm. I knew that if I didn't lie down soon, I would be worthless. Already, a sick feeling was spreading in my stomach as the trauma of the past few hours caught up with me.

We bumped down the asphalt roads back to our neighborhood. I was half curious to see my house but also filled with unease. What did it feel like to return to nothing? All at once, I pictured Hale, making the same drive back home after getting the call Ruth had been on the bridge. After going out to the little park under the bridge, standing for hours while search crews combed the scrubby beach and scuba teams launched themselves into the choppy bay waters, he came home again alone and fearing that the night would fall and he would still be there, waiting.

Hale turned onto our street and looked over at me. "I was thinking you could shower at my place while I run out and get some food. Later, if you're up to it, we can go see your parents at their hotel."

Taking a deep breath, I said, "What was it like to come home that first day, the day Ruth died?"

Hale pulled up in his driveway and coasted to a stop. He cut the headlights, darkening the driveway and the neat stand of bougainvillea. I kept my head turned to the side so I wouldn't have to look at the hole where my house had been. It would be right over the bougainvillea, past their heavy vines and dark green branches.

"I've actually thought a lot about that day in the past few

hours, once we knew March was missing. It's funny how much Ruth has been on my mind today. It's not like I don't think of her every day, of course I do, but as I was getting more and more involved with your sister, it was like Ruth was taking a backseat."

"I guess that's normal, right?"

Hale nodded. "Totally, regrettably normal. I've moved through all the stages and now I'm segueing into some sort of new life." He laughed, a short laugh that was quietly sad. "Nice life, huh? Here I am, running off my first girlfriend."

"Don't say that, Hale. That's a move out of my book. Blame yourself for everyone else's problems."

Hale pocketed the keys and leaned back in the seat. Turning his head toward me, he said, "You're right, you're right. But it was so strange to be in that position again. The sheriff, the sirens, the walkie-talkies. I think a couple of the deputies looked at me like, 'Oh, here's that guy. Maybe we had him figured wrong. He's not the sympathetic widower. No, he's much more dangerous than we imagined.'"

"I guess I hadn't thought of it like that, but it does look kind of bad."

"Luckily, your sister showed up, healthy and ticked off because she wasn't going paragliding."

I rolled down my window, eager to hear the ocean. I felt cut off from it these past few hours. Instead of the familiar tang of salt, however, all I smelled was dank and smoky air. I rolled the window back up. "Oh, that's gross."

"We all thank you for the new neighborhood perfume."

"Thank me? Thank my landlord. She's the one who kept the house up to code for 1912. It's not like I left some candles burning or something."

We were quiet then, the night air layered in salt, smoke, and the silence that's comfortable between friends. A car swished by on the main road, its headlights bouncing off of the houses on our end of the island.

Clearing his throat, Hale spoke. "So, since you asked, I'll answer your question about Ruth. I don't talk about her enough. Think about my deceased wife? All the time. It's just more difficult to put it into words."

Tapping his fingers on the steering wheel, Hale said, "It was hard to drive back home that first night. Of course, I never believed Ruth was dead right away. I thought it was someone else who had foolishly climbed the old bridge. It was another woman—any other woman, dear God, not my Ruth—but someone who looked remarkably like her. I kept up that fantasy into the night until sometime around dawn, I tore the house apart looking for clues to where she might have gone."

I waited, silent and still. My breath came in shallow sips. Another car went by on the road, but this one slowed to a stop. Gawkers.

"I read it all, her work journals, her personal journal, her grocery list. I winced while I did it, but I was also driven by a sense that maybe something horrible had happened and it was up to me to figure it out, like a detective, because everyone else thought she was out there, in the water. I was ready for anything—that she had left me, that she was tired of our marriage, that she'd run off and joined the circus. I was strong, I could take it.

"And then, when the sun was cheerfully rising despite the fact that my wife had not come home, apologetic for working all night at the theater costume shop without calling, I ran out of things to search. Her cell phone contained no unknown numbers. Her e-mail account—both home and work—was empty of anything sinister or shadowy. So I stopped looking. And I had to start living like she was gone from me forever."

Hale got quickly out of the car and I followed. We walked up on his porch and stood, looking toward the ocean. The heavy cloud cover gave little light to the darkened beach. But over the sea oats, the white tumble of surf fizzled and bobbed in a dark gray haze.

"It was weeks, of course, before I really accepted that she was dead. That she wasn't wandering around, unsure of us, or irritated by life. That Ruth hadn't developed amnesia and was trapped in an institution saying my name over and over again, making no sense. Ruth was the woman on the bridge, and I'll never know what happened that day. Never."

I leaned into Hale, and put one arm around his waist. The salty air, tinged with smoke, lifted our hair, rearranging the slight strands into a pattern all of the wind's design. I thought of how I wasn't supposed to be here, not really, and how March shouldn't be in her hospital room staring at the television screen without seeing it. And I thought of Ruth, and her thin, graceful body, and how she should be tucked inside the bungalow steps away, scratching absentmindedly in her sketchbook while Hale worked, contented and in love, painting on the other side of the living room.

No, none of us should be here, smelling smoke, salt, and antiseptic. None of us should, but here we were, all of us, beside the sea. We turned to walk into the house and I straightened my shoulders. As the waves crashed behind me out on the darkened beach, I knew it was time to go find my sister, March.

NINETEEN

Morning gave me a first look at my home's devastation. I don't think I had ever been that close to a burned-out structure. Even though the house was destroyed, a lot of things remained. It wasn't all a heap of ashes. Some things, like the creaky front steps I never used since they led to the front part of the house, still stood, creaky and dangerous as ever. A watering can from the back porch was melted into a little gray puddle. Wide wooden joists, pocked with smoldering ash, stood over the former kitchen, propped up by a black skeleton of studs.

"Hey! I found my old flip-flops!" I laughed, picking them up from the back deck steps. Most of the deck was charred but still in one piece. The firefighters had attacked the wooden planks aggressively, as they were the closest thing burning to Hale's house.

Thankfully, his neat and tidy bungalow had sustained no damage whatsoever.

Hale shoved his hands in his pockets. "Mae Wallace, I have to ask you something, and I feel terrible even bringing it up, but was Ruth's green notebook in the house when it burned? I was hoping maybe you brought it back to my bungalow and I just hadn't noticed." He looked down at the ground, kicking some crushed shells with his toe.

A guilty flush rushed across my face as I pictured the broken notebook. "Oh, Hale. I'm so sorry!"

"It's okay. I think I knew it was gone."

"No, no. It's safe. I mean, the notebook needs to be repaired, but it was in my car. I was planning to have this woman at the Villas fix it after I dropped it the other day, but then March got mad at me, and you got mad at me, and well, it was still in my car when the house burned."

"You're kind of talking crazy, you know." Hale smiled at me, relief all over his face. "Let's get out of here before the OFDs start coming over and chatting us up," he said, glancing toward the road. "The last thing we want to do is get stuck talking about fire codes."

"Agreed." I grabbed my ratty flip-flops with the nine lives and carefully walked around the deck, trudging through the sand. Yellow caution tape surrounded the house and deck.

A solid night's sleep in Hale's guest room, combined with food and a hot shower had revived me so that I almost felt like a real person again. My chest still hurt, and I coughed a little bit, but I was ready to face my parents and March. Hale opened the passenger door of his car. "Let's jet. This heap of burned house isn't going anywhere. It's probably not healthy to stare at it endlessly."

"I wasn't staring. I was fascinated."

"Whatever. You looked like you were getting a little misty-eyed out there. Miss your lovely home?" Hale backed out of the drive onto Sea Street.

"Thanks, Mr. Sensitive. Have a heart, I just lost the place where I lay my hat."

"Yup, you did. Now, on to other things. What are you going to do next?"

I secured the seat belt, and leaned back against the fabric headrest. It was too early for decisions. I had to make it through my conversation with March and my parents. After all, they had come down here to fix my mess.

"I'm waiting," Hale said in a falsetto voice, keeping his eyes on the road.

"If you must know, I hadn't really planned all the next steps. First, I'll talk to March. After that, who knows?" I closed my eyes, suddenly tired of thinking.

Hale glanced over at me. "You know what I mean. Where are you going next? Back to Atlanta?"

I sat up, my heart pounding. That wasn't even an option. I had March to think about, plus I had to find a new place to live here on Langdon. "What about Atlanta? What's there for me?"

"Well, your old job, for starters. It sounds like from what you've told me, you could have it back in a second."

In my mind, I could see the World Matters headquarters building. I could almost hear the click-clack of my high heels on the granite floors of the lobby, and feel the cool pulse of air-conditioning. It was always such a relief to walk inside the tall building after being outside in the city's muggy heat.

Shaking my head, I looked out the window at the green and brown island landscape. "I can't think of that right now, I can't."

Hale drove in silence, but I could almost hear his brain gears whirring. We passed the Shop All, the Laundromat, a few weath-ered bungalows, and then I said, "Okay, say what you have to say. Geesh."

Smiling, Hale turned on his blinker at the entrance of the Sea Villas. "Well, it just seems like a lot has happened in the past few days. Your sister flew the coop, your parents arrived back on the scene, and you lost your house to an entirely poorly timed but yet completely foreseeable conflagration. Sounds like a day for new beginnings, am I right?"

We pulled into a parking spot near the front entrance, so I was saved from having to make a sarcastic reply. Of course, Hale was right. If there was ever a time to make a new or different start, this was it. He didn't mention it, but he was days from moving into Charleston. I would miss him, of course, but there was the larger question at play: where did I fit into March's life now? And did I want to be there in the first place?

I stepped out of the car and stretched. The morning sun was partially obscured by stretchy, thin clouds. A slight breeze lazily lifted the white Villas flag standing near the circular driveway.

Every manicured hedge and shrub stood silent and ready. There were no excuses anymore. I had to talk to March, and I had to do it in the next five minutes before I lost my last nerve.

Hale paused, his hands on the steering wheel. "I'll say my good-byes now. The moving truck is coming tomorrow and I haven't packed a lick."

I walked around to his window. "I totally understand. I have to face the dragon alone, I get it."

"Not alone. Your folks will be there. And for lunch, I propose we all go grab a bowl of she-crab soup. You, your parents, March. My treat."

I felt tears pooling in my eyes. Hale was such a true friend. He had spent all of yesterday looking for my sister, then taking care of me. And now, he was planning a family reunion meal. All that was missing was the fried chicken and sweet tea to make it truly a Southern moment. "You are something else, Mr. Hale."

He put the car in drive. "That's what all the ladies say, ma'am."

I smiled, blinking back tears, and walked inside. The receptionist Alice waited behind the counter, as always, and when she saw me, she pressed her lips into a mean little squiggle. Nodding her head to the uniformed police officer standing a few feet away, she whispered, "Your sister gave us quite a scare, yes sir, she did. That's right. We had the police running all over this place. Not at all the type of environment we like to project at the Sea Villas."

The officer glanced at me and apparently detecting no particular threat, looked away. Alice primly tapped a folder on the counter and stared at a spot just over my head. My chest ached, and I coughed slightly. The fluorescent light fixture above my head buzzed intermittently.

I opened my mouth and the new Mae Wallace waltzed right over. "Alice, you are the worst part of the 'environment' at the Sea Villas. You are judgmental, angry, and the most unwelcoming person here or maybe anywhere on Langdon. I hope you or one of your loved ones never need the services here, but if you do, you'd be hard-pressed to find someone more insensitive than you manning the front desk day after day."

The officer's head snapped up, and I may have imagined it, but I think he placed one alarmed hand on his holstered gun. I rolled my eyes, taking in Alice's unbelief and swept into the waiting elevator. Inside, my heart pounded, but it was in a good, clean way.

March's floor was fairly quiet. A young teenage girl I had seen only once or twice wheeled silently past, the scars still visible on her scalp but quickly becoming covered by a thin layer of light brown hair. She kept her eyes down as we passed each other. March's nurses nodded at me, a bit warily. I wondered if they thought I blamed them for letting March get away. If only they knew, I thought. When March wants something, she wants it all the way.

I paused at the door to March's room. It was slightly ajar. I knocked softly and heard my mother's voice welcoming me in.

"Oh, baby. Are you okay?" Mom stood up from the corner chair and folded me into a soft hug. She smelled great, like Mom always did. Her hair and makeup were perfectly polished, too. "Hale called last night and said you were in the hospital all afternoon. We didn't know." Stroking my hair, Mom said, "We called your cell once we heard about the fire, and couldn't reach you. Dad drove out last night looking for you, but he had to return once we found our little lost sheep here." Mom gestured toward March.

I took a deep breath and looked at my sister, who was sitting up in her bed. Her hair was neatly brushed into a thick ponytail and she wore lip gloss and a pale blue tracksuit. "Hi, March. How are you doing?" Then I held my breath.

A wicked smile slid across March's face. It was a look my sister—the old March—might have made. "Oh, I'm all right," she said in a somewhat guarded tone. "But I'd rather be parasailing."

"March! That's not funny." Mom sat on a chair and frowned. "You scared us all, especially Hale."

"What did I say? Can't a girl make a little joke around here?"

"Where's Dad?" I made a stab at changing the subject.

"Your father is in the business office, going over the incident with the director. Your sister may be going home sooner than later." Glancing down at her hands, Mom reached into her tote bag for a silver tube of hand lotion.

"You're getting kicked out?"

March nodded modestly. "It seems I pose a very high insurance threat at present. The management at the luxurious Villas has prepared a letter requesting that I vacate this lovely room." She gestured grandly. "What a pity. What will I do without all of my pals like Susie Shotgun Mishap and Diving Board Bennie?"

Mom rose quickly and shut the door. "March Ivy Anders, that is enough. There are patients right outside your room. What if they heard you?"

March wants them to hear her, I thought. For a second, I was tempted to fall into my old role of room straightener and hair brusher. But then, I squared my shoulders and inhaled deeply. I had come here to tell my sister some things and I was going to do it whether March was in a snarky mood or not.

"Mom, do you think you can give us a few minutes? I have something I want to talk to March about."

If Mom was surprised, she didn't let on. "Sure, doll. I need to get some decent soap and shampoo. You know how drying those motel no-label brands can be. I'll just pop over to the little gift store and look around." Leaning in to kiss March, Mom whispered, "Be nice. Your sister loves you."

After Mom left, March rolled her eyes. "Thanks for calling in the calvary. They've done nothing but be on my case since they pulled up in their private jet."

I felt a flash of anger. The old Mae Wallace would have taken every word March dished out, but no longer. I calmly sat down in the chair Mom had vacated. The pleather seat was still warm. "For your information, sis, it's not all about you. At about the time I was notified you were officially missing, my lovely firetrap of a rental house was burning to the ground. If it had been a few minutes later, I would have been inside. As it was, I was a little busy inhaling smoke and then being carted off in an ambulance to the hospital. So, no, I didn't really have time to rat you out to Mom and Dad. You can blame that on the Sea Villas."

I paused, unsure of how March was going to take the new me. I looked at a spot of dried oatmeal on the floor. Was she going to scream at me? Lob her water glass at my head? I had no way of knowing. March had ceased to be the sister that I knew and had become instead a whirling, angry globe of something all tangled together. She was a twine ball, a mash of soap pieces, an enigma.

"Nicely done, big sister, nicely done. I was wondering where your spine had run off to."

My head snapped up. We looked each other in the eye for the first time in months. Outside the room, a cart rattled by. A young girl laughed, and in the distance, I heard another voice yell, "No, no, no!"

"March, I want to say something." I held my gaze.

"I'm listening." Her arms were crossed, but there was a softness to her mouth. For once, it wasn't ringed in a snarl.

"It seems like forever ago, but the last time I saw you, at lunch here, you said something that was true. I didn't realize it at the time, but what you said about me not talking to you was right. Hale tried to get me to see it. Vince tried to get me to see it, but I wouldn't listen. I was so upset about the accident that I thought if I just took all your anger and sadness, that it would make you feel better."

"That was stupid," March said helpfully.

Sighing, I leaned back in the armchair. "I know that now. But I couldn't see it when I was in the middle of things."

"I never asked you to move here and take care of me," March said, tugging at the elastic that was holding her ponytail. Her long, dark hair fell over her shoulders as she shrugged. "Mom and Dad may have asked you to, but I didn't."

"I know I didn't have to move down here, March. But I thought if I helped you, then—"

"Then you wouldn't feel so guilty that I had the accident."

March rolled her eyes. "Classic stuff. Moon Fairy told me so in one of the group sessions. Yours is apparently a typical response: throw yourself into a new role so you don't have time to mourn."

I sat up, scratching the corner of one eye. "But you're still with us. I didn't need to mourn you."

"Moon Fairy means mourning my impairment and the loss of our formerly close relationship." She scratched her nose. "You know, I'm actually sorry I made so much fun of her behind her back. She's really quite good."

I shot March a quick look. "Made fun of her to her face was more like it."

Biting her lip, March silenced a giggle. "Oh, I am so awful. How do you stand me?"

A low tone sounded outside the door and then we could both hear the sounds of padded feet running down the hall. I shivered, wondering what might have happened to a patient. I also wondered what March meant. How could I not stand her, even at her worst? She was my little sister. I felt the tears start but I wasn't embarrassed. "I was able to put up with your nastiness because I remembered the person you used to be," I told her. "And I'm not talking about your legs. I'm talking about you, March. I missed you and wanted you back."

I put my hands up to my face and hid under them for just a minute. I was sure March would have something biting to say. And I would have to get up and leave, because I was finished being the outlet for her frustration.

There was a shuffling and I could hear March moving in the bed. I dropped my hands in time to see March sitting up and swinging her legs off the bed, one at a time, using her hands to cradle and lift her thighs. She looked at me and patted the rumpled cream bed covers. "Will you sit beside me? Please?"

It took me a split second to get from my chair to her side. We sat there, shoulder to shoulder, facing the window overlooking the bay.

"So, what will you do?" March asked.

"What do you mean?"

"My days are numbered at the Sea Villas. Are you going to go to Atlanta and try to get your job back? Or stay here?"

I swallowed hard. It was impossible to think of Langdon without Hale, March, or Ruth. When Hale decided to move into Charleston, I was the model of denial and I never really accepted him leaving. Even if he did, I knew that I would always have March at the end of the island. Now, they were going. Both of them were moving on.

"I really don't know what I'll do. I was supposed to start that contract work for World Matters. I called Hans and he said the job would be waiting for me when I was ready. I guess I could find a new house on Langdon. You know, stay here and befriend the next widower who moves into the neighborhood." I put on a brave smile.

"You know what I think you should do?"

"What's that?"

"Try to get Vince back. I know he's been out of your life for a while."

Stunned, I sat back on the couch. We didn't discuss Vince. Vince was off limits. March seemed to sense my shock.

"Oh, I'm over Vince, Mae Wallace." March sighed dramatically. "You don't have to look so puritanical. I beat that dead horse too long, according to Moon Fairy. And I shouldn't have. Vince and I were never in love, we broke up, and you and he fell for each other. It's okay, really. I'm sorry."

"It's just that you seemed so mad at me for so long about Vince."

"I was, I admit it," March said, looking at me. "I couldn't believe that my serious, save-the-world sister could attract one of my boyfriends. Vince and I were never that close, but I didn't want you to have him, either. I think I just got in the habit of being mad at you. And then, all this happened." She gestured to her legs.

I blinked back tears. "Don't you know the reason I followed you down here was because I didn't know how to tell you that I was sorry you were hurt? That a part of me was thrown away when you fell off that horse?"

March began to cry. "I know. Or at least, I think I did know it deep inside."

"If I could be where you are now, I would change places with you." I meant every word I said to my sister. A fierce love for her seized my heart, making it almost uncomfortable to breathe.

"But you can't, Mae Wallace," March said, her voice soft. She grabbed my hand and clung to it. "Believe me, I wanted everyone to take my place those first few months. I was looking for someone, anyone, to step forward to take the blame. But at the end of the day, it was just me. I was the one who took out a horse and didn't pay attention. Careless riding and stupid bad luck. That's it."

I balled up my fists in my lap. "You don't know how many times I have blamed myself for not talking to you the night before the accident and clearing the air about Vince. You were mad at me, and I had decided to take it until you moved on to some other interest. I think part of me even wanted an excuse to slow things down with Vince so that you wouldn't be bothered. So, I didn't go knock on your door at Mom and Dad's house." My tears came fast, followed by gasping sobs.

March leaned her head over on my shoulder. She smelled like honey and powder. "I could have done the same thing, sister. Instead, I took a stroll out to the barn and decided to take a little ride." She paused. "Do you know I can still see the orange and yellow of the field? In my mind, I replay the glossy feathers of the blackbirds. I see the steam coming off of Butter's coat. And then, I'm flying, me and Butter, hoping you'll see me from the kitchen window and regret not being my best friend. I wanted you to be jealous—me astride the horse and you inside, cut off from me. My thoughts that morning were mean and spiteful."

We sat there for a while, hearing murmurs outside in the hall combined with the normal hospital noises. There was the sound of carts and equipment rolling by, wheels squeaking. Mom had been gone a while. She was probably waiting for some sign from us that we were okay. I thought we would be. If not today, then someday soon.

I closed my eyes, hearing March's breathing. It was slow and steady and I wondered if she had fallen asleep.

Suddenly, March sat up. "Oh, you remember how Hale got

ticked off at you the other day because you were pushing him to contact that gallery in New York? You know, move on with his life and all that stuff?"

"Yes, I remember, and no, I didn't say it like that," I said with a little sniff.

"Well, he ended up calling her. Lark's her name. Some big shot."

I sat up, excited for Hale. "I read about her—she's huge. Not that I know anything about the art world."

"When he got her on the phone, it turned out she was already in South Carolina. Someone had shown her that awful story Friday, and the next day, she turned up on Hale's doorstep. I was there—it was a few hours after our cozy lunch. I think the humidity didn't agree with Lark. She looked a little wilted."

"So, what happened?" My heart was beating fast. This was amazing. I was sad I hadn't been there to see it happen. And Hale hadn't breathed a word of it the entire time I was with him last night and today.

"It was so artsy-fartsy. They talked about motivation and inspiration and all of this lame art mumbo-jumbo. I was so ill. I was like, 'Offer him some money or something, and get the hell back to New York.'" March sighed, her every gesture dramatic.

"You did not, you liar."

Laughing, March met my eyes. "You're right. I served sweet tea and nodded politely."

I laughed, too, enjoying the story. It was like we were in college again, and my sister was telling me about one of her adventures.

"So anyway," March said, "the upshot of it all was that Lark offered Hale a one-man show in her Chelsea gallery next year."

"Wow, what did Hale say?"

"He was stunned and excited, all normal things, I guess."

I bit my lip. "But isn't he a little bothered that everyone will see the bridge paintings and everything?"

"I think he was upset about that at first, when the newspaper story came out. You know, you were there." She shifted on the bed. "But now, he says he thinks it's like Ruth helped him. Not in a ghostly way or anything, but that her influence, even in death, urged him to create good work. And he's okay with that."

"Hale's gone through a lot in the past few days. I wish I had been a better friend to him."

March squeezed my hand. "You helped him more than anyone, Mae Wallace. When he got mad at you, he told me he figured out pretty quickly that he was really mad at himself."

"Why?"

"For one thing, he was afraid to call Lark and the gallery in New York. It seemed too big, too scary that someone wanted his art. Life was comfortable here on Langdon. He had his best friend—you—and a new girlfriend . . ." March squeezed my hand again and then released it, "That's me. And he had his memories of Ruth. It was hard to think about everything changing."

"I can't believe we won't be neighbors anymore. At first, it was because he was moving to Charleston. But now, it's because my house burned to the ground."

"Yeah, you never liked that place," March said, nodding seriously. "So, did you throw a match on it?"

"Why does everyone think that?" I jumped up from the bed and walked over to the window.

"Kidding, kidding, big sis. But you quiet types are always up to something. It's a theory."

"Changing the subject. Since you're getting bounced from this Shangri-La, have you and Hale made plans to see each other once you're back in Henderson and he's down here?"

March nodded and then smiled slyly. "We have some tentative long-distance romance things in the works. Although, I wonder if he might end up in the Upstate after too long, if I have my way."

This was the sister I remembered. "So, you think there's a good future between you two?"

"Yeah, if he can get over that dead wife of his." March sucked in her cheeks.

"March! That's awful. Ruth means the world to Hale."

"Look, Mae Wallace, I'm all for Ruth. Go Ruth! Ruth is great. But I'm here to say that Ruth is no longer with us. It's because of Ruth being dead that Hale was available to pal around with you all the time. He was able to paint awesome paintings of junk floating in the bay. Good for him. But don't you get it? It was because of Ruth cartwheeling off that bridge that all of this happened. If she were still alive, you wouldn't have become Hale's friend and I would have never started dating him."

I looked over the bay toward the new bridge. "You have a point, I guess, but I still think you need to tread lightly. I mean, she's not been gone that long. He still hurts, you know."

Glancing over at me, March said quietly, "I know a thing or two about hurting." She lowered her eyes. "And I also know the best way to stop hurting is to start living again."

Then we were quiet with our thoughts. For once, I didn't think of Ruth, but of Hale, surrounded by art admirers. I pictured him striding through our parents' house, opening the cupboards in the kitchen. I saw him walking down the lane between the fields.

"Mae Wallace?" March's voice was soft, tentative.

I turned away from the window. "What?"

"What do you think happened to Ruth? I mean, really happened on that bridge?"

Exhaling, I gathered up my thoughts. Everything I knew about her had been gleaned from Hale and his memories. There were a few letters and her notebooks, of course, but for the most part, Hale drew the picture of who Ruth used to be. I would never know what drove her to climb that bridge the day she died. So I said, simply, "I'm not sure. But I hope for Hale it was an awful mistake. I hope she had planned to be back in the bungalow that evening, cooking dinner for her husband."

March pulled her hair back into a ponytail. "Yeah, I hope that, too. Even though I never met her, she sounds pretty great. I would hate to think she walked around with a heaviness that could only be solved one way."

I knew that March was thinking of her own depression and anger. I said a silent prayer of thanks that my sister was still with us. Even though I had gone about trying to save her in a bumbling manner, a small part of me rejoiced that March always knew I was trying to help. She might not have wanted me there all of the time, but I had stayed and tried.

"Uhm, can you go tell Mom we're good here? She's probably had time to purchase the entire gift shop."

"Are we good? Really?" I stood at the foot of her bed.

My sister smiled at me. It was a genuine smile, with warmth and love behind her eyes. "We are. I'm sorry I have been such a jerk of a sister."

Turning to open the door, I blinked back tears. Somehow, the little strands of my life were being repaired. I leaned out into the hall and saw Mom sitting on a bench a few rooms down. She searched my face for answers and I gave a huge smile in return. Walking quickly toward me, Mom pulled me into a hug.

"Oh, I knew you could work it out. I always did. I was wondering why it was taking so long. You two are both so stubborn." She held me tightly and then swept inside to embrace March.

I followed her. "Oh, I almost forgot in all the family bonding that Hale wants to take us to lunch. She-crab soup, Mom, your favorite."

My mother looked over at March. "Is that fine with you?"

"Absolutely! Let's blow this pop stand."

I walked over to the door. "I'll call Hale and tell him we're getting ready to go. Crab Hut in thirty minutes?" March nodded and Mom grabbed a brush. I was glad they were getting along. Mom and Dad would be good for March. They could dote on her at home, at least until they drove her crazy. I didn't know what would happen after that. As I walked, I tried Hale's cell phone. There was no answer.

I ran into Dad at the elevator. His face looked fairly grave.

"Is March history at the exclusive Villas?"

"The clock is ticking even now. We're to vacate her room immediately."

"Yikes, this is a family first."

Dad said dryly, "I'd have to say so."

I told him about the lunch plans. "Do you mind if I take your rental car? Hale's not answering his phone. He's probably deep in moving boxes. I'll swing by his house, pick him up, and then head to the Crab Hut."

"That works. I have permission to use the Sea Villas' van one last time, for a trip to the airport. I don't see why we can't make a lunch stop on the way."

I grabbed the keys and then pushed open the stairway door. I didn't feel like facing Alice, and this way, I could duck out the side exit to the main building. Within minutes, I was pulling up to Hale's house. His car was in the driveway, but his bike was gone. Still hopeful, I knocked on the door and tried his cell again. No answer. So I hopped back in the car, cranked up the engine, and tapped my fingers on the wheel as I faced the ocean. Carefully keeping my gaze away from the burned-out house next door, I tried to figure out where Hale had slipped away to and then it hit me.

Hale was hours from leaving Langdon, the place of so much happiness and then heartrending sadness. Yesterday's search for March no doubt brought up all kinds of horrible feelings. Even though he seemed okay when I saw him, I had a hunch Hale was hurting right now.

I backed out the drive and started down Sea Street. A storm was coming in; the wind swept over the pavement, scattering rust-colored leaves and grass clippings. I drove at a fast clip toward the bridge, passing the fancy beach houses painted peach and pink and powder blue. A few late-morning bikers pedaled down the roadside paths, their heads bent into the wind.

I pulled up into the weedy lot under the old bridge and leaped out of the car. Out on the bay, the shrimpers steamed for home and pelicans flew fast and hard above the churning sea. Heavy, gray clouds loomed over the water.

I surprised Hale, who was walking back toward the impromptu parking lot, head down and his hands in his pockets. I suddenly felt shy. "Hey, friend."

His head snapped up and Hale looked startled. "How did you know I would be here?"

"A good guess, I suppose." My hair flipped up and over my face with a gust of wind. I glanced nervously toward the bay. "I would hate to be out on the water today."

"Tell me about it," Hale said, turning his back to the wind. "Let's get over by the bridge piling. I'd hate for something to blow off one of the cranes and rearrange our skulls."

I glanced up at the old bridge and saw the cranes again. It seemed like so long ago that I drove across the bridge after my disastrous trip to see Vince and arrived home to find March missing. But it was just a day and a few hours. So much had changed. I took a deep breath and faced my best friend.

"There's so much I want to say. It's hard to start, so I'll just begin with how much I am going to miss being your neighbor. And how wonderful it was that you took care of me yesterday when I had nothing. And even though we really didn't talk about it, I am sorry for how I treated you the other day. Pushing you to call the gallery when you weren't ready—that wasn't right. I'm sorry.

"And I wanted to tell you how happy I am you and March are doing whatever it is you are going to do." The wind howled, this time bringing with it staccato droplets of cold seawater. "Not that it's any of my business what you do or don't do with her. Because I've always thought you were amazing, and what happened to you and Ruth was horrible and wrong, and I have wished so many times I could take her, and shake her, and tell her not to climb that stupid bridge. But she did and here you are, with me and March. We made up, by the way. I have my sister back."

Hale grinned as two long raindrops crossed the bridge of his nose. "I figured as much because you seem happier and you're talking a mile a minute."

"I know. It's funny, isn't it? I swallowed so many words for so many months and now I just seem to have a million things to say."

"Mae Wallace, I'm sorry I got mad when you were trying to help. I was so mired in missing all things Ruth that I was terrified to move on in any significant way. That's why I'm down here right now. I needed to say good-bye to Ruth before I took this next step: moving to Charleston, painting for the New York show, and seeing where things go with your sister."

I punched him on the arm. "So, are you going to be my brother-in-law?"

"Actually, we're eloping tonight," Hale said with a shrug.

"Hale!"

"I'm kidding, I'm kidding. Just a joke to lighten things up."

"You have no idea how that is not funny. March used to bring home fiancés regularly."

Wrapping his arms around his shoulders, Hale nodded. "She mentioned something about falling in love rather easily in the past."

"I'm glad she's being honest with you."

"And what about you? Are you finally telling her everything you wanted to but didn't know how?"

I brushed hair out of my eyes. "Yes, although it seems like I couldn't have said the things I said to her this morning yesterday or the day before. I was so stuck on feeling guilty and sorry."

"It was like you had one setting: tragedy," Hale said. "And that's from someone who operated for a long time in that limbo."

A ship churned past under the bridge. Spray shot over the bow as men in yellow rain slickers worked on the deck. The rain continued to fall, first in small droplets, and then in huge, wet dollops. We ran for my car. Once we were inside, I started it up and cranked on the heat. "Fall's coming," I said.

"Yeah." Hale looked out the window toward the bridge, his hands on his knees. "I'll come back later and get the bike. I don't want to shove it into your folks' rental car. It would make a mess."

"Is it strange to leave her?"

"Ruth?" Hale clasped his hands together and looked down at the floor mat. "It is. It's harder than I thought it would be, too. Packing up this morning, I put so many pictures and memories into boxes. It's one thing to do that when you are living in the house you shared with your dead wife, but it's another when you pack up that house. A lot of those boxes I know I won't be opening again."

I waited, listening to the rain splatter the windshield. I thought of March back at the Sea Villas with our parents, who were fawning over their youngest daughter.

"I keep thinking that Ruth would mind being reduced to a few boxes of memories, journals, and photos. That she's looking at me right now and saying, 'You're screwing this up, husband.'"

"From everything I have heard of Ruth, that's the last thing she would say. Look, you've kept her memory alive in your paintings and with people like me, people who only know her through you. You've maintained a relationship with her theater, and you would have been close with her family, but they're kind of strange."

"I guess it just doesn't seem like enough. How do you know when it's enough?" A tear slipped down Hale's face.

I took a deep breath. I thought of everything I did for March, or tried to do, and I thought of all that Hale did for Ruth, all the time not knowing what had caused the end of her life. "Maybe looking at it like there's some bar you have to achieve to let your Ruth rest peacefully is the wrong way to go about it." I stared out the window, watching the sheets of gray rain fall across the span of the new bridge. "Instead, maybe you have to realize what it is that you can do to rest peacefully. We don't know what Ruth was thinking and we'll never know. And she can't tell us the best way to honor her."

"So, I'm left with making up a life," Hale said simply. "Deciding what to do, day in and day out. Make coffee, walk on the beach, buy paint, eat pizza."

"Right, and you've done all that really well. The next part is the hardest: you're entering a world without Ruth. A new house, a new career. New friends."

Hale laughed out loud. "You know, I kissed your sister last night. I thought I would never kiss another woman as long as I lived. I had forgotten what it was like to be nervous, to wonder what the woman was thinking, all that. But it happened, and it was okay."

"You really don't have to tell me all of this."

"Whatever. I thought you were my best friend."

"I draw the limit on hearing about my sister's kisses. Have some taste, man."

Hale smiled, his first since I found him under the bridge. I turned down the heat and looked over at him. "So, are you the darling of the New York art world now?"

"Apparently."

"Well, I'll take my ten-percent cut when you start selling those paintings."

Hale pulled on his seat belt. "Actually, all the credit goes to my dear landlord, Mr. Forrester. He was the one who got this started with his breaking-and-entering."

Putting the car in drive, I set the windshield wipers to the fastest setting. "True, true. But if I hadn't urged you to call the Chelsea gallery, then you wouldn't have entertained Ms. Feauto when she arrived on your doorstep."

Hale rubbed his face. "It was so weird to open my door and find her standing there. I can't believe that woman would get on a plane and come down here."

"I'm really proud of you." The car bounced over the pothole-strewn park road. "Just promise to remember the little people when you're a famous art snob."

"I've already forgotten your name. It's Maggie, right?"

"You want to walk home in the rain?"

"Not really."

We drove the short distance back to the Crab Hut, the wipers pulling hard through the deluge. The rainstorm felt like fall, chilly and gray, rather than the warm showers of summer. Life was moving on. I turned the car toward Langdon's short commercial strip.

"Did March get ejected from the Sea Villas?" Hale leaned down and found a crumpled paper towel on the floorboard. He wiped his face, staring out into the water-logged landscape. Palmetto trees sagged with wind and rain, and alongside the street, thick rivers of excess water chugged toward sewer drains.

"She sure did. Now she's my parents' problem. I told her I was firing myself as her case manager."

"It's about time, if you ask me."

"Thanks, as always, for your candor."

Hale scrunched up the paper towel. "You know I'm telling the truth. And now I have to let her go, apparently. Back to Henderson."

I parked in front of the Crab Hut. The place looked deserted as the rain streamed down. "Not necessarily. There are always visits and letters."

Making a face, Hale shrugged. "I'm a little past the summer-camp phase, Mae Wallace. I think I'm going to have to make an honest woman of your sister before too long."

My heart clammered in my chest. For the first time in my life, the prospect of March getting engaged didn't terrify me. If the groom was Hale, I welcomed it. It would be the best thing to happen to her—and to him—in a long time. I took a deep breath and tried to act nonchalant. "That's cool. Whatever."

Laughing, Hale reached over and lightly punched me on the arm. "Nicely played, big sister. You've already got the wedding shower planned in that well-mannered brain of yours."

"And I've decorated the nursery for your triplets. I'm thinking a nautical theme."

Hale leaned forward, his hand on the door handle. "I'm not sure if entering this family is a good idea or pure madness."

"We'll be good, I promise." I smiled over at him.

And then Hale was out of the car and bounding into the rain. Before he dashed under the Crab Hut's faded blue awning, I saw his eyes widen as he caught a glimpse of March being wheeled down the sidewalk by my father. Mom walked beside them, carrying a huge umbrella. Hale splashed through the standing water on the sidewalk until he was in front of March's chair. Bending down, he planted a firm kiss on her surprised mouth. Water streamed down his face and onto hers. They parted, laughed, and kissed again. I saw my parents exchange glances, but it was a loving look they shared just between them. I sat up in the driver's seat, keys in one hand, as I inhaled deeply.

I realized the constant tightness in my chest was gone. That companion of worry and anxiety over my sister had flown. Instead, I felt the warmth of family and gratefulness for new and old love. Behind the Crab Hut, the ocean waited in the gray fog and rain. It had become like a friend to me, almost an easy presence taken for granted from time to time. And although I could not see the bridge, it waited, too, hovering incomplete and unloved, while the shiny new bridge held court over the stormy bay. Cars and trucks traced the old bridge's pattern even now, in rain and water, and where the shadows fell. I opened the car door, feeling the rain splash down on my head. The air smelled of salt and sea. If I timed it just right, I would reach the door at the same time as my family. For now, it was enough, and I ran forward to greet them.

EPILOGUE

People swirled around the gallery. Huge bouquets of flowers sat on low tables and people wearing dark, expensive clothing sipped glasses of wine. I adjusted the collar of my new navy blue dress and stepped over to the bartender to refill my glass.

"Amazing, isn't it?" March said, nodding to the crowd clustered around each of Hale's paintings. Most were sold, but that didn't stop the well-heeled art buyers from stopping the gallery staff to inquire about new work and commissions. Lark had told us to be ready for quite the sensation when she debuted Hale. I guess she knew her stuff because the review in the *Times* was superpositive, even downright giddy.

"I can't believe this turnout. Hale must be in heaven."

March looked around the gallery, searching for her fiancé. "I'm not sure. I think he's overwhelmed. Who wouldn't be?" A sparkly diamond sat on her left hand, which she casually draped on the arm of her wheelchair just so.

"Does he need anything? Should we kidnap him so he can go to the bathroom?"

Giggling, March laughed. "Oh, there he is. Look, that woman with the long nose is going on and on about his work. He's trying not to laugh."

I looked over in time to see Lark deftly steer Hale over to a couple with graying hair. Even yards away, they appeared imposing. Poor Hale, I knew he would prefer to be miles to the south, back in Charleston at his loft.

March said, "Hale's had it up to here with these art phonies. They all want to chat his ear off about his motivation and his angst. He just painted what he was seeing and feeling, but that's not what they want to hear."

I drifted away from March to look at the paintings once more. We had flown up to New York seven days ago. My father footed the bill for a week in the city for March and me. World Matters didn't pay me enough to drop that kind of cash on hotels, plays, and dinners.

While we played, Hale had been busy at the gallery, supervising the uncrating of paintings and helping the staff hang the art. Mom was getting a jump on early Christmas shopping and exploring museums, something Dad and his short attention span would never want to do.

The Chelsea gallery space showed off Hale's work perfectly. The soft white walls and the rich wood floor gave the paintings a modern setting while subtle lighting made the art almost pop off the wall. I stopped in front of what was probably my favorite. The piece was called simply, *At Her Cottage.*

It was a portrait of March in front of the Sea Villas. Her head was turned to the side, and she looked over the ocean. A few strands of hair lifted away from her face and up into the air. The hair looked so real, as did the slight blush of March's skin and the gleaming brown of her eyes. The artist had captured March in love, almost serene. It was beautiful.

And then, if the viewer was very observant, she would look over March's shoulder to see the faint background. Far, far in the distance, stood a bridge. It was not the nightmare bridge, the old bridge that was featured so prominently in the other paintings.

It was the new bridge, shining and efficient. Carrying passengers to and from without regard for whimsy or nostalgia. The old bridge, its constant companion for nearly five years, was nowhere to be seen. It had been finally torn down and was now a memory that the artist had chosen to leave behind.

I tilted my head and gave the painting one last look. It was my sister, frozen in time, but somehow still alive on the canvas in delicately rendered strokes of oil. I exhaled, drinking it in one more time.

"I know. It's something else, isn't it?" A voice shook me out of the scene far away on a South Carolina island.

"What?"

"The painting. There's a lot of power there." The speaker was a man maybe a few years older than me. He wore a black suit and carried a bottle of water.

"You're right. It's a whole story in one simple portrait."

"I'm Karl Pembrook, by the way." He stuck out his hand.

I shook it, noticing Karl's straight, white teeth and handsome smile. "Mae Wallace Anders."

"I detect a touch of a Southern accent. Are you by any chance a friend of the artist?"

"I am, and he is engaged to my sister. That's her in the painting."

"So, I'm guessing that since you're from the South, your first name is Mae Wallace."

That got my attention. "Wow! Usually people think 'Wallace' is my middle or last name."

Karl smiled and took a quick sip of his water. "I'm from Connecticut, but I went to school in Nashville, so I learned a thing or two about Southern traditions."

"What did you think of our South?"

Smiling, Karl said, "It was lovely. I'm hoping to get back down there sometime."

We walked from painting to painting, and I told him parts of our story. I knew now that what March, Hale, and I had all been through, together and apart, were chapters of a rich and complicated story. It was a story that I would have never known how to tell when I was in the midst of it. But now I could stand back and look over those months before Langdon and after, weighing what I said and did, and how I cared for those I loved and was beginning to love.

We came to the last painting, one that was smaller and tucked onto a side wall away from the main gallery. It had been sold that night and was bound for a stranger's wall somewhere. I would never see it again.

Karl and I stopped. We were alone, the crowds steps away in front of the larger paintings.

"That's you," Karl said simply. He turned from me as he spoke.

Hale had asked me to sit for him one day. I was game, so I tried to pose without fidgeting too much. The park under the bridge was deserted, the teen couples temporarily absent from their marathon makeout sessions. I sat in the sand, the roaring cars traveling on the new bridge overhead, beating out a constant rhythm. Hale sketched and sketched, his pencil scratching the rough paper.

I never saw the finished product; I felt shy about asking. So, it was a huge surprise to see the painting once we arrived in New York this week. I still could barely look at it—it seemed so open and vulnerable.

Hale painted me sitting on the ground. I remembered all the trash strewn about my feet, the plastic bags and fast-food wrappers. A plastic gallon jug or two. But those discarded items were gone in the neatly framed painting in front of us. Instead, I sat there, arms resting lightly on my folded legs. The bay and the bridge pilings were in the background. And all around me, under me, and piled up beside me were flowers. Gorgeous, fragrant, blooming flowers. Against the gray of the bridge, their colors blazed bright and clean. The title said it all: *My Neighbor at the Bridge, Quick to Save.*

"You must have been a good friend to him," Karl said quietly.

"We kind of all helped each other." The crowd noise dimmed slightly. The party would be over soon.

"I am glad I heard your story. It will make it all the more special when I look at this painting over the years."

My eyes widened. "You bought it?"

Karl smiled. "I hope you don't think it's rude to tell you. But when I saw it, I felt all the love the artist had for his subject. I had to have it. Luckily, it was still available. Most of them were sold. And then, I saw you in the gallery and I wanted to meet you."

"I usually don't sit on heaps of flowers, you know."

"That's okay. It could be an expensive habit, if you think about it."

"Would you like to meet the artist?"

"At some point," Karl said. "I'd prefer to learn more about you, to be honest. Do you miss Langdon? It sounds like a place that meant a lot to you and to your sister. Or am I being too nosy?"

I pondered his question for a moment. What was Langdon? It was an island, it was Ruth, it was pain and healing. It was my sister, March, back to me, hopefully forever. I didn't think I could tell this new stranger all of that, and yet I felt instantly that I could.

"Langdon," I said finally, "was a lot of things, and I know I'm not going back there anytime soon. When I crossed that bridge"—I nodded toward the painting—"I left a lot behind. And it's better and more beautiful that way."

Karl leaned toward me. We were just a few inches apart. "What is more beautiful?"

I looked up into his friendly, open face. "Everything, everything," I said.

We turned away from Hale's painting, now Karl's, and walked

back into the main gallery. Hale glanced up and caught my eye. He looked tired but happy. I gave him a thumb's up and he rolled his eyes. I laughed and slipped my arm through Karl's. Then we walked across the room toward Hale together.